PR   Creasey, John
6005   Dangerous quest.
.R517
D35

MAY   '77   APR   19 6
APR   '77
                FEB   '82

KVCC   KALAMAZOO VALLEY
       COMMUNITY COLLEGE
       LIBRARY

24838

DANGEROUS QUEST

DANGEROUS QUEST

A
DOCTOR PALFREY
THRILLER

JOHN CREASEY

WALKER AND COMPANY
NEW YORK

Revised Edition © John Creasey 1965
All rights reserved.
No part of this book may be reproduced
or transmitted in any form or by any means,
electronic or mechanical, including photocopying,
recording, or by any information storage and retrieval system,
without permission in writing from the Publisher.

All the characters and events
portrayed in this story are fictitious.

First published in the United States of America
in 1974 by the Walker Publishing Company, Inc.

Published simultaneously in Canada
by Fitzhenry & Whiteside, Limited, Toronto.

ISBN: 0-8027-5282-9

Library of Congress Catalog Card Number: 73-83308

Printed in the United States of America

10 9 8 7 6 5 4 3 2 1

To
F. A. COWLING
*In appreciation of his help
and co-operation*

1 : The Pleasure of Dr. Palfrey

Through the wide streets of Rome there walked a tall Englishman. He had a slight stoop, a diffident manner and sensitive lips which occasionally parted in a smile of ineffable contentment. He wore a lounge suit of light grey with which his shirt, collar, tie and socks toned admirably, and his toney-brown shoes were brilliantly polished.

He stopped at the corner of a narrow street, which had no pavements. There was a group of barefooted, grimy children playing at the far end, military traffic was passing, a single-decker bus lumbered by, and citizens of Rome walked leisurely to and fro.

Dr. Stanislaus Alexander Palfrey, Sap to his friends, turned down the side street and sauntered towards the children who, on seeing him, immediately broke off their play and stared. Some of the bolder spirits pushed their grubby hands tentatively forward.

'*Inglese, signor,*' one said, doubtfully.

'English, yes,' said Palfrey, surveying them with a widening smile and putting his right hand into his pocket. Immediately, they crowded round him in silent supplication, the most backward child now holding out a hopeful hand.

There were seven children. Palfrey took out a handful of *liras*, carefully counted seven, and placed one in each small hand before him. He saw their faces glow with pleasure, listened to their chorus of thanks, and walked on.

The street was narrow, smelly and dirty. The heat was intense and doors and windows were open, allowing the odour of cooking, with its invariable accompaniment of garlic, to permeate into the street.

Palfrey saw a German sign painted on a wall, weather-worn but not effaced. He did not sigh, for he had never expected to find the Italians thorough; traces of the German occupation of Rome would last for years, as would the proclamations of *Il Duce*, side by side with the V-sign and the scrawled welcomes to the *Inglesi* and the *Americanos*. On the darker side, accidents from German mines and booby traps were still too frequent.

He was here on a brief respite from work which had been excessive for the past months, but the rest was not of his own choosing. While awaiting instructions from London, he was extracting the last ounce of pleasure from walking freely about the streets of the first city of Italy. He had last visited Rome early in 1943, when, being an English agent, he had been in constant danger; the contrast now added greatly to his enjoyment.

He found himself in the *Piazza di Spagna* and strolled towards the Spanish Steps.

He walked slowly up the steps, twiddling a spray of mimosa which he had bought for no particular reason from an enormous flower seller. He stood at the top for a while, idly watching the view.

Free, free, *free*! The whole city, soon the whole country.

Palfrey heard a stealthy footstep behind him and swung round. A man shorter than he, thin, wiry, wearing a suit of exaggerated cut, a bright blue shirt and a spotted bow-tie, stood grinning crookedly at him.

'Alex!' exclaimed Palfrey.

'So you aren't dead on your feet?' greeted Alex Conroy.

Their hands gripped, Palfrey's long and well-shaped, the American's squat, with spatulate fingers and a powerful grip; Palfrey's looked white against the other's brown. 'Well, well!' exclaimed Palfrey, inanely. 'So you've arrived, Conroy. How long have you been in Rome?'

'Just three hours,' said Conroy, 'and I'm fine.'

'Oh, lord, I knew I shouldn't have stayed out so long,' said Palfrey, 'but I thought your plane would probably be late. I was just going back.'

'If they told the truth at the hotel,' said Conroy, 'you'd be back before nightfall—maybe! "You'll find him near the Spanish Steps," they said, "he's always hanging around them."'

'How do you like being back here?'

Conroy pursed his lips, considered, then said: 'It gives me one hell of a kick!'

'I wish——' began Palfrey, hesitatingly.

'You wish the others were here,' said Conroy. 'Sure, so do I. Is there any chance of them coming?'

'I don't know,' said Palfrey. 'Not for Drusilla, that's

certain. Brian might turn up. I don't think Stefan will get here, it looks as if he's booked for Moscow from now on. A pity, but'—he shrugged—'most of the work's finished.'

'You mean, we're all washed up?' asked Conroy, and then added with a ferocious scowl: 'Our work isn't finished and it won't be finished for a long time, and if any dumbwit in Washington, London or Moscow thinks it is, it's time someone put a cracker under him. Finished!' repeated the American, derisively, 'why, it's hardly started. *Someone* has to clear up the mess.'

'Oh, I don't know. Even if you're right, is it our job? I quite expect to be recalled.'

'There's something biting you,' Conroy said decisively, 'you're not yourself. If they break up our party—oh, shucks!' He changed the subject abruptly. 'I'm hungry, do you think you can stagger on?'

Palfrey smiled. 'I suppose it is getting late,' he admitted.

They strolled back towards the *Via dell'Impero*. They were staying at the *Hôtel de Péra,* which was neither large nor small, luxurious nor squalid—they were accustomed to staying in such hotels, for they were less noticeable here than elsewhere.

With Conroy, Drusilla Blair, Brian Debenham—the last two English—and the Russian, Stefan Andromovitch, Palfrey had formed the nucleus of a party once unique in the war. They had worked on and off for three years in neutral and enemy-occupied countries.

Occasionally, Palfrey admitted that the word which described them was, simply, spies. He had always had a sneaking regard for spies—men without honour in any country—even before he had dreamed of becoming one, yet at times he had felt the yoke of the short, ominous word heavy on his shoulders. He did not now.

Their original work was nearly finished, because the need for it was gone. Stefan had been recalled to Moscow, presumably to take up a post of some importance. Drusilla, to whom Palfrey was engaged, was working with Brett in London, putting the finishing touches to post-war plans made a long time before. He, Conroy and Debenham had been given an assignment in Ankara, that of ousting a number of restive Nazi elements.

So, the tide of espionage and counter-espionage had passed its flood; what work remained, Palfrey reflected a little sadly, would probably be done by the innumerable regular agents who had been disparaged if not despised before the war. The special qualifications which he and his friends had brought to bear on their particular problems seemed no longer necessary.

He had received word from London to go to Rome and wait for Conroy and Brian Debenham; in Rome, they were to receive instructions. Later, the Marquis of Brett had sent word that Brian might return to England direct from Cairo. Palfrey took it for granted that they, too, would be told to return and report on the Ankara assignment—and then, retirement.

Since Conroy had expressed himself so strongly, Palfrey began to wonder afresh whether more heartening instructions might be received. He was silent throughout the meal.

'Something's wrong with you, Sap,' Conroy said suddenly. 'I give you two words—war guilt.'

'Oh,' said Palfrey. He sounded blank but his heart leapt. 'What about it?' When Conroy did not answer, he added: 'Or do you mean the punishment of war criminals?'

'You know darned well what I mean,' said Conroy, irascibly. 'Sap, let me give you some facts. There are ninety-seven thousand four hundred and eleven Nazis rubbing out all the black marks against their names, and preparing beautiful alibis for the War Guilt and War Crime trials. There are some of them skulking in Germany and sweating blood in case they're found out. There are plenty in Rome, too. Those who haven't changed their names mighty soon will. They'll be up to any dirty trick to cover themselves, and there's plenty of work picking out the worst of them and preparing them for the hangman. Work? It would take us the rest of our lives to finish it properly!'

Palfrey looked thoughtful.

'Ye-es. I've thought of that, but the War Crimes Commission, or whatever they call it——'

'Will want help,' Conroy said, 'and if you were half the man you used to be you would have written to Brett and said so. Recall be damned! When I heard it whispered I got on long-distance to Washington—did I let off steam!' He grinned, sourly. 'Yes, sir, I told them plenty and if I thought they'd listened I would be a durned sight happier now.' His smile faded, and he grew more intense. 'Sap, would Brett put a word in for us?'

'Odd thing, Alex, I had wondered along the same lines. I

dropped Brett a note about it, as a matter of fact. Mind you——'

He broke off.

Conroy's back was to the door, but Palfrey could see everyone who entered. He stared at a short, silvery-haired man with handsome features and an air which brought the plump head-waiter hurrying towards him.

The head-waiter said: 'Yes, milord,' and led the way.

'What's biting you now?' Conroy demanded, turning his head. Then he exclaimed aloud, as he pushed back his chair and stood up, while Palfrey rose to greet the Marquis of Brett, who had loomed so large in their thoughts and discussion.

2: Of Great Minds, Thinking Alike

The sincere pleasure with which Palfrey and Conroy greeted the Marquis brought a smile to the old man's lips and eyes; they were fine eyes, retaining the glow of youth. His quiet, mellow voice was invigorating, yet Palfrey admitted he was more excited by the reason for Brett's appearance in Rome than by his company for its own sake.

The head-waiter brought up a chair with his own plump hands and inquired humbly whether milord had dined.

'Yes, thank you,' said Brett, 'but I have heard that you have some Armagnac in Rome.' He raised an eyebrow. 'If so, perhaps——'

'Of course, milord!' The man's voice fell to a whisper. 'An 1870, milord.' He made his stately way from the table, speaking to a waiter as he passed; glasses and a methylated spirit lamp were brought; the lamp was lighted and glasses warmed.

'Quite an occasion,' murmured Palfrey.

'An occasion for what?' asked Conroy, eyeing the Marquis.

Brett smiled. 'You don't beat about the bush, Alex, do you? I hear that you've had things to say to Washington.'

'Are you telling me that someone listened?' demanded Conroy, incredulously.

'And listened to good effect,' said the Marquis, looking at Palfrey. 'And I had your letter.'

Palfrey shrugged, self-deprecatingly.

Brett smiled. 'There are a large number of Nazis and Fascists in Europe doing their damnedest to hide themselves, and to change their identity. Most of them will be found without much trouble, as there were never so many people prepared to inform against one another! But there are a few who have made plans very carefully, over a long period, so that they can step out of one identity into another—it's particularly true of Germans.'

'The cult of thoroughness,' Palfrey murmured.

'How much do you know about the War Trials Commission?'

'The great Panjandrums are still thinking about it,' Conroy interpolated.

'It's gone further than that,' said Brett, 'it has been working at pressure for some time. It has representatives from all the Allied Nations, but its immediate work is concerned only with Europe. That is one of the things I wanted to know. If you work on this, you will be under the auspices of the War Trials Commission, not Allied Intelligence. There is one particular faction which is worrying us more than any other. We know that there are still Huns who dream of the next war. What is firmly established is that some of the big industrialists and some of the militarists will refuse to accept defeat in this war as final. While they remain at large and unknown, there will always be danger. There are rumours of one particular faction, no longer in Germany, which has been safeguarding itself against defeat since the start of the Russian war. One is Kurt Schlessing——'

Conroy said sharply: 'He's dead!'

Brett smiled: 'Is he?'

Palfrey began to toy with a strand of hair, slowly coiling it about his forefinger. According to neutral sources of information Kurt Schlessing, one of Germany's armament kings, on a par with Krupp, had been found dead in a room of his luxurious country home in the Black Forest.

'There is a rumour that he has been seen since his "death",' said Brett, 'and we want to make sure. Moscow is particularly anxious about Schlessing; the first intimation that he might be alive came from Russian agents. Schlessing is—or was—rich, powerful and clever, a dangerous combination. And one of his closest friends was Kurt Bruckner.'

'He was caught in Genoa and shot trying to escape,' Conroy said, quietly for him.

'We thought he was,' corrected the Marquis. 'The man

who was shot had Bruckner's identity papers, looked like him and was identified by the widow and children, but rumour, again emanating from Moscow, says that he has been seen with Schlessing.'

Bruckner was the man who had superintended the fortifications of the outer defences of the Reich.

'Who else?' asked Palfrey.

'Zukmayer,' said Brett, quietly. 'He was supposed to have been shot by S.S. men when trying to get into Switzerland, but now we aren't so sure. Schlessing, Bruckner and Zukmayer between them make a useful trio, don't they? Steel—fortifications—aircraft. They were always close friends. They were amongst the earliest influential industrialists to adopt the Nazi party. If they are alive, it isn't accidental, but probably the result of a long-term and carefully prepared plan. We want them, if they're alive, and we want to know whether they have any plans for counteracting Allied measures for Germany,' Brett said. 'Your first assignment will be to get them.'

'Where do we start?' asked Conroy.

'In Moscow,' Brett said.

Conroy looked puzzled. 'Don't say they're in Russia!'

'The most likely men to give you information about them are there,' said Brett, 'and Moscow is anxious that the United States and ourselves should be *au fait* with what's happening —they're anxious to make sure that we don't think they are raising an unjustified scare! You'll be with friends,' Brett added, smiling. 'Stefan will work with you, we were able to arrange that.'

'Well, well!' said Conroy, beaming. 'The old brigade again! What about Brian?'

'I hope to send him, but he's gone back to England *via* Cairo,' Brett said, 'his mother is ill, and I was able to arrange a passage for him. I think he'll be anxious to join you, and as soon as he's free, I'll speak to him.'

'Ah,' said Palfrey, slowly. 'Drusilla?'

The Marquis eyed him steadily.

'Is it a job for her, Sap?'

'Er—no,' mumbled Palfrey. 'No, it probably isn't. Although I'd hoped—oh, it doesn't matter.' He smiled, brightly. 'How is she? When did you last see her?'

'Yesterday evening,' said Brett. 'I came by air. She's very well—you needn't worry about her, and I'm keeping her busy! I've a letter for you,' he added.

'I'll give you one to take back, if you don't mind,' Palfrey said. 'Nothing else? I mean, about the trio.'

'Probably there'll be nothing more until you reach Moscow,' said the Marquis, slowly. 'Except—as far as I am concerned, and I speak for the Commission—you have *carte blanche*. If you get into trouble with neutral countries you'll have to get yourselves out, although I don't think it would have serious consequences. Provided none of the trio learns that you are looking for him, you should have a fairly easy job at first.'

'We need to make sure they're alive,' Palfrey reminded him. 'Intriguing situation, anyhow,' he added, smiling his gentle smile. 'I shall be quite glad to get to Moscow.'

As he spoke, he glanced sideways at a small man whose chair seemed nearer than it had been when Brett arrived; it was as if he had shifted it to get a better view of the room. Palfrey could only see the back of his sleek head. The man had finished eating, and although he was smoking and drinking he did not appear to be relaxed but seemed to be on the alert.

On the word 'Moscow', Palfrey thought the man's head moved, but when they left the room, Brett going ahead of them, the solitary diner appeared to take no notice.

When he was alone in his room, he pushed his suspicions aside. He fingered the letter which the Marquis had brought, but did not read it until he was in bed, with the bedside lamp switched on and the pillows stacked behind him. He wanted to extract every possible moment of pleasure out of word from Drusilla.

He felt a curious reluctance to open the letter and break the spell of anticipation, and his mind began to wander back to his imaginings.

He kept the letter in his hand, without opening it, and stared at the end of his bed—it was a large, double bed in a long narrow room. The curtains were drawn, for Rome was still blacked out. He could hear the rumble of traffic outside, and the occasional drone of an aeroplane.

Schlessing, Bruckner and Zukmayer were names carrying a note of loathing coupled with fear. Those of the Nazis who were enclosed in their battered fortress had lost most of their power to frighten even those who remained in bondage, but any who contrived to escape and remain free would be doubly dangerous because their safety depended on their cunning. Such men would be prepared for any attempt to trace them, and might even think Brett a likely hunter. The sleek head kept appearing in his mind's eye.

He opened Drusilla's letter. Soon, he began to smile.

3 : Inquiries Begin

As the Marquis of Brett had other business in Rome, he spent little time the next day with Palfrey and Conroy. Even his influence, however, and the efforts of well-intentioned red tabs, could not obtain seats in the transport plane going to Moscow *via* Ankara that day; the best that could be promised were seats for Friday—it was then Tuesday.

With that, Palfrey had to be satisfied.

Conroy received the information with a scowl, but Palfrey did not think that he was greatly disappointed. Palfrey himself welcomed the opportunity to test his suspicions, which he kept to himself. He declared to Conroy that they could talk about the new assignment as well in Rome as in Moscow.

'When in Rome, why remain idle? Bruckner was known to have been here just before Mussolini faded out. Schlessing probably came as far south after he'd toured the northern cities; and I had a vague idea that someone was listening to Brett last night.'

'You mean, you know there was a snooper?' Conroy demanded, sharply.

'I wouldn't say that,' dissented Palfrey. 'It was an idea which set me thinking, that's all. I don't seriously think that we can learn anything here, but we can keep our eyes open. I wanted a word about it with Brett, but he's never in the same place for five minutes at a time. Astonishing man,' he added, evasively, 'he——'

'When are we going to start looking?' asked Conroy.

'Here and now,' said Palfrey, 'for we may be followed. But we won't be wise to make our suspicions obvious. Think, Alex! Is the reason for Brett's visit known? If so, who's most likely to be interested in it?'

'Bruckner and company,' said Conroy, softly, 'but I don't follow your reasoning.'

'Brett wasn't followed from London—high priority is

required for a seat on a transport aircraft. So a message was sent to have him watched. It's a guess, I know, but why should anyone trouble about watching him in Rome?'

Conroy said: 'Go on, Sap.'

Palfrey smiled. 'Friends of Bruckner and his party would want to know he had even mentioned one of them by name.'

'It needs working on, anyway,' Conroy said. 'Is there anything else?'

'I can't get my mind clear of an idea that I've heard some story about Bruckner, in Rome,' Palfrey admitted. 'Something he did or saw, some trifle that probably doesn't mean a thing. I was thinking that we're out of practice, for there's an obvious place to start. Where do they keep the Fascists who didn't get away?'

'Those awaiting trial, you mean?' Conroy said.

'Yes. They must be somewhere near, but probably not in the local jail,' murmured Palfrey. 'Perhaps an internment camp, and some of the more distinguished will probably be housed in palatial quarters, on the theory that no one is proved guilty before a trial. We can find out. Bruckner was an expert on fortifications. I wonder who the Fascist chief of fortifications was? He might know something about it.'

'Have you forgotten our own Intelligence Bureau?' asked Conroy.

'I suppose they might help,' conceded Palfrey. 'But if we go to see them and are followed, we'll give away the fact that we're after something.'

'We'll take a chance,' said Conroy.

'I hope we see Brett first,' Palfrey said.

By good fortune, they saw the Marquis at luncheon. He was returning to London by an afternoon plane and sent a message asking them to lunch with him at the *Hôtel di Russi*.

But he looked startled when Palfrey confided in him.

'I wasn't followed from London,' he said, 'that's quite certain. If we were watched last evening——'

'It means that someone probably heard of your arrival, perhaps even of your departure from London.'

Brett nodded. 'There are leakages, we can't always avoid them, but it's expected. You've noticed nothing since?'

'No.' Palfrey felt that the other was not being wholly frank, but did not press the point. Instead, he raised that of trying to find Bruckner's confidants in Rome.

Brett agreed that it was worth trying, and spent half an

hour making sure that they were given facilities for interviewing ex-Fascist officials, many of whom were now interned in a large house on the outskirts of the capital.

'You can't go today,' Brett told Palfrey, after a brief telephone conversation, 'they're taking in another contingent from the Balkans, but it will be all right tomorrow. The man you will probably learn most from, I'm told, is Biagni, Leonardo Biagni, Minister of Fortifications in the last days of the regime.' The Marquis wrinkled his nose. 'You won't like Signor Biagni, but he will tell you anything he knows; he's prepared to swear his own son's life away to save his own!'

They saw the Marquis off at the airfield and watched the great transport aircraft out of sight, before being driven back to the centre of the city. The officer who was driving them was in a hurry, and asked whether they would mind being dropped near the Spanish Steps. Conroy grinned.

Palfrey bought a spray of mimosa and held on to it firmly. Turning from the flower seller, he looked up sharply, hearing a faint click.

A well-groomed man, standing near him and holding a camera, smiled widely.

'It is Dr. Palfrey, isn't it?' The man looked English and his accent was flawless.

'Who are you?' Palfrey demanded.

'Murray of *Unity Press*,' said the other. 'I had a flash from London that you were in Italy, and a lot of people would like to know why.'

'I've nothing useful to say, I'm afraid.'

'If you can't tell me why you're here, you can at least say what you've been doing and where you've been,' said Murray. 'You do work with Brett, don't you?'

'Brett?' echoed Palfrey. 'Brett—oh, the Marquis!' His smile was extravagant. 'One of my oldest patients,' he said. 'I see him whenever I can.'

'I know you've reserved seats for the Moscow plane on Friday,' Murray insisted.

Palfrey put his head on one side and regarded him levelly.

'Oh, well, truth will out,' he conceded. 'One or two people at the Kremlin rather want to consult me, people in high places not very fit. Conroy's holding a watching brief for the Rockefeller Institute. No more than that.'

'I'll have to take your word for it,' said Murray.

After dinner, they retired early to their rooms and Palfrey suggested that it might be wise to try to slip out early next morning and escape the attentions of Murray or anyone else who was curious.

At six they were up, at seven they had breakfasted—an English breakfast, as food was not scarce at the *Péra*. Conroy left the hotel first and Palfrey followed him ten minutes afterwards.

Palfrey strolled along the wide street, already astir, with some of the cafés open, and reached the first corner, where he saw a car standing with a chauffeur at the wheel. He looked behind him; Murray was not in sight, but a short, sturdy fellow whom he had seen talking to Murray at the bar the previous evening, was ambling in his wake.

'*Sap!*' called Conroy.

Startled, Palfrey looked round, to see the American's face pressed against the back window of the car. The chauffeur got out and opened the door, and Palfrey climbed in. As the car moved off, he saw the sturdy man standing at the corner, scowling.

Palfrey laughed. 'How did you manage it?'

'I fixed it with the hotel manager,' Conroy said, 'that ought to rile them!'

They were due at the internment camp at nine o'clock, and having plenty of time, they decided to walk the last mile, which led them along the muddy banks of the Tiber. There were no early morning mists, and they could see the hills rising ahead of them, and the shadowy outline of the mountains beyond. There was a regular flow of traffic from the small farms outside Rome; donkey-drawn, gaily-painted carts ambled along loaded with garden produce, sometimes with oranges, but more often with potatoes and vegetables.

They drew within sight of the villa where the ex-Fascist internees were held. It was an ugly, two-storied building, camouflaged green and grey, standing in extensive but untended grounds. There were sentries on duty, both U.S.A. and British, as well as one or two Italians. The fence was reinforced with barbed wire, and at intervals were sentry-boxes, all in need of paint.

Palfrey and Conroy reached the main entrance, and showed their passes. An American escorted them to the office of the Camp C.O. He was a middle-aged, leathery-looking American whose slow drawl placed him as a Texan.

In spite of his drawl, his manner was brisk as he sent for an escort.

An American sergeant, obviously from the north, arrived to guide them, and they followed him from the C.O.'s office. They were surprised to find so many passages and doors. The place was spotlessly clean, the floors boarded, the walls cemented and distempered; there were no carpets, and their footsteps rang out clearly, sending echoes up and down the passages. Palfrey absorbed it all before they reached the door of a room where the guide stopped. He admitted that he would not be able to find his way back unescorted.

The sergeant rapped on the door; there was no immediate reply, and he shot a wide grin at Conroy.

'These guys can sleep! Get up, there!' He shouted and knocked again, but when there was still no answer, he took his revolver from its holster and banged with the butt, also without result. He scowled, took a pass-key from his pocket, and opened the door, muttering under his breath.

He pushed it wide and stood aside for them to enter—so that Palfrey was the first to see the body of Leonardi Biagni, lying on the floor, with his head lolling back and his throat cut.

4: Why Kill Leonardi Biagni?

Palfrey stood still on the threshold; the sight was horrid in itself, and its unexpectedness heightened the effect. He felt his stomach heave as he moved slowly forward; Conroy and the guard pushed past him.

Palfrey recovered quickly, and studied the dead man. There was no sign of the knife which had killed him, and it was obvious that he had not committed suicide, for his hands were empty. The slash had bitten deeply into the carotid artery.

The guard's jaws clenched together; he pressed a bell by the door, before breaking the silence.

'Squealing didn't save him, I guess.'

Palfrey cleared his throat. 'No, it certainly didn't.' What absurd, pointless things words could be! 'When—when was he last seen?'

'I'll find out,' the sergeant said. 'Last night, most likely.'

Footsteps clattered near and he barked at the newcomer: 'Fetch the Colonel and keep your trap shut.'

Palfrey caught a glimpse of a man's startled eyes and then heard the footsteps receding. Conroy brought out a packet of Camels. Palfrey coughed as the smoke bit at his throat, but was glad of the distraction. They waited for what seemed a long time before the Texan Colonel entered the room. He caught sight of Biagni, and pursed his lips as he stepped forward and stared down.

'That was one way,' he said, with no trace of regret in his voice, 'but it wasn't the right way. There'll be plenty of trouble from now on.' He looked into Palfrey's eyes. 'Did you want to see him about any particular thing?'

'No,' said Palfrey, 'just general items.'

He had to lie, but the Texan had revived a disquieting thought which had already sprung to his mind. *Was* it possible that Biagni had been killed in order to prevent him from betraying Bruckner?

Conroy looked eager to talk, but they had no opportunity to discuss it as they walked back to the C.O.'s office.

'What you want on this is a Federal Bureau man.'

'Surely,' said the C.O., sarcastically. 'I guess I'll send for one.'

'I'm from F.B.,' Conroy said. 'I'd like to look around.'

Palfrey doubted whether he would get permission, although he remembered that Conroy had been transferred from the Federal Bureau to Z.5. He had never seen Conroy in action on such a task, and wondered how he would tackle it.

'Surely, there's nothing to stop you looking around,' the Texan said at length.

Conroy's eyes brightened. 'You mean that?'

'Go ahead,' invited the Texan, 'I want the man who killed Biagni, and I want the men who allowed the killer in. I want them mighty bad, mister.'

'That's dandy!' exclaimed Conroy 'Come on, Sap!'

'No job for me,' Palfrey said. 'Carry on.' He did not move as Conroy stormed out, but looked into the Texan's eyes. 'Do you mind if I stay here?'

'I guess not.'

'You're being very good,' Palfrey said.

'You're no stranger, and I had instructions to be good,' said the Texan, smiling. 'I guess I've heard of you, Dr. Palfrey.'

'Oh—really,' said Palfrey, genuinely startled. 'When?'

'Two-three times,' said the other, carelessly, 'there was talk about you at the bar of the *di Russi* last night, some war correspondent threw a party.' He smiled, mirthlessly. 'They thought you were after something in Rome. I guess they'll be sure after this.'

'Who did most of the talking?'

'A smooth guy named Murray.'

'Did anyone try to guess what we're doing here?'

'They reckoned you'd been switched from Allied Intelligence to War Trials,' the other told him.

Palfrey smiled. 'It's bad guessing.'

The Texan laughed. 'Do I pass that on?'

'Well, I can't stop you,' said Palfrey, owlishly.

Conroy put his head round the door.

'Those damned Italians!' he said. 'One of them says he's "lost" a key. He's being questioned.'

The head was withdrawn.

Palfrey smoked another cigarette and accepted an invitation to coffee. Men came and went, with reports on what had happened the previous night. The coffee was hot and good. The Medical Officer came to confirm that Biagni had died from a single knife wound in the throat, severing the carotid artery.

Palfrey began to wish he had gone with Conroy; an hour passed since he had seen the American.

The telephone on the Texan's desk rang and he lifted the receiver swiftly.

'Yes,' he said, and then after a pause: 'Colonel Willis speaking.... Who?' He listened and cocked an eye at Palfrey, forming a single word with his lips. Then: 'Yes, Murray, that's right.... Yes.... Oh, I guess not, it looks as if he killed himself.... I said so, didn't I?' He laughed. 'Haven't you got enough sensations? ... Who? ... Spell it, will you? ... *Pal*frey, isn't that the man you were talking about last night? ... No, I haven't seen him around. ... No, I haven't time right now, later I'll see as many as you want to send.'

He replaced the receiver and cocked an eye at Palfrey.

'You took that in?'

'Most of it,' admitted Palfrey, his eyes very hard. 'Colonel Willis, I must say that I admire your discretion!'

'Aw, shucks,' said Willis, slumping down in his chair and thrusting his hands in his pockets. 'Some one will get bawled out over this. Just how bad is it?'

'I don't know, yet,' admitted Palfrey.

'Which means it could be mighty bad,' said Willis. He looked at the door hopefully, for there were hurried footsteps in the passage.

After a perfunctory tap on the door, Conroy came in, by himself. He looked hot and dishevelled, but his expression was elated.

'The wop didn't lose any keys,' he said. 'He sold them!'

Palfrey snapped: 'Do you know who bought them?'

'I guess I know,' said Conroy, taking out his paper packet of Camels, lighting a cigarette and letting it droop from the corner of his lips. 'If we move fast, Sap, we might catch up with them. Are you ready?'

Palfrey stood up eagerly.

'You wait a minute,' said Willis, 'I want——'

'One of your men was with me all the time, he took notes and he'll be along,' said Conroy. 'What we want is an auto, and we need it right now. Can do?' he asked abruptly.

Willis said, slowly: 'Surely, I can fix it for you.'

Not until five minutes later, as they were driving away from the villa, did Conroy begin to explain what he had learned.

5: The House at Tivoli

'It didn't start until yesterday,' Conroy began. He was driving a Ford V-8, and accelerated as they passed a corner and reached the wide main road to Rome. 'Yesterday, after five o'clock,' he went on, 'the rat was approached by a man—an Italian—who offered him a thousand *lira* for his keys. He accepted. He told the buyer how often the fence was patrolled and how to reach Biagni's room. The man who bought the keys is named Antonio Gagliani,' Conroy said, 'a reputed anti-Fascist business man, living at Tivoli.'

'It's a long way from help,' Palfrey said, 'it might have been wise to tell Willis. But no, you're right,' he went on more briskly, 'we want this unofficial for the present, so that we can have a shot at Gagliani before we let Intelligence question him.'

He drove through the outskirts of Rome, and soon they saw the picturesque town of Tivoli spread out beneath them.

'The Villa Menton,' Conroy said, 'that's all I know.'

He pulled up the car with a squeal of brakes outside a little shop on the outskirts of Tivoli, and dived into the shop—a post office. He was inside no more than three minutes before he came out.

'Okay,' he said, 'it's not far from here, up on the hill—a big house with a blue roof. Newly built and near the first church.'

Palfrey saw the spire of a church not half a mile ahead; Conroy turned round the corner and then the Villa Menton, a large, impressive-looking house, appeared before them. Curtains were drawn at large, semi-circular windows on either side of the front of the house, making Palfrey frown as Conroy pulled up, with a further squealing of brakes.

They climbed a short flight of shallow steps.

Conroy rang the bell. The door was painted white, the bell and fittings were of black bakelite material. They could hear the bell ring faintly, but there was no immediate response.

'Seems like they've flown,' Conroy said. 'Shall I look round the back, Sap?'

'I'll go,' said Palfrey, and hurried round the house; it took longer than he expected, and the exertions made him warm. A closed door, with small glass panels, looked as if it led to the hall and ran right through the house to the front door. Conroy seemed to be keeping his thumb on the bell, for the ringing was insistent; then the American started knocking.

Palfrey shook his head and murmured: 'That won't help, they've flown.'

Suddenly he heard a new sound.

He thought at first that it was Conroy, trying to get in at a window; but decided that he would not have been able to hear it from where he was. He strained his ears; it came again, a faint scratching noise, which might have been a cat or dog pawing on the other side of the door. He tried the handle, but it did not open, and, standing back and looking about him, he saw a small window, through which he would be able to climb. He picked up a piece of white stone which edged a path and, from a distance of a few feet, tossed it at the window. The crack was loud and splinters fell in all directions, but mostly on the inside.

He wrapped his handkerchief over his fingers and began to take out the slivers of glass that remained in the frame. As he cleared the last large piece away and put a leg over the bottom side, he heard Conroy's footsteps behind him.

Palfrey stepped into a small cloak-room, bright with

chromium, and smelling faintly of disinfectant. The door was closed but the key was on the inside. He went into a wide hall, which ran from the front of the house to the back. Conroy joined him, licking at the back of his hand, where he had scratched himself on a piece of glass left in the window. The faint sound he made was the only thing Palfrey heard for several seconds. Then the scratching noise came again, making Conroy jerk his head up.

'Do you hear that?'

'Yes,' said Palfrey, 'come on!'

Conroy took his right hand from his pocket, and Palfrey saw the squat shape of an automatic.

Quickly, they went into every room on the ground floor, but found no one. Returning to the hall, they mounted a staircase which led to a gallery on the first landing.

The faint scratching noise grew louder as they mounted the carpeted stairs. On the landing they paused and peered in turn along three passages, one running to the right, one to the left, and the third and widest straight ahead of them. The walls were panelled and painted white; tall, flower-filled vases, ultra-modern in design, stood at every few feet. The flowers were drooping.

'This way, I think,' murmured Palfrey, leading the way down the widest passage. He paused outside the first door and listened, but heard nothing. Conroy reached the second door, and shook his head. They approached the third together, to find that the scratching came from that room.

Conroy was about to step forward, but Palfrey stopped him with a warning glance. Conroy grinned, then pressed himself close against the door and edged into the room, holding his automatic in front of him, ultra-careful now that he was warned.

From his profile Palfrey judged that he was at first startled, and then angry. Palfrey stepped past him, only to stop and stare, at first astonished, then filled with sharp anger.

It was a well-appointed bedroom, and, because the windows were closed and the fan switched off, extremely hot. By the wall near the large window was a cot, and in the cot lay a child. Someone had tied a scarf about its face which had loosened a little, though not enough to allow the child to cry out. Tiny hands and feet were tied, and the little body was moving convulsively, with tears flooding its eyes. The movements shook one side of the cot, which was fitted so that it could be lowered; the metal fittings made the scratching noise, which continued as the two men approached.

Palfrey, inwardly raging, unhinged the catch which kept the side up, and slid it down slowly. The child was a little girl, with dark, curly hair, whose crying increased and whose breath came in choking gasps because of the scarf. Conroy took out a knife and, while Palfrey kept the dark head still, cut through the scarf, then the string at wrists and ankles.

About the child's lips were red marks, where the scarf had chafed. She was too exhausted to scream; her sobs were silent, but shook her little body.

There was a bleak expression in Palfrey's eyes as he said: 'Get some water, will you?'

Conroy nodded, and hurried out of the room.

He returned almost at once, and Palfrey spooned a little water into the parched mouth. The sobs grew less, and the tears began to slacken. Gently, he wiped the child's eyes, and, after about a quarter of an hour, she was sitting upright on his knee and looking at him. There was no childish serenity in her dark brown eyes, but a shadow which was akin to horror.

He spoke to her softly, in Italian.

'You are all right, little one, we shall look after you.'

She did not try to answer, but after a moment her lips quivered, and she began to cry again.

Palfrey said to the child: 'Where is your mother, little one?'

The tiny lips quivered again, but no tears came, she had cried herself dry.

'They took her away.,

'Did they?' said Palfrey, gently. 'She will be all right.'

It would be folly to question the child now, lest she went into hysterics. Some scene, perhaps of horror, combined with fear at being unable to move, had caused the shadows in her eyes.

'Have you a nurse?' he asked.

'Yes. She went away, yesterday, *signor*.'

'You don't know where?'

The child said: 'There was such trouble, *signor*, Maria wished to stay.'

'Are you hungry?' Palfrey asked.

'*Sì, signor!*'

'Then we will go downstairs, and find something for breakfast,' said Palfrey, lightly. He stood up, lifted her to his shoulder, and carried her down the stairs, saying to Conroy in English: 'Is there anyone outside, Alex? Willis will have sent word to Rome an hour ago.'

'I saw a couple of cars coming up the hill,' said Conroy. 'I expect they're heading for us.' He still looked angry, but had an enforced outward calm which Palfrey shared. 'Why?'

'We'll have to find the nurse, who might give us some information. She'll be better able to handle the child, anyhow. Try the neighbours as soon as you can.'

In the kitchen, which they found without trouble, there were oranges and grape-fruit, bread, butter, and milk—the last two in a refrigerator. Palfrey set them out on an enamel-topped table and pulled a high-chair up for the child, who drank orange juice, followed by milk, then ate heartily, smearing the butter on the bread herself.

Cars drew up outside; she stopped eating as she heard them, looking startled, or perhaps afraid.

'Keep 'em off for a few minutes,' Palfrey said, 'and don't forget that nurse.'

Conroy nodded and went along the passage, his heels ringing on the parquet floor. He opened the front door as Palfrey said to the child:

'You will be all right now.'

'They took my Mama away in a car,' she told him.

'Did they?' asked Palfrey, grave yet hopeful.

'*Sì, signor*. There were two men, they made her leave here. She wished to take me, but they would not permit it. My grandfather——' she looked very serious, but there was a spark of anger in her eyes.

'Is he Antonio Gagliani?'

'That is right.' She clenched her fist. 'He hurt Mama! She cried out, but he hit her many times. I tried to hit him, *signor*, but the others stopped me!'

Palfrey dared a question: 'When did this happen, little one?'

'It was night-time,' she told him. 'My Mama was in bed, they came and took her away.'

The child—whose name, she told him, was Amata—knew none of the reasons for what had happened. Palfrey wished it were possible to fix the time of the visitation, but he did not harass her too much.

Conroy came in, with a tall, leathery-faced English Colonel.

'Look here,' said Palfrey, hurriedly, 'we've got to find the nurse, and we mustn't question the child until we've got the woman. She left here yesterday, after a row.'

'Two men are making enquiries,' Conroy said, 'we'll have word soon.'

Palfrey nodded, and the Colonel and Conroy went out again.

Palfrey pacified the child as well as he could, reassuring her and promising her that she would not be left alone, but he gave only half his mind to Amata.

There must be a good reason for the dismissal of the nurse, and the quicker they found her the better the chance of getting information. That was not all; there was evidence of haste in all that had happened, and men who could murder Biagni so cold-bloodedly would not necessarily stop at him.

The Colonel returned, with Conroy, who said quickly: 'The nurse lives in Rome, Sap, we've got her address.'

'Can we phone her?' Palfrey asked, then sharply: 'No, better go to see her. Colonel, if you can find her telephone number, will you call her and tell her to wait for us!'

'Why——' began the Colonel, and Palfrey said impatiently:

'She's been away from here for too long to be safe. Look after Amata!' He smiled at the child, and patted her cheek; she looked frightened when he disappeared.

As they drove off Palfrey said: 'The house might have been watched. If we were seen, they'd know we'd find the child and be after the nurse. If the nurse knows anything, to shut her mouth they'll probably murder her. What about some speed?'

Conroy put the V-8 through its paces, and the few miles to Rome were covered in little more than a quarter of an hour. Conroy, who had the address of the nurse, at a café near the Pincio Gardens, knew the city well enough to find the gardens without asking for directions.

The café was open, but no one stood or sat beneath the gay awning, and no one was visible inside. Palfrey, jumping out of the car before it stopped, hurried through the doorway with Conroy close on his heels.

There was a sound, as of someone moaning. It came from the rear of the café, and they hurried through. There was a stout old woman lying unconscious on the floor by the door, but she did not look badly hurt; an old man was sitting up and moaning, with his hands at his temples; there was a streak of blood on his right cheek, and in his eyes was an expression of sheer terror.

'Maria!' he gasped. 'Maria, save her——'

Palfrey forced himself to speak quietly.

'Where is she, now?'

'They—they took her,' stammered the old man, pointing towards the garden beyond.

Palfrey did not wait to hear him, but ran into the garden, turning right and motioning to Conroy to go the other way.

Suddenly they heard a sharp oath and a cry, from a woman.

Fifty yards away, near the far wall of the garden, was a fat woman, lying on the ground; above her two men were standing indecisively and looking towards Palfrey. One was armed and Palfrey saw him raise his gun and point towards the woman.

From Palfrey's side came the sharp report of a shot; Conroy had fired first, and the man by the gate reared up, dropped his automatic, and turned to run; his right hand was dripping blood.

His companion was already through the gateway.

Palfrey turned towards the woman, and Conroy raced towards the gateway, through which the second man disappeared. Palfrey was sure that this was the nurse, and when he went down on one knee beside her she opened her eyes. Her mouth was already open, and she was drawing in great gasps of air; then she saw Palfrey and a scream started from her lips.

'I have come to take you to Amata,' Palfrey said, quickly.

She stopped short, her breathing grew steadier, and she tried to sit up. Palfrey helped her.

By then, the old man was coming from the café. He stopped at sight of the woman and crossed himself, uttering a prayer of gladness.

Palfrey said: 'Take care of her, and remember that Amata needs her quickly.'

He left them together, but when he reached the gate he saw Conroy coming towards him, frowning disconsolately.

'They had bicycles,' Conroy said, 'and I couldn't see them properly for the trees.' There were chestnuts and almond trees beyond the café grounds.

'One of the swine won't be able to use his right hand for a long time, anyway,' Conroy went on.

Officials of the *carabinieri* had arrived, after hearing the shot, and Palfrey saw no reason in refusing any explanation. Conroy and the old man described the assailants, and the police promised immediate action. They were impressed by Palfrey's card of authority.

Both the nurse and the old woman, who was her mother, had recovered by the time the first formal inquiries were over, and Palfrey and Conroy took the nurse back with them. She sat in the back seat, perched forward on the edge, uttering Amata's name over and over again. Palfrey had decided that she was in no frame of mind to be questioned, yet.

As soon as they reached the villa, Maria rushed from the car towards the front door. A startled Intelligence man said that the child was in the garden, walking with the Colonel. Maria hurried along the hall, and into the grounds, still calling Amata's name.

She saw her, smiling happily up at the leathery-faced Colonel.

'*Cara mia!*' she cried. 'My precious one, my lovely one!' She almost stumbled as she rushed forward and raised Amata in her arms, crushing her to her large, soft bosom, tears springing to her eyes.

Palfrey waited ten minutes before beginning to question her.

With many gasps and exclamations she told how she had nursed Amata from the day she had been born, had also nursed her mother, the lovely Madalena, who was married to the only son of Antonio Gagliani. Such a man! A Fascist, even now he fought with the Germans! Father and son had quarrelled, or so it had been said, and Madalena had stayed on because she had nowhere to go; her parents had been killed years before, when the Fascists had looted their house in Foggia; Madalena's father had been half Jew.

Palfrey managed to put the story in proper sequence.

On the previous afternoon, Antonio had told the nurse she must go. He had given no explanation, but had offered her money, which—she said—she had flung into his face. Maria had flounced off, going to her own home, in Rome, where her parents kept the café near the Pincio Gardens.

Palfrey said: 'Have you no idea why Signor Gagliani wanted you to go, Maria?'

'No, none, I have none at all, I have been faithful always. It is shameful that I should be so treated!'

'It is,' Palfrey admitted, 'but there must have been a

reason, Maria. Has Signor Gagliani been—shall I say—frightened recently? Has he been different?'

'He has been short-tempered, *signor*, yes.' The large, flabby, good-natured face was set in concentration. 'Since two days, he has been very sharp, addressing me as I am not accustomed to being addressed.'

'Did anything happen that day?' Palfrey asked.

'There was a visitor, I recall.'

'An old friend or acquaintance?'

'I did not know him, *signor*, but they talked as friends would talk.'

'Did you hear his name?'

'No, *signor*.'

'This visitor to Signor Gagliani—was he young?'

'No, *signor*, a man of your own age, perhaps.'

'An Italian?'

'Of that there is some doubt,' said Maria, unable to be definite, or to give even the slenderest of clues to help trace the man.

'Was there anything unusual about him, Maria?'

'He was a man of good looks, and well-spoken. There was one thing which might, perhaps, be of interest to the *signor*.'

'What was that?' asked Palfrey.

'He had but one arm, *signor*, the right arm.'

'Did he, by Jove!' Palfrey allowed his satisfaction to show, and Maria gave a crow of delight. 'I need worry you with only one more question, Maria. When they talked, did they discuss other people?'

'Why, indeed yes, *signor*!'

'Listen carefully, please,' said Palfrey. 'Was the name Bruenning mentioned? Or Zukmayer? Or Schlessing?'

'I regret, *signor*, I cannot recall the names. None that you have mentioned was used, of that I am sure.'

'Try just once again, Maria, about these names. Does that of'—he paused—'Bruckner mean anything?' He softened the name, pronouncing it as Italians would do. 'Does "Bruckner" appear——'

He felt himself growing excited because of the sudden gleam in her eyes.

'Bruckner, *signor*, such a name was mentioned, I am sure, because Herr Bruckner'—she scowled—'visited the house one day, long ago. When was it, now? While *Il Duce* remained. A little man, is that not so? Short, fat, with no hair—Bruckner!'

He discussed the problem of Amata, agreeing with Maria that the child could not be left at the villa and allowing Maria to suggest that she should take her to the café.

He travelled in the car with Amata, two great cases filled with her clothes, and Maria. The child had recovered and was almost normal, except for the gravity of the expression of her eyes when she spoke of her mother.

Palfrey, anxious to learn more, returned to the house in Tivoli. It was being searched by Intelligence officers and men, and Palfrey, not surprisingly, found himself in the way.

He sauntered through the house towards the bedroom.

Staring down at the cot, he thought of the child and her tears and the faint noise which had attracted him.

He peered into the cot, which was dishevelled, with the pillows still slightly damp from the child's tears. The blankets were thrown over one side.

Absent-mindedly, he straightened the clothes of the cot. The mattress, a hair one, was pushed a little too high, and he tried to put it right; it jammed between two rails at the head of the cot, and so he raised it—and then he stood with it in his hands, staring at what he saw lying on the wire springs of the cot.

Papers—and more than papers; there were *blue prints*.

He dropped the mattress and picked up the prints. They seemed new. They were just prints, not original drawings, and he knew that there might be dozens of copies. He examined them closely, but could make nothing of them. They seemed to be the plans of some building, with passages and rooms clearly defined, but there was nothing to explain them; there were letters and numerals, but not a single explanatory note.

He folded them in two, thrust them beneath his coat, and hurried downstairs. Before long, he was poring over them with Conroy, but he too could make nothing of them.

They took the prints to the Intelligence Office. An Engineer officer was called in, and remained silent for so long that Conroy began to grimace with impatience.

'Can you make anything of them?' Palfrey asked.

The officer looked up.

'I'm afraid I can't—they're comprehensive plans of some kind, but there's nothing to indicate measurements—they might be for a small place or a large one. Each print might represent a floor of a building—there are indications of stairways and lifts—but I can't even be sure of that. I'll go over them more carefully, if you'll leave them with me.'

'Can you get copies made?' asked Palfrey.

'Yes, that'll be easy enough.'

'Have a dozen done of each, will you?' asked Palfrey, and the man promised that he would, and that they should be ready within twelve hours.

When they were prepared, Palfrey despatched them to Brett, with a covering note and the somewhat dismal admission that no one in Rome could make anything of them. He even began to doubt their importance.

6: *The Interest of Charles B. Murray*

On Thursday morning, there was a message to say that there would be no room in the plane going to Moscow that day, but seats would definitely be available on Friday; they were to be at the airfield at nine o'clock.

Late in the afternoon, Palfrey decided to go up to his room.

As he entered the hall, a curtain moved at the door leading to the bedrooms. He paused, frowning, and wished suddenly that he had followed Conroy's example and carried a gun; his automatic was in his suit-case, upstairs. He passed two servants *en route* for his room, and as he drew nearer his door he heard a sharp exclamation and a thud.

The handle of his door turned, then stopped, and another thud followed, echoing along the narrow passage.

'Confound you!' a man said, in English.

Palfrey's heart steadied as he turned the handle of the door, alarm fading in relief, and, he believed, understanding of the situation. He thought that he recognised the voice, and Conroy, inside his room, put the matter beyond doubt.

'It's time you stopped stalling, Murray.'

'There's nothing——' Murray began, only to stop as Palfrey entered. His coat was rucked about his shoulders and his hair was dishevelled. He brushed it back and glared at Conroy, who was standing squarely in the middle of the room, holding his automatic.

'Look here, Palfrey, there's no need to read anything sinister into this,' Murray said, with commendable self-possession. 'I came up to see you and as there was no answer to my knock, I opened the door and came in. Conroy seems to think that I came with malicious intent.'

'I don't trust Mr. Charles B. Murray,' said Conroy, very gently.

Murray opened his mouth and looked on the point of losing his temper. Then he forced a smile and spoke lightly.

'For Pete's sake don't make a major incident out of it!' He took a gold cigarette-case from his pocket and held it out. 'They're not poisoned,' he added, seeing Palfrey's hesitation. 'What *is* biting you people?'

'Inquisitive war correspondents,' Conroy said.

'Why are you so interested in who knew Brett, Palfrey? Had you asked me who listened-in to your interesting conversation I could have told you.'

'Could you?'

'Since you ask so nicely, I'll tell you,' said Murray, ironically. 'It was a French correspondent, named Gruvel—a little, sleek, black-haired fellow with a long nose—do you remember him?'

Palfrey said: 'No,' mendaciously.

'He was next to your table, with his back to you,' said Murray. 'We threw a party that evening and I tried to make Gruvel open out, but he kept silent about it, pretending that he hadn't recognised Brett.'

'Where is he now?' asked Palfrey.

'That's what I thought would interest you,' said Murray, smiling. 'He disappeared yesterday morning—the same morning that Biagni was found dead and Gagliani disappeared.' He was blandness himself as he told them that he knew of the latter. 'Remarkable, isn't it?' he added.

'Very,' said Palfrey.

Murray laughed. 'When I heard where you were going— to give medical attention to those in high position, the Russians have no specialists, of course!—I managed to get assigned to Moscow. I should imagine,' continued Murray, eyeing them with unveiled amusement, 'that Moscow would be a very interesting place to visit just now. I was there in '41—it's probably changed a lot.'

Conroy said: 'I give up!'

'What an admission!' Murray lowered himself into an easy chair and crossed his legs. 'I'm sure I could help, you know.'

'I doubt it,' Palfrey said, wary again. 'When are you going to Moscow?'

'Tomorrow, by the morning plane.'

'Supposing we leave this over until we see you in Moscow?' suggested Palfrey. 'I'll have had time to think about it by then. Meanwhile, I'll promise you to say nothing to other newspaper men.'

Murray stood up briskly.

'Thanks, I appreciate that a lot. I'll see you in the shadow of the Kremlin, then!' He went to the door and smiled back at them, moving very quickly, as if glad to get away. 'I won't worry you any more now.'

Palfrey and Conroy exchanged glances as the door closed.

Conroy declared that he was going to have a shower, and went into his room. Palfrey stepped into his own.

He, too, felt in need of a shower. He sat on the bed and took off his shoes, undressed leisurely, put on a summer-weight dressing-gown of pale blue, and went to the bathroom. Conroy was just coming out.

'Don't be long,' he pleaded. 'I'm hungry. I'll wait in my room for you.'

Palfrey did not dawdle, but had a hot shower, then a cold, towelled himself but not too briskly, and went back to his bedroom, feeling limp. He began to dress slowly.

He had nearly finished and was knotting his tie in front of the dressing-table mirror, near the window of the long room. The bed was a long way removed from the window, which overlooked the main street.

Someone tapped at the door.

'Hallo?' said Palfrey, then hastily, 'Come in!'

He did not know what he expected, but again he wished he had his gun in his pocket. He even had time to remember that he must carry it in future, before the door opened. A maid, thin and sad-faced, came in.

She spoke in Italian; she wanted to turn the bed down.

Palfrey turned to the mirror. He could see the maid's face, long and gloomy, an unusual type for an Italian. An *unusual* —he turned abruptly, not quite knowing why; the maid was taking off the bedspread. She folded it neatly, giving all her attention to the humdrum task; there was nothing suspicious about her behaviour. He looked back at the mirror and adjusted the knot of his tie. The maid pulled back the folded blankets.

She screamed!

Palfrey heard it, before there came a sharp, tearing explosion and a sheet of flame and smoke. Something flew past him and crashed through the window, something else struck against the mirror. He was deafened and breathless, for the blast had winded him, and he stood doubled-up and gasping by the hole in the window. The door was flung open and Conroy stormed in as Palfrey fought for breath.

7: A Welcome for Palfrey

Murray sat some way ahead of Palfrey, whose elbows rested on the comfortably upholstered arm-pieces of his seat. The steady, pulsating beat of the aircraft's engine lulled him to a state of apathy, he had been inert for nearly a day and a half. Conroy was coming later, but Palfrey thought he would not be long.

He had adhesive plaster on his cheeks and the back of his hand, but apart from that he showed no signs of the explosion at the *Péra* Hotel; but there were scars on his memory. He could not rid himself of the sight of the unhappy face of the maid, and her scream echoed in his ears. She had seen the fiendish thing and known what it was for a split-second before it had exploded.

Afterwards, when he had gone to her, she had been quite unrecognisable.

Inquiries had been put in hand, but they had led to nothing. Murray had been early on the scene, but he appeared to be acting in good faith, for none of his colleagues looked in, although the story of what had happened to the maid must have gone the rounds. Palfrey was inclined to think that Murray had given out that it had been just another booby-trap, discovered by accident.

Palfrey thought that Murray knew the truth.

The plane droned on, until someone said aloud:

'There it is!'

Eagerly, men who had not seen the Russian capital before craned their heads to look out of the window, Palfrey among them. He saw farmland immediately beneath them, cultivated fields stretching about little buildings. Moscow itself, a sprawling dark mass, was no different from any other large town approached from the air and seen from a long way off. There was silence in the cabin as the onion-shaped domes of the churches showed up against the sky-line.

'The place has a queer fascination for me,' said Murray. 'From my point of view, it's ugly. I don't like their system, or their hotels, or the way they push everything aside for the army, but—it has a curious appeal. You'll probably know what I mean if you stay here a week. That is, if you intend to stay so long.'

'It will depend on how I find my patients!' smiled Palfrey.

'There it is,' said Murray, suddenly. 'The Kremlin!'

Palfrey followed the other's gaze, and saw a building which, even at that distance, appeared to have pink walls. He looked beyond it and saw, very tiny from their height, an open space which he thought might be Red Square.

'And there's Red Square,' Murray said, pointing.

'Thanks,' said Palfrey. 'Where are you staying?'

'At the Metropole, I expect,' said Murray, 'our Moscow man should have booked a room for me. But there might be a crush, I may have to come wherever you're staying! Which is——' he paused invitingly.

'Do you know, I haven't the faintest idea.'

'Now I know you're an optimist! If you're stranded, come and see me,' Murray went on, 'we can always find room for just one more!'

The plane did not circle for landing but went straight in, and came to rest not far from the single-storey wooden buildings about which a few dozen people were clustered, mostly airport officials.

Palfrey looked with surprise at the people nearby. Two were bare-footed, and only a few of them, whom he imagined to be important officials, were well-dressed. Most of them had patched trousers, few had a complete suit, and the discovery gave him a shock.

He felt keenly disappointed, for there was no sign of Stefan Andromovitch, who must surely have had his cable.

'No luck?' Murray asked, joining him as he stepped from the plane. 'You'd better come with my party.'

Palfrey realised, also with a sense of shock, that the well-dressed members of the welcoming party were war correspondents.

After he had been authorised to leave the wooden building, where his papers had been examined, his first concern was to get to the centre of the city; without Stefan, moreover, he had to face the problem of getting accommodation. There was still no sign of the Russian, and no message, but Murray was standing by and grinning with satisfaction. He made no effort to introduce him to the other newspaper men, all of whom eyed Palfrey curiously.

When a car came into sight, driven at some speed, he eyed it hopefully. The driver pulled up gradually, and Palfrey saw a small fellow with a wide, friendly grin, and then——

'Hello, Sap!'

A deep voice greeted him from the back of the car as the door opened. A massive figure emerged, bent double at first and then standing upright and towering above the car and the driver, who was a man of medium height made to look like a pigmy.

'Hallo, Sap!' the giant repeated, warmly.

Palfrey's eyes glowed as he reached the other and they shook hands, Stefan's dwarfing Palfrey's, his grip powerful, even painful. They appraised each other for a moment, both grinning widely. Stefan's large, kindly face, with its broad cheekbones, hinting of the Slav or the Mongol, and his friendly eyes, had a pleasing familiarity. Palfrey had come to regard the Russian as one of his closest friends.

Unlike most of the other men, Stefan was admirably dressed in a well-cut brown suit; it had been made in Savile Row.

'And so, you've come to see me at home,' said Stefan. Pleasure radiated from him, and he looked as if he could burst into loud hurrahs. 'How was the journey? Good?'

'Wonderful!' exclaimed Palfrey. 'Everything was wonderful. If it hadn't been for the unpunctual Russian——'

'I had great difficulty in getting away,' Stefan told him.

'I don't mind. Why the munificence? I mean——' He pointed to the car, a Rolls Royce. 'Surely only the famous are allowed to travel like plutocrats?'

Stefan laughed. 'It goes, my friend, that is all that matters. I will tell you a secret. It once belonged to a member of the German Embassy and it has now become the property of the Supreme Soviet. They had to let a large man have a large car,' Stefan added, resting a hand on Palfrey's shoulder and leading him to the Rolls, 'and this was the only one available. The car and the chauffeur are at our disposal. Where is Alex? He is all right, I trust?'

'Oh, yes,' said Palfrey. 'He stayed behind to clear up one

or two odds and ends, and he'll be along as soon as he can get another plane.'

Stefan opened the car door. 'The Gorki, please.'

Palfrey climbed in and relaxed on the comfortable seat. The upholstery was badly worn and the interior had a most dilapidated appearance.

'Now,' said Stefan, as the car was driven off, 'tell me, what is the mystery of Alex?'

'There's been trouble in Rome,' Palfrey told him. 'I'm sorry and I wish it were not so, but in the long run it might help. How long will we be getting to the hotel?'

'You are not going to a hotel, you are going to my flat,' said Stefan. 'It will take about twenty minutes.'

'Oh,' said Palfrey. 'Well, in that case——'

He embarked upon a résumé of the story, starting from the time Brett had arrived.

When he finished, Stefan eyed him steadily.

'At least there is one consolation,' he declared. 'There is no doubt now that Bruckner and the others are alive. We have never doubted it here, but in England and America there were sceptics.'

The story had subdued the Russian's high spirits, and they fell silent until they turned into a wide street, the Gorki, and the Rolls pulled up outside a tall, narrow house. The chauffeur leaned out and opened the door in the manner of a London taxi driver, beamed at Palfrey as he climbed out, and drove off.

Palfrey stood in front of the house, with Stefan towering beside him.

'It is too early for you to try to get impressions,' said Stefan, smiling, 'you need a good night's sleep after dinner, and in the morning I will show you a little of Moscow.'

They entered the house, the front door of which was unlocked, and walked up two flights of stairs. There were no carpets and the passage was gloomy, for the windows were boarded-up except a pane at each landing, through which came a cold wind, making Palfrey shiver. On the second floor, Stefan unlocked a door and stepped aside for Palfrey to enter a narrow passage with doors leading off it.

Stefan switched on electric light in one room—there was no shade but the light was soft and mellow—and Palfrey saw traces of a past era. The house had been owned by someone of standing in Tsarist days; the ceilings were painted and ornate, the walls, soiled now, and old, were panelled. A large desk, a beautiful example of the Louis Quinze period, stood in one corner. In front of it were two wooden chairs which looked as if their maker had not had time to finish them.

Stefan chuckled.

'The truth is, there is not enough of anything to go round,' said Stefan, 'but before we leave Moscow I will show you some of the best places! This is where I work,' he added, 'and there are two bedrooms. The other rooms are storerooms for documents.'

'Documents about what?' asked Palfrey.

'Amongst others, there are dossiers on those who are wanted for war crimes,' Stefan said, simply. 'That was to be my major task, Sap, assisting in the preparation of a list of wanted men. Then the affair of Bruckner was considered important and I was transferred! There is much to clear up before I go.'

'Do you know where we're going?' Palfrey asked.

Stefan said, very quietly: 'I think so, Sap. At least I know where we are going to start. I will tell about the beginning of the story.'

8: Of the Russian who saw Bruckner

A Russian prisoner of war, working on the vast fortifications in Poland during the latter part of 1943 and the early days of the terrible January of 1944, had escaped, said Stefan.

Behind that simple story Palfrey guessed a great deal that Stefan did not put into words. The world knew of the agony which the cold had brought to Europe in that dread winter, when a Russian soldier had escaped. He had found sanctuary with a party of Poles in wooded country some fifty miles north of Warsaw. The men had lived in holes dug in the ground to keep themselves warm, and during the winter they had been close to starvation. The object of the party of Poles was to act as guerrillas, but they had only one gun between them and a little ammunition.

The Germans, occupying a village five miles away, had not been prepared for the paralysing blasts of arctic winds and, in desperation, they had been compelled to try to get on terms with the few old folk who remained in the village. They had been promised help; but actually, their clothes had been stolen and they had frozen to death.

Stefan, talking steadily as they ate hot vegetable soup and coarse bread, said a great deal in a few words.

'So the little party took over the village, and with the store of German arms and ammunition felt that they could do something useful. They could have escaped towards the West, and perhaps, in the winter, they might have got east, to Russian lines, but they preferred to organise themselves for the assault when the Russians broke through—all except Vladimir Roshki, the prisoner of war.'

Palfrey nodded.

'Roshki came from the Orel district, and his family, he knew, had been driven back into Poland,' Stefan continued. 'He believed they were in Warsaw, if they were alive. He went not only to look for them, but also to try to find out the circumstances in which the civilians were living. He is a man of some education and by no means a fool. His German uniform enabled him to reach Warsaw without great difficulty. He could speak German and he carried civilian clothes in his pack.

'In Warsaw, he received help from the Poles who still fought on—and they were many—and he heard something of the horrors inflicted on them as well as on Russians who had been forced into slave labour with them. They collected hundreds of names and items of proof of German atrocities. Something of what they discovered has already been published, but the rest has been kept secret—much is in this house,' Stefan added, waving a hand about the room. 'They were in touch with underground newspapers, naturally, and one way and another they did well, but Roshki was not wholly satisfied. He was confident that the winter offensive would bring the Red Army near to Warsaw, if not beyond it, but there remained work to be done in Germany itself. You will remember that he was particularly interested in the fate of his own relatives and, naturally, others who had been driven out of Russia. He heard of some parties which had been taken into Germany and, thanks to his efforts, was able to give details of where they were and what they were doing. But some disappeared. Most of the slaves driven into the hinterland of Germany or Poland were half-starved, but now and again small parties were seen, well-fed and well-cared for, and sometimes even given transport. It is not known where they were going, although often it was towards the north. There are rumours that some of them were shipped to Norway, to help in the fortifications there, but—*would* the Germans take men across the sea and up the coast to help in such work?'

'No-o,' admitted Palfrey, puzzled, 'but how does this affect us?'

'I have wondered if those parties of men, all very strong and well-cared for, were sent to a particular place to do special work,' Stefan said. 'I do not know for certain, none of us can know for sure, yet—but at least it is interesting.'

'Work for Bruckner, you mean?' Palfrey said.

'Bruckner would surely only be employed on building projects. You have said that Gagliani was a building engineer, with expert knowledge of tunnel-drilling. Building needs labour. These are ideas, Sap, which may not be of any great importance, but they are worth keeping in mind.'

'The Germans don't often take much care of their prisoners, especially civilians. What more did Roshki discover?'

'A great deal of interest. What is more important, he started a line of inquiries which our agents have been following up. The results have made us sure that Bruckner, Zukmayer and Schlessing are at liberty. They were seen near Breslau and then reports came from our agents of one or the other being in Danzig, Königsberg and Lübeck. They all disappeared again, but Roshki pressed his inquiries. Rumour said "Nordia".'

'It's reasonable,' Palfrey conceded. 'But we haven't much in the way of clues, have we?'

'We shall find them.'

'Ye-es. The anxiety of Gagliani and the man with one arm is helpful, if nothing else,' said Palfrey; 'but'—he raised a hand helplessly—'Moscow seems a million miles from Rome! It's a different world.'

Stefan shrugged.

'I ask myself what such men as Bruckner, Zukmayer and Schlessing would do and I tell myself that they, above all others, would fight until the last to make sure that Germany had a chance of creating chaos again in thirty years' time. Their freedom worries me, Sap. It worries others in Moscow, too. Sometimes, I think more is known than I have been told.'

'I had an impression that Brett was keeping something back,' said Palfrey, frowning.

He had hardly noticed the food—fried eggs and bacon

had followed the soup, and a raw white wine had been served to him. Stefan drank vodka. There were peaches afterwards, followed by raw liqueurs which made Palfrey grimace, although he swallowed them bravely.

It was dark outside when they finished their meal.

Palfrey still felt tired, and soon after nine o'clock he was lying on a comfortable bed, with clothes piled on him. The conferences were being held downstairs in the same house, Stefan told him, so he would not be alone. He lay awake for a while, his thoughts confused, until he went to sleep and slept soundly.

Soon after seven o'clock next morning, he was disturbed by a sound at the door. He opened one eye, to see Stefan smiling at him.

'How the English sleep!' exclaimed the Russian. 'Sap, I cannot get you morning tea, tea is a rarity in Moscow.'

'You're not even civilised!' Palfrey said, as he sat up, yawning.

'But there is a bath,' said Stefan.

'That's more like it,' conceded Palfrey. 'How did the pow-wow go?'

'Well, my friend! I have to go out for an hour, but I will have breakfast sent in to you in half-an-hour's time. A waiter will bring it. Then I will be back and I will begin your Russian education!'

'Is anyone else here?'

'Downstairs, yes. In this flat, no. I have very few visitors, Sap.'

'Good,' said Palfrey. 'Don't be any longer than you can help.'

'I won't,' Stefan assured him. 'The bathroom is at the end of the passage, I will leave the door open.'

Palfrey got up, stretched himself, rasped his fingers across his stubbly chin and hoped there would be hot water for shaving. He took his kit to the bathroom and found a small electric kettle, already switched on and singing. The water ran lukewarm in the bath. He bathed, tied his dressing-gown about him and enjoyed a shave, looking into a gilt-framed mirror which had a wide crack across the middle of it, splitting his face in two. Palfrey amused himself looking above and below the crack, seeing the upper half of his face separated from the lower.

He laughed at himself for his childishness as he went back to the bedroom. He opened the door and went in, with no thought in his mind except breakfast—and then he stood quite still, blinking, more astonished than alarmed, at a little, sleek, dark-haired man sitting on the foot of his bed. Not until the man spoke did a memory spring to Palfrey's mind— Murray's description of the French war correspondent, Gruvel.

'*Short, dark, with a long nose.*'

Such a man sat looking at him, with his right hand in his pocket, and a sardonic smile on his face.

9: The Presumption of M. Gruvel

'Good morning, Dr. Palfrey!'

'Er—oh. Good morning,' said Palfrey. He did not feel as vacant as he sounded, but he was weighing the chances of this being Gruvel and of there being a gun inside the pocket.

'Er—how are you?'

'I am very well,' said the other, softly. 'Come right in and close the door, Dr. Palfrey.'

'Don't you think——' Palfrey began.

The man moved his hand from his pocket; he did carry a gun. 'Come inside and close the door,' he repeated.

'Well, if you insist,' said Palfrey.

The man's English was excellent, but Palfrey thought he had a French accent and he felt certain that this was Gruvel.

'Sit down by that wall.'

'Thanks,' said Palfrey, sitting on an upright chair.

'Do you know me?'

'I could make a guess.'

'Murray told you, I suppose?'

'Murray?' asked Palfrey, looking puzzled.

'It does not matter,' said Gruvel, his identity now established beyond all reasonable doubt. 'Doctor, you should have stayed in Rome, you would be much safer there.'

'Oh, I don't know,' said Palfrey. He had been confident that there would be no immediate danger in Moscow, yet they were here, on his heels. He must have been watched from the airfield or—and more likely—Stefan's house had been under observation. It could only mean that the organisation had regular agents in Moscow.

'As you have come so far,' said Gruvel, 'I have a piece of advice for you, Dr. Palfrey. After we have finished our discussion, find some urgent reason for returning to Rome or London—I am quite indifferent where you go.'

'Accommodating of you,' murmured Palfrey. 'Oh, by the way—where's Madalena?'

Gruvel said: 'Listen to me, Palfrey——'

'I *am* listening,' Palfrey said obligingly.

The man's face grew darker; Palfrey glanced apprehensively at the gun, although the first shock was past and he felt more composed. This man was not a fool, but there were many things he lacked, and he seemed a strange emissary from so powerful a trio as Bruckner, Zukmayer and Schlessing. The thought persisted as he looked blandly into the man's eyes.

'Whom are you looking for?' demanded Gruvel.

Palfrey said: 'Who do you work for?'

'Palfrey, if you don't——'

'Now listen to me,' said Palfrey, sharply, 'I am not going to tell you the truth and I am not going to lie, so you may as well finish what you came to do, and get off with you. You are an anachronism in Moscow, don't you realise it?'

'You are inviting trouble,' Gruvel said.

'Exactly what do I have to do?' inquired Palfrey.

'Return to Rome or London.'

'It wouldn't surprise me if I have to, eventually,' Palfrey said, 'but I'd rather spend a day or two looking round Moscow. For you.' He smiled.

'You are insane!' snapped Gruvel.

'I'm beginning to think so,' admitted Palfrey, 'but this must be a particularly vivid delusion—you *are* real, aren't you?'

'I am real, and so is my gun!'

'Oh, threats!' said Palfrey, disparagingly. 'Gruvel—why have you come?'

'I came hoping that I could persuade you not to be foolish any longer,' Gruvel said, 'it looks as if I have wasted my time. Palfrey—what papers does Andromovitch keep here?'

So that was it, thought Palfrey; he felt almost gay with relief. The earlier talk had been to frighten and mislead him, so as to reduce him to an amenable frame of mind.

'I don't know,' he said.

'Palfrey,' said Gruvel, softly again, 'I have given you ample warning. I want to know what papers Andromovitch keeps here and what papers he has about your particular quest. If you don't tell me where they are, *quickly*——' he paused, and his eyes narrowed, the gun came even further forward—'quickly,' he repeated, 'I shall shoot you.'

Palfrey thought: 'I think he means it.' He felt surprisingly calm, although he was afraid. There was no chance of knocking the gun from the man's hand, and if he tried he would only precipitate the shooting. He wondered whether he could invent a plausible story to cause delay. His earlier doubts returned—he was not yet sure of the real motive behind the visit; but of the grim intent of the threat he had no doubt at all.

He said: 'Gruvel, I——'

'*Quickly!*' snapped Gruvel.

Palfrey shrugged. 'If you——'

He stopped, and gasped.

A hole appeared in the wall behind Gruvel, so suddenly and with so little warning that he could not stop himself from betraying his amazement. Gruvel frowned. The hole in the wall widened, but there was no sound. A man with a grinning face—Stefan's chauffeur!—stepped softly into the room, carrying a vast revolver, which looked heavy enough to weigh him down.

'Such tricks will fail, there is no one behind me,' Gruvel sneered. 'I will give you one more chance, Palfrey, and if you refuse to tell the truth, I shall shoot you without compunction.'

'Well, if you won't take a tip,' said Palfrey, 'what can I do about it?'

Standing a yard behind Gruvel, the chauffeur raised his gun and, using the barrel, struck the side of the Frenchman's head. Gruvel had been glaring at Palfrey, still convinced of a clumsy effort to distract his attention. Then as he swayed sideways, the chauffeur simply bent over and plucked his gun from his fingers. Gruvel struck against the foot panel of the bed and lay still, with his eyes open and an incredulous expression on his thin face.

'Good?' demanded the Russian, hopefully.

'Very,' said Palfrey.

'Good!' said the Russian, and prodded Gruvel with his right foot. He wore a pair of highly-polished patent-leather shoes with snaky, pointed toes. 'Bad,' he said.

'Very,' concurred Palfrey, wholeheartedly.

'Good!' declared the Russian, and it began to dawn on

Palfrey that the man's English was limited to 'good and 'bad'; quite a comprehensive selection, when all was considered. Perspiring with relief, Palfrey sat down heavily, then stood up and went to the bedside table for a cigarette. He offered one to the chauffeur, who beamed but shook his head.

Gruvel said: 'Palfrey, if you let me go——'

'Oh, don't be silly!' snapped Palfrey.

'If you let me free I will give you information about Bruckner which will help you,' said Gruvel, speaking swiftly, 'I must not be caught by the Russians, they——'

'Frightened, are you?' asked Palfrey. 'I don't know why I should set your mind at rest, but if you talk freely, they won't hurt you. No, Gruvel, you've finished your little game, I think I'm beginning to understand why Stefan went out and left me here alone.' He smiled, very cheerfully, took off his dressing-gown, and drew on his singlet and trunks, then heard foot-steps in the passage.

'Hello, there!' he called. 'Is that you, Stefan?'

'You're all right?' asked Stefan, pushing the door open, and stepping in, his smile wide but a little anxious. 'I was afraid they might act before Josef could get in,' he added, 'I am sorry to have had to use you for a bait, Sap.'

'So I should think!' said Palfrey. 'You did expect him?'

'After what you told me, I expected someone,' said Stefan. 'Do you know him?'

'It's the Frenchman, Gruvel.'

'Gruvel? Oh, the man of whom Murray told you. This is progress! Did he say much?'

'He said that Bruckner was dead, like others,' said Palfrey, drawing on his shirt, 'and that if I let him go free he would tell me all about Bruckner, alive, so perhaps it's a matter of reincarnation. I don't really know why he came,' he admitted. 'He wanted to know what papers we had about the present business, and also what other papers you keep here. He also wanted me to go back to London or Rome. If you ask me, he's loco.'

'I doubt that,' said Stefan, 'they are not fools, they have proved that. Josef——' he spoke in Russian, and the chauffeur bent down, and gripped Gruvel's lapels, dragged him to his feet, and hustled him towards the door with fine vigour.

Palfrey said: 'Is it time to send him away, yet?'

'It will do him good to wait,' said Stefan, 'he will get more frightened. Someone who speaks French will tell him of the tortures we have invented for spies, and by the time he is questioned he should be very garrulous—that is the right word?'

'Precisely right,' said Palfrey. He finished dressing, and said, ruefully: 'He worried me, Stefan.'

'What you want is some breakfast!' declared Stefan. 'I am also hungry, so let us go. As he was seen to come in, I did not send food round, so we will go to a restaurant, you will have all you want there, and you will be able to see a little more of Moscow.'

Palfrey said: 'You know, you're taking this very calmly.'

'Why should I do anything else?' asked Stefan, reasonably. 'We have captured a man who is working for the enemy, simply that.'

'I'm puzzled,' said Palfrey. 'Why did he come to see me? He wasn't even consistent.'

'Everyone makes mistakes.'

'Bruckner and his brood don't make that kind,' said Palfrey.

'Perhaps not,' agreed Stefan, 'but I tell you that you will feel much better when you have had breakfast!'

Palfrey was mystified almost as much by Stefan's attitude as by Gruvel's visit.

He was hungry enough to appreciate the food, and to deplore the execrable coffee. He noticed, with interest, the remarkable mural decorations of a vast room, which was nearly empty. Stefan told him that it was not open to the general public—particularly to foreigners—until the evening, but for certain people it was available for all meals. There were eggs in great abundance, ample butter, cream—which helped to make the coffee palatable—fruit and sugar. Palfrey began to feel the contentment induced by food.

Palfrey looked about him, at first paying no particular attention to any individual, but, after a while, he watched a bearded man sitting in a corner beneath a subdued electric light. There was nothing peculiar about the man at first sight, but Palfrey found his gaze continually wandering towards him. Not once did the bearded man look in his direction, but applied himself to the food. He was a good trencherman, who ate with steady deliberation rather than enjoyment. His movements with the knife and fork were stiff, however, and almost mechanical.

Palfrey's eyes narrowed; he looked away from the man and stirred his coffee.

'Stefan,' said Palfrey. 'In the corner, there is a bearded man. I think he's wearing an artificial arm—the right one.'

Stefan said softly: 'You are very observant, my friend, I congratulate you. Is he far on with his meal?'

'Not so far as we are,' said Palfrey; they had nearly finished. 'Why?'

'I will try to get inquiries made,' said Stefan, 'everyone who is now in the building should be known.' He beckoned the waiter and asked for more coffee, and as the man was bending over him to take the tray, added a few words which Palfrey did not catch. The waiter glanced towards the bearded man, at whom Palfrey was looking; the suspect's gaze was riveted on the wall opposite him.

The waiter went off, and Stefan said:

'We have a system by which all arrivals in the country are checked. Few are unobserved for more than an hour or two, unless we have good reason to trust them. If that man is a foreigner, we shall soon know who and what he is supposed to be.'

Palfrey nodded, too intent on the bearded man to speak. His beard was black, but streaked with grey, and his hair looked black. It was impossible to see his features clearly, but they seemed to fit in with the description of the one-armed man in Rome. He was sure that the fellow had an artificial arm.

After little more than five minutes, the waiter returned. Beneath the coffee pot was a folded slip of paper. Stefan took it; his back was towards the man in the corner, so he was in no danger of being seen. He read it quickly, before looking up with a smile which told Palfrey that his suspicions were not entirely unfounded.

'According to his papers, he is a representative of the Yugo-Slav guerrillas, of the section most favourably inclined towards the Soviets,' Stefan said, 'he is supposed to have come from Zagreb, which is a most convenient stepping-stone from Rome. It is his first visit to Russia, and has not yet met anyone who is acquainted with him. Of course, he may be a genuine Yugo-Slav on a genuine mission, but he is well worth watching. It is good that you noticed him, Sap. Has he looked this way?'

'Not once,' said Palfrey.

'That tells us nothing,' Stefan said, 'we will leave, and see whether he follows us. Don't worry, he will be very carefully watched from now on, and will present no danger.'

Palfrey finished his coffee, and pushed his chair back.

'Good!' he said. 'I'm ready. I hope——'

'Of course, we both hope that it is your man,' said Stefan.

10: The Statement of Pierre Gruvel

Once they were outside, having passed but aroused no interest in the bearded man, Palfrey said:

'What are you going to do?'

'Do? Just walk!' said Stefan.

'But——'

'He is closely watched, as I say, although I do not think he realises it. If he shows any interest in us, we shall learn it in good time. If we show too great an interest in him, he will probably be warned, and that is the last thing we want. He is better at large and shadowed, than in prison and silent. I think Gruvel will talk, but will this man?'

After half an hour, there was no sign of the bearded man.

Stefan led him along, smiling with satisfaction, until they reached a square of great proportions. There were many people in it, and a great deal of traffic, mostly military, although there were also cyclists and horse-drawn vehicles with market produce piled high. The people were poorly dressed, but they looked well-fed and there was an atmosphere of cheerfulness which could not be mistaken.

Palfrey was too preoccupied to take much notice; he was still absorbed in the visit of Gruvel and the apparition of the one-armed man. He could trust Stefan and the Muscovites to take all precautions. But that took second place to the problem arising out of Gruvel's visit.

The more he thought of it, the more purposeless it seemed. Their conversation had been pointless. Gruvel had talked as if he had wanted only one thing—to gain time.

Stefan had stopped, and Palfrey looked vaguely about him.

'So you are not impressed?' asked Stefan, sadly.

'Impressed?' asked Palfrey. 'I——'

He looked at the tall buildings. Nearby were the domed pinnacles of buildings within a pink wall, which looked as if it were made of icing coloured with cochineal. The walls were plastered unevenly, as if the man with the trowel had slammed the plaster on and smoothed it over hurriedly, without trying to get a good surface. On one side of the square was a building, completely hidden by sandbags which were bedecked with colourful posters.

'Great Scott!' exclaimed Palfrey. 'The——' he looked at the pink walls, like giant stockades of a fairy palace. 'The Kremlin?'

'The Kremlin,' Stefan told him.

'You know,' declared Palfrey, 'I must have been daydreaming!'

Stefan laughed. 'I wouldn't be surprised! How does it strike you?'

Palfrey said: 'Impressive, definitely impressive.' His lips curved as he regarded the Russian. 'Have I blotted my copybook too badly? I mean, how many black marks?'

'Oh, you will be forgiven,' Stefan said. 'This way.' He led the way across the Square, and Palfrey kept at his side. Everyone appeared to be smiling, he heard exchanges of cheerful greetings and the lilting note in rough voices. This was a happy city, if a poor one.

They reached a tall, massive building, and Stefan said:

'Gruvel should be here.'

'Where are we?'

'If you wished to re-open old wounds, you would call it the headquarters of the Ogpu,' Stefan said. 'The secret police. Now they are Beria's security police, and most of them are working on the War Crimes problem. That is enormous; I sometimes wonder whether London and Washington know how involved it is.' He led the way into a darkened building —windows were boarded up everywhere—and to a lift. They went up several storeys before Stefan opened the door and they stepped into a wide, stone corridor, where their footsteps rang clearly. Outpacing Palfrey, Stefan reached a door which he opened without knocking and Palfrey went in first. There were a dozen desks, at all of which men or women were working. None of them looked up.

The second room was smaller. In it there were three men and a woman. The woman was sitting at a large desk at one corner, as if she were in authority. Palfrey was surprised. She was nearer sixty than fifty, he judged, was dressed poorly, and wore glasses, over the earpieces of which her grey hair fell untidily. She looked up as Stefan approached her and smiled. 'Good morning, gentlemen.'

'I would like to introduce our very good friend, Dr. Palfrey,' said Stefan, in English.

The woman looked at Palfrey, and smiled.

'Madame Crikov,' Stefan said, 'is——'

'*Comrade* Crikov, Comrade Palfrey,' corrected the woman. Palfrey felt still more uncomfortable, and did not know whether to shake hands. He put his out, indeterminately. She took it and, looking into her eyes, he saw that they were very calm and self-possessed—and smiling. Confound it, she was laughing at him, the 'Comrade' had been for his benefit! He warmed to her.

'You are favoured, Sap,' said Stefan, 'only those high in the Party are called "comrade"!'

'How else could we honour so distinguished a guest?' demanded Madame Crikov. 'Besides, do not the English expect to hear the title? But, seriously, you are very welcome, Doctor,' she went on. 'You have had a busy morning, I understand?'

'It had its moments,' admitted Palfrey.

'Yes.' She looked at Stefan. 'Gruvel has made a statement, he would not wait, I have never known a man more frightened!' She laughed, and Stefan smiled.

Palfrey said, thoughtfully: 'Frightened, yes.'

'What do you mean?' Both the woman and Stefan stared at him.

'Frightened,' repeated Palfrey, 'of course. That was the trouble with him at the flat, he was frightened all the time, in spite of his gun and his braggadocio. Stefan, I'm slipping, I didn't see it before.'

'That is curious,' said the woman. She selected a piece of foolscap paper, covered with typewriting. 'Gruvel declares that he was forced, against his will, to visit Palfrey. He was told exactly what to say. His task was to spread doubt as to the continued good health—' Madame Crikov's lips curved sardonically—'of Herr Bruckner. He received his instructions in person from a man whose name he does not know, and who visited him at his hotel.'

'What hotel?' asked Palfrey.

'The *Metropole*.'

'Oh. A big place?' Murray was there, Palfrey remembered.

'Yes. We are endeavouring to find who visited Gruvel there,' said Madame Crikov. 'We shall, eventually. His secondary instructions were to inquire about the papers at the house, but his primary task was to spread doubt about Bruckner.'

'You believe him?' asked Palfrey.

'There is no doubt that he is telling the truth,' said the woman. 'I have seen him myself, his fear is real, he is not pretending. He states that he first made contact with these people in Rome, through the medium of Antonio Gagliani, whom he frequently met. That he was at your hotel—the *Péra*?——' she waited for Palfrey to nod agreement—'in order to watch you. He overheard your conversation with—' her eyes positively sparkled—'Comrade Brett.' She paused, eyeing Palfrey in keen anticipation.

Palfrey repeated, dutifully: 'Comrade Brett—yes, I know him.'

Madame Crikov stared at him, puzzled, and then Stefan smiled, and all of them laughed together. As he recovered, Stefan said:

'Madame Crikov, you will find him proof against such things, he is reputed to have an answer for everything!'

'I am beginning to find it out,' admitted Madame Crikov. 'So! Gruvel was watching you and the American, Conroy, and he reported what he heard to Gagliani. From what I know of events in Rome, the rest followed, as was to be expected.'

'Ye-es,' said Palfrey, 'except——' he broke off.

'You were about to say, Doctor?'

'Er—thinking aloud, I'm afraid,' apologised Palfrey. 'I was wondering whether we *can* take everything Gruvel tells us for granted? I don't like it one little bit!'

'Nor do I,' said the woman, dryly. 'It has been done for a definite purpose, there is no question of that. Yet nothing he has confessed, or said to you, indicates what it is. They——' she used the 'they' disparagingly—she was the embodiment of confidence, and Palfrey liked her matter-of-factness more every moment—'wished us to form conclusions, but they omitted to indicate *what* conclusions. Isn't that your opinion?'

'It is very involved,' said Stefan.

'Involved it may be,' said Madame Crikov, briskly, 'but one thing is certain. There are a number of men in Moscow who know more than Gruvel, and we must find them. That is the first task. You have already noticed this one-armed man who calls himself Danilo. That may help.'

Palfrey said: 'I don't know his name.'

'He is being followed,' she said.

'Wrong!' said Palfrey, decisively, and then stopped. 'That is, I mean, I don't agree that he should be. I've been thinking——' he began to feel awkward, for the woman looked askance, she might be affronted. 'I spoke out of turn, perhaps,' he added, hastily.

'Doctor, we did not invite your help in order to silence you,' said Madame Crikov, smiling again, but looking intently at hin. 'Why were you so emphatic? Why is it the wrong thing to do?'

'They want us to stay in Moscow, to look for the other agents, of course. They've made reasonably sure that we will. But why should they? Because they prefer us to be in Moscow! Again, why? Because there's nothing really worth finding here. I mean—it does stand to reason, doesn't it?'

He looked from one to the other, not sure of their reaction. He thought Stefan would be convinced. The woman might be doubtful, and those doubts might be sufficient to make them stay indefinitely in Moscow. Hers was the authority, and there would be no appeal. He was suddenly quite sure that he was right, for there could be no other explanation of Gruvel's behaviour, and now that he considered that problem solved, he was eager to go on to the next obvious move.

'I think you may be right,' said Stefan.

The woman nodded. 'I agree. What else do you think Doctor?'

'That's the trouble,' said Palfrey, 'there isn't much to think about, except—they want to keep us here because they *don't* want us to go elsewhere. Where don't they want us to go?'

Stefan said, very gently:

'Nordia, of course.'

'Precisely,' said Palfrey. 'We know Nordia might be the seat of the trouble. They know we know it, so they want to keep us away at all costs.' He wound hair about his finger again, and smiled upon the woman. 'How soon can we start, Comrade?'

11 : The Man Who Threw a Knife

'There is no doubt that you created a good impression on her,' Stefan said, as they walked away from the Red Square. 'She is no fool, Sap; in fact, in that head of hers she carries some remarkable information—she has a memory second to none in all Russia. Also, she has often been rather impatient with the English. You can consider it a triumph.'

'That's all right as far as it goes,' said Palfrey, 'but she didn't tell us how soon we can start.'

'She will send word,' Stefan assured him, 'for she is persuaded that you are right. Now I can see how obvious it is! That one-armed man—in my opinion, he was sent to the restaurant in order to make us think that he is the Italian, heavily disguised. Another bait to keep us in Moscow, wouldn't you say?'

'Probably,' admitted Palfrey. 'I wish——'

Something flashed past his eyes and made him stop.

He thought at first that it was the reflection of the sun, already bright, on the windows of a passing car, but then he heard a sharp noise. Stefan swung round. Palfrey, looking towards the sound, saw a knife fall to the sidewalk. It had crashed against the wall of a house and was broken in pieces.

Stefan plunged into the road.

It was a wide thoroughfare, near Red Square. About a dozen people were walking on the opposite side of the road, and one man was running. No one tried to stop the fellow. Palfrey, about to follow Stefan, drew back as a motor-cycle roared past him. He felt impatient, but knew that it was wise to stay where he was; Stefan would return to him there.

He realised that the knife had missed him by no more than a foot.

A crowd gathered about him, mostly of children and old men and women. No one spoke, but all gazed at him curiously. After a while, a policeman came up, asking questions in a leisurely manner, and appearing to take interest in everyone except Palfrey, who was duly grateful.

At long last, Stefan came in sight.

At first Palfrey thought he was alone, but, when the crowd cleared, he saw that Stefan was holding a little fellow by the scruff of the neck. The victim wriggled, and danced, and hopped, and skipped—it was so comical that Palfrey could not repress a grin. Squeaks of protest emerged from the diminutive creature's mouth—a wide one, which twisted into all manner of grotesque shapes.

He was not so very small, thought Palfrey; only Stefan's size made him look a dwarf. He was very thin, however, and had on one shoe and one boot, and the rest of his clothes were little more than rags. He danced like a marionette on a well-played string, his squeaks like those from a ventriloquist's doll.

Stefan put him down, but did not release his hold. The fellow fell silent after casting a single, indescribably cunning glance at Palfrey.

'The culprit?' Palfrey asked, mildly.

'The scoundrel!' said Stefan, smiling faintly. 'Yes, I saw him as he threw it, Sap. A peculiar specimen, isn't he? Shall we take him home, and see what he has to say, or revisit Comrade Crikov?'

'Must we see her?' asked Palfrey.

'I think we can postpone it,' said Stefan. He turned, and beckoned one of the silent men, who approached promptly and faced him without smiling. Stefan spoke to him in Russian, his words swift and decisive. The man answered, turned, and hurried off.

Palfrey watched the messenger disappear.

'What did you say to him?' he asked.

'I sent him to the Crikov, and told her what we are doing,' said Stefan. 'Come, little one!' He jerked the fellow up by his coat collar and, without any apparent effort, walked with him towards the end of the street. Soon they were outside the corner restaurant. In the rush of events, Palfrey had forgotten the bearded man, and now he was thinking of Stefan's decision to refer the matter to Madame Crikov.

All the time, the little man in Stefan's grip danced and wriggled. Stefan held him so that he could just walk, and he took running steps, then held back, or sprang into the air. Sometimes he pretended that he had lost consciousness, and allowed himself to be dragged along, heels scraping on the ground. Stefan took all this with remarkable aplomb, but Palfrey, after the first amazement, felt its absurdity.

Arriving at the house in the street named Gorki, he closed the street door; the chanting laughter of the crowd filtered through.

'Don't you like publicity?' asked Stefan.

Palfrey drew a deep breath, and dabbed at his forehead.

'Why did you bring him like that, confound you?'

'How else could I have brought him?' asked Stefan, regarding the little man curiously. 'A freak, Sap.'

'"Freak" is right,' agreed Palfrey. 'Well, here we are, and we've got him. You're sure it's the fellow who threw the knife?'

'Oh, yes.'

'Has he said anything?'

'Nothing intelligible,' said Stefan, 'he is busy pretending that he is a half-wit, but I doubt it very much. However, we will find out.' He raised the man, put him over his shoulder, and carried him up the stairs, thrusting him into the arms of his waiting chauffeur.

'I wonder——' began Palfrey, as they sat down in Stefan's shabby room. 'The little fellow reminds me of a comic ballet dancer.'

'A ballet?' said Stefan, incredulously.

'Only guess work, I know, but if you want to find out where the little customer came from, try the ballets. *Is* there one with such a character? I don't know them very well.'

'What a mind you have! There is a new ballet, and in it there is a character such as you say, a fool at the Court of Peter the Great. It is a skit on the Tsarist *régime*, a kind of musical comedy ballet.'

Palfrey felt a surge of excitement at the trend of events, and the possibility that, after all, there was a direct line to the source of the trouble in Moscow. The new ballet *could* be the centre of the subversive faction.

'It isn't really likely,' Palfrey said, 'it's senseless to jump to conclusions.'

'I will go and get the fellow,' Stefan said.

Left alone in the room, Palfrey lit a cigarette. He thought about Nordia.

The small Baltic state had clung desperately to neutrality, just as Sweden had done, and as successfully. As its boundary on the one side was Norway, on the other Finland, and on the South—only a short frontier—Sweden, and the sea, it had been independent mostly in name only, until the change of the fortunes of war had forced the Nazis further and further into their inner fortress. It had not even been a hotbed of espionage like Portugal, and, to a lesser degree, Sweden. Goebells and his yes-men had breathed threats of fire and steel now and again, and yet it had been allowed to remain neutral.

Palfrey frowned as he drew on his cigarette.

'Why?' he asked himself. 'I wonder why?'

The room was silent; he could not even hear the sound of traffic from the street. No one appeared to be in the other room of the flat, and Stefan had been gone some time.

Oddly, he thought of Amata Gagliani; and he smiled.

He put the thought of the child aside. Gagliani might have some important part in the plans that were being made, but Palfrey suddenly realised that the events in Rome might have been deliberately designed to focus attention on the Italian capital, just as he believed events in Moscow had been so planned. The blue prints might be part of an elaborate scheme. The underlying strategy of the Bruckner faction would be to keep Palfrey and the others away from the real centre of operations. It might not be Nordia, but——

'It probably is!' Palfrey said, abruptly.

His reflections were interrupted, for he heard a door bang and footsteps along the passage. Stefan came in, pushing the little man ahead of him. The fellow's mouth sagged, his eyes were wide open and he rolled them horribly, showing the whites and making Palfrey frown; he was an objectionable little creature. When Stefan spoke to him, he poured out a stream of gibberish.

'And that is all I can get out of him,' said Stefan.

'He's not been recognised?'

'There are papers in his pockets which say that he comes from a village on the outskirts,' said Stefan.

'The village idiot?' asked Palfrey.

'That is implied, yes—the papers are like the disc that in England you tie on a dog. "If lost, please return to . . .!" Is that not what you do?'

'Ye-es,' said Palfrey. 'So I'm wrong.'

'Not necessarily. The normal procedure, when seeing his papers, would be to release him, or take him back to his village. He would probably be sent by train or by a coach, and no one would ask questions. All that need be arranged would be for someone to meet him at the village, probably the halfwit's father or mother. There would be nothing to tell us that our assumption was wrong, and no suspicions would be aroused. Of course, it might be genuine,' Stefan conceded, 'we shall see. I wonder how quickly our people will go to the theatre?'

He was looking at Palfrey, but Palfrey saw him glance

swiftly towards the little fellow. If the idiot-face altered, Palfrey was too late to see it.

'They won't lose time, surely,' said Palfrey.

'I don't think so,' said Stefan. 'What an idea of yours, Sap! I should never have thought of the ballet.'

This time Palfrey was looking at the man, but the latter gave no sign that what had been said mattered to him.

'What theatre?'

'The school is at present at the old Regency Theatre,' said Stefan, 'but it was to have moved to the Theatre Royal for the winter season.'

'Can't we go?' asked Palfrey wistfully.

Stefan smiled. 'I suppose we could, but it will not be left to us, we are wanted for serious things!'

'I'm not sure that I like the method,' said Palfrey. 'Put this little customer somewhere and take me to the ballet, Stefan, I'm restless.'

'All right, my friend. Come, you!' He spoke in Russian to the little creature, who shrunk away from him, still mouthing. Stefan shrugged, went forward and stretched out a hand.

'Wait!' the man cried.

His voice boomed out, filling the room, and Stefan was so startled that he drew back. The little creature had stopped cringing, and stood up to his full height. There was an air about him which impressed Palfrey deeply; he had been acting the part of a *cretin*, but in that moment he was seen for his true self, a man of intelligence, perhaps of authority.

'You are wise,' he cried, and he spoke in English, with only a slight accent. 'You are wise to stop and listen to me, you will be wiser to go from Moscow, to cease searching, because, if you should find what you seek——'

He paused; neither of the others interrupted him.

'If you should find what you seek,' the man went on, 'you will bring upon yourselves and upon others horrors which you will never forget. I am warning you. Go no further! You are free men, you have done your duty, no man has a right to take such risks as you will take if you continue to search in Moscow for——'

He broke off, shaking his head, and crouched down again; the brief, compelling speech might not have been uttered. Palfrey stared at him as he crouched, as if in fear of his life. Stefan turned to Palfrey.

Then the man sprang up, and into his right hand there flashed a knife. Palfrey had no idea where it had come from, the transformation was too abrupt. He cried aloud, and the cry gave Stefan a vital second of warning. The knife, used dagger-fashion, flashed past his neck. Stefan swept his arm round, catching the fellow on the shoulder. The *cretin* was flung against the wall with a thud which shook it, but he was not knocked out; he slid to the floor, still holding the knife, and jumped up again like a spring-heeled-Jack, his face now wholly evil.

Palfrey stepped hastily out of the way. He shot out his foot but the man skipped nimbly over it, reached the door, then turned and flung the knife at Stefan, who was starting after him. Stefan dodged to one side, and the knife whistled past him, but in dodging, he struck Palfrey, who was going towards the door. In the collision, Palfrey felt as if he had come up against the side of a hill. He reeled back, losing his balance, and fell.

He banged his head on a corner of the desk, and his senses reeled.

He was just aware of Stefan disappearing through the doorway, and thought he heard the heavy thud of footsteps. A black mist clouded his eyes, the blood was roaring in his ears. He did not try to get up, but lay there for what seemed an age, until his head began to clear and the noise of footsteps had stopped.

When he pulled himself to his feet he leaned against the desk and buried his face in his hands; then he bent double, forcing his head between his knees. He did that three times, until he felt able to straighten up, gasping. His head ached and he winced when he felt the back of it. There was a smear of blood on his fingers.

He walked unsteadily to the bathroom. There was only the cracked mirror, and he could not see the back of his head, but the wound was bleeding freely.

'Oh, well,' he said, philosophically, 'it's better than a knife cut.' He bathed it gingerly until it appeared to have stopped bleeding before drying it on a hand towel. Although it felt very tender, the actual breakage of the skin was probably negligible. He lit a cigarette and returned to the main room, walking much more steadily.

Some ten minutes passed before Stefan returned.

Eagerly, Palfrey said: 'Did you catch him?'

Stefan said, gruffly: 'He is dead, Sap.'

'Oh,' said Palfrey, blankly.

'The house was watched, of course, and when he realised

59

that he could not get away, he ran straight into an army truck.' Stefan shrugged his great shoulders. 'I do not think that such a man would have talked, so perhaps it is no great loss.'

Palfrey said:

'He said too much for my liking.'

'You mean that he echoed Gruvel's words,' Stefan said, thoughtfully.

'He did more than that!' Palfrey said, sharply. 'He put over an act damned well, and Gruvel did the same. Neither was based on imagination, the devils have got something up their sleeves. There are moments when it frightens me,' he added, soberly.

Stefan said: 'Are you sure that you are not paying too much attention to words?'

'I don't think I am,' Palfrey said, emphatically. 'Oh, I don't pay much attention to his "don't go on with it", he had a mentality which can't understand that talk like that will make us hot up the pace.'

'One thing we know,' Stefan said, 'is that your theory about the ballet is the right one.'

'Do we?'

'Yes, of course! The little fellow changed so abruptly when he heard us talking of the ballet. I have no doubt that he tried to get away to warn them, but I hope they will be rounded up before they can do more harm.'

'Would they be at the theatre at this time?'

'Probably,' said Stefan, 'they might be rehearsing, and the chorus would be working, anyhow. But I don't know whether all the leaders would be there. How are you feeling?'

'Dizzy,' said Palfrey.

'I was afraid for you, I heard the way your head cracked against the desk,' said Stefan, 'but I was anxious not to allow the little brute to go.'

'Ye-es,' said Palfrey. 'Well, shall we go?' Stefan nodded. 'Do we walk?' asked Palfrey.

'I have the car,' said Stefan, 'the Regency Theatre is some way off.'

Outside, on the opposite pavement, Palfrey saw the little man's body. They had not covered it and there was no doubt that death had been instantaneous. An ambulance was arriving as Palfrey stepped into Stefan's Rolls. Stefan pushed the sliding roof back and Palfrey was glad of the keen, fresh air. They drove across Red Square and then towards the suburbs. Palfrey could not forget the man who had pretended to be a *cretin*, and the cunning he had shown. He did not doubt that the whole incident had been yet another effort to detain them. He wished they had mentioned 'Nordia', to find out the man's reactions, but he thought it would probably have drawn a blank.

The drive seemed unending.

They went along wide roads with wooden buildings on either side. Brick buildings were few in the suburbs, although now and again, flanking the road, were vast blocks of workers' tenements, comparable with any blocks of flats in England. The roads were dusty and dirty; the sidewalks were crowded, but the shops did not seem to be busy.

Stefan stopped the Rolls in a narrow street, on the corner of which was a tall, domed building. Outside it were painted pictures of the ballet, some photographs, a few remnants of tawdry decorations, and empty lamp sockets and shades of coloured glass.

'A guard is around the place already,' Stefan said. 'I imagine they have been warned to expect us.'

As Palfrey climbed out, he saw the soldiers with fixed bayonets at every entrance and every window. The doors were open and led to a foyer which had no carpet and little decoration on the walls. The lights were on and, a few moments later, when they entered the auditorium, he saw that the lights were also shining there. Armed men stood about, but Stefan appeared to be recognised and no one stopped them as they made their way towards the wings.

There were more soldiers, as well as some frightened girls, and also a monstrously fat woman who was gesticulating violently and hissing at an officer who stood gravely in front of her.

Stefan smiled. 'The ballet mistress sounds offended!'

'So they haven't gone?' Palfrey was hopeful.

'This is only the chorus,' Stefan said.

He interrupted the flow of words which they had taken to be abusive and asked whether any detentions had been made. The officer turned, saluted, and spoke rapidly in Russian.

Stefan turned to Palfrey.

'Only the girls were here when the men arrived—the old dame is telling him about it.'

'Oh,' said Palfrey. He listened to the sibilant voice, and glanced at the girls, all of whom were huddled together and looked scared. An old man, presumably a caretaker, was in a corner, looking on nervously.

The woman stopped at last.

Stefan said, slowly:

'They were too late, Sap. Everyone was here an hour ago, there was to have been a full rehearsal. The dancers, the stage director, the musicians—everyone. Filov himself, the author, was also here. There was to be a special performance this evening, for foreign Embassy staffs. Then the manager, a man named Boroskin, told them all to go.'

Palfrey said: 'Is that all?'

'A messenger came and spoke to Boroskin, after which there was much alarm among the important dancers,' said Stefan. 'I am afraid that we were just too late, my friend. Obviously, the little fellow was watched. They saw him caught and whoever saw it came back and gave the warning. But there will be a search for them, and few of them will get away.'

The car stopped.

'Hallo, home again?' said Palfrey, then saw that they were in Red Square. 'Oh, no! Where are we going?'

'To see Comrade Crikov!' said Stefan. He climbed out first and, when they were walking together through the narrow passages of the big building, asked with a smile:

'Many deep thoughts, Sap?'

'Yes,' said Palfrey, crisply. 'Guess what about?'

'Drusilla,' suggested Stefan.

Palfrey laughed. 'You'll do!'

Madame Crikov—Palfrey could not really make up his mind how to think of her or even to address her—was even more untidy and her clothes might have been slept in. Her hair was escaping from a few clips which looked as if they would fall out if she were rash enough to shake her head; yet her eyes were calm as she greeted Palfrey.

She said: 'So you have not been satisfied, Doctor?'

Palfrey stared. 'With what?'

'Our busy morning. You had to do more.'

'Don't blame me,' said Palfrey hastily. 'Blame the others, I didn't start anything!'

She smiled again. 'You would not, of course!' She took a sheet of paper from the desk but made only a pretence at reading it as Palfrey and Stefan sat down. She went on: 'I have the report of what happened in the street, of the detention of the dancer, Blik——'

Palfrey said: 'So you've identified him?'

'Did you not suggest who he was?' asked Madame Crikov.

'Of his escape and his death—I would like a further report on that.'

'The homes of the members of the ballet who were not at the theatre, and the others, are being visited. There are no reports in yet, but before the day is over I hope there will be news in plenty.' She tapped her stubby fingers on the desk. 'They are slow in coming,' she complained.

'Hardly slow,' protested Palfrey.

'I think so.' The hint of reproof in her voice passed over Palfrey's head. 'Now, what are you going to do?'

Palfrey put his head on one side and said deliberately:

'Prepare for a journey, Comrade!'

She stared at him owlishly, then laughed.

'He is persistent, Andromovitch! Yes, of course, you will need to prepare, and you will also need sleep and rest, judging from your pallor and your eyes, which look tired. You hurt your head, I understand. Be careful with it, it is a precious possession!'

Palfrey's hand strayed to his hair.

Stefan asked: 'Are there any instructions?'

'At the moment, no. Oh—one point of interest. Danilo was arrested when the raid on the theatre was started. He *is* a Yugo-Slav. He has confessed to having been bribed by someone, whom he does not know by name, when he was in Zagreb, to come here and to follow you about, Doctor! It was clever, you see—they wanted you to imagine that he was the one-armed man who talked with Gagliani.'

Palfrey said, thoughtfully: 'Yes, nicely done. Does he know Gagliani?'

'He knows nothing,' she said, 'nothing of importance. Blik must have known more, but he was a fanatic, who would not have talked. Now—I suggest that you rest during the afternoon, Doctor. I will have word sent to you if there is any news of interest.'

'Good of you,' murmured Palfrey.

They left at once for Stefan's apartment, where Palfrey admitted the wisdom of the woman's advice. He did feel tired, less from lack of sleep than from the blow on his head and the hectic rush of events. He allowed Stefan to bathe his head and put iodine on it, grimacing as the antiseptic stung. They had some sandwiches and coffee, which was quite as bad as that he had drunk on the previous night, and with less cream.

Palfrey shrugged his shoulders, kicked off his shoes, unfastened his collar and tie, and lay down on the bed. He woke up, some three hours later, feeling stiff and sore. The house was very silent, and it was nearly six o'clock. He sat up, lazily, finding that his head no longer ached, but was stiff at the back. The stiffness reached half-way down his neck, numbness rather than pain. He yawned—and heard footsteps approaching.

He sat quite still.

Then he relaxed, for Stefan came in.

'So you are awake?' he greeted.

'Have I been asleep?' asked Palfrey, naïvely.

'I have been in four times,' Stefan told him, 'and each time you were snoring, my friend! I shall have to warn Drusilla!' In spite of his brightness he looked worried, Palfrey did not anticipate good news. 'How do you feel?'

'Curious,' said Palfrey.

'Naturally,' said Stefan. He leaned against the wall and thrust his hands into his pockets; his head nearly touched the ceiling. 'It is a remarkable thing, Sap.'

'I knew it,' said Palfrey, swinging his feet to the ground. 'I should never have gone to bed!'

'You could have made no difference,' Stefan assured him, gravely. 'Filov, the author of the ballet, all the higher members of the—what is your word?—cast, the cast, yes, the producer and everyone who might be able to give information——'

'Gone?'

'Gone,' concurred Stefan.

Palfrey raised one eyebrow. 'So it can happen here!'

'It has,' admitted Stefan, 'but I would never have believed it. Obviously, they had planned escape beforehand, but it is very disturbing.'

Palfrey pursed his lips, but said nothing.

'Not even one man was caught,' marvelled Stefan. 'I would have called it impossible!' He gave Palfrey the impression that he was both restless and alarmed. Then: 'But I am forgetful again! I have other news. Conroy is safe and on his way to Nordia, although he has no further information,' said Stefan, 'and Brian is also going there from London, a cable reached us an hour ago. And, my friend, we have been busy! Accommodation has been booked for all of us, in Sven.

Reports are already coming from our agents there and in the rest of Nordia.'

'Well, well!' said Palfrey, greatly cheered. 'Action at last, and Alex is all right? Do you know when he'll arrive?'

'He should be there tomorrow morning,' said Stefan, 'and he will probably pick up the same plane as Brian, so they may arrive together. Now—we will go out for the evening, there is nothing much we can do. You feel better?'

'Much!' declared Palfrey.

By the time he had bathed, shaved and changed, he felt buoyant and fresh. The news of Brian and Conroy cheered him up as much as the knowledge that there would not be a long delay in starting for the capital of Nordia. He whistled softly to himself as he walked from the bedroom towards the living-room, but stopped when he heard voices. He tapped and went in.

Stefan was sitting on an upright chair; Madame Crikov, her plump stocking-less legs crossed, was sitting back in the easy one. She looked at Palfrey and smiled with a preoccupied air.

'I am glad you have come, Sap.' said Stefan, quietly.

'News?' asked Palfrey.

'Yes, news of consequence. We have reports from agents in Sven that the Italian, Gagliani, and Madalena, his daughter, arrived there yesterday, but have since disappeared.'

12: The Beginning of a Journey

Palfrey sat down on a companion chair to Stefan's. He had been half expecting such news, it was the early confirmation which surprised him most. Then he began to smile; the last doubt of the significance of what had happened in Rome was dispersed.

He said: 'Could there be any mistake?'

'No,' said Madame Crikov. 'Photographs of the woman and the man were sent to Sven, and there has been a lookout for them. They went to a leading hotel, but left without a trace.' She shrugged her plump shoulders and smiled wryly —'What can happen in Moscow can happen much more easily in Sven.'

'When your other friends have arrived, you will start, that has been arranged. You will go by air on the ordinary passenger liner. Provision for you has been made in Sven, and Andromovitch knows upon whom it will be safe to call for help. There are the English and American agents, of course, who will perhaps be helpful, as well as the consulates. You will not conceal your presence at first.'

Palfrey frowned.

'Is that wise?' He knew that his objection was partly due to a faint resentment at being given arbitrary instructions. The restrictions which had made themselves felt so much in Moscow must not be allowed to operate in Sven.

'We do not wish to antagonise the Nordian authorities,' said Madame Crikov, quite sharply.

'Fiddle-de-dee!' said Palfrey, as sharply.

They eyed each other, the woman frowning, Palfrey smiling and hoping that his attitude would not precipitate any kind of a crisis. Stefan sat back and said nothing; had Palfrey glanced at him, he would have seen a faint smile at his lips.

'You do not agree?' demanded Madame Crikov, more quietly.

'I do not, comrade!' declared Palfrey. 'If we advertise our presence in Sven, we tell the other side that we've got that far. I'd much rather they thought I was in Rome!'

She frowned. 'Are you serious?'

'I mean, I'd like to be able to put in an appearance in Rome,' said Palfrey, 'or anywhere but Sven, just to fox them. I wonder if we could allow it to be rumoured that we have been assigned to'—he paused—'well, anywhere you like, but not Nordia. And whether it would not be wise to go into Nordia by sea or ferry, and not *via* the airport, which will probably be watched.'

'I begin to understand,' admitted Madame Crikov.

'Good!' smiled Palfrey. 'A difference in method, that's all. Possibly they know that we suspect a Nordian angle, but they can't be sure. So—entry by stealth, I think. That's if you don't mind.' He looked anxious.

Stefan's smile widened.

'It had not occurred to me,' admitted the woman, pursing her lips as she finished and staring at him thoughtfully. 'It should have done, of course, it was careless. I saw only one aspect. So—you may have your own way, comrade!'

'Thanks very much,' murmured Palfrey.

She laughed, and said to Stefan: 'I think perhaps it would be helpful if the doctor lived here for a year!'

'He would doubtless cause another revolution,' said Stefan, gravely.

'One thing is certain,' said Madame Crikov. 'I shall refuse to allow him into Russia at any time without a clear understanding of his reason for coming! Now I must go. I will make the arrangements—they will be careful ones, Comrade Palfrey! Among them, the unfortunate detention of the correspondent, Murray, whose papers will be queried. He must not be allowed to worry you.' She hoisted herself from her chair and Palfrey stood up, but she made her way to the door and opened it, flinging: 'Good night!' over her shoulder. She closed the door with a bang and padded along the passage.

Stefan laughed.

'Is she annoyed, but being nice about it?' asked Palfrey, anxiously.

'No, no, my friend! If anything, she is amused. She is probably going to relate to her husband the story of the arrogant Englishman, but she will say nothing of the circumstances, of course.'

'Who is her husband?' asked Palfrey, curiously.

Stefan's eyes crinkled at the corners.

'He is a driver on the *Metro*.'

'Great Scott!' gasped Palfrey. 'You mean——'

'Is it so surprising?' asked Stefan. 'Each one does the work for which he is most suited. But you put your finger on one of the weaknesses of Comrade Crikov, she is a little too prone to see only one side of a problem. Her ingenuity is stupendous, but—dare I say it?—perhaps a little automatic.'

'Possibly. She's a good sort,' Palfrey said.

'High praise,' said Stefan. 'Talking of the worthy Comrade Crikov, masculine—reminds me that I have not yet shown you one of our under-ground stations. We will travel by train for a short journey. It is only two stations, but it will be worth it.'

Palfrey said: 'Travel where?'

'You must have one night out in Moscow,' said Stefan. 'We will go to the Kafkaz. Have you heard of it?'

'No,' admitted Palfrey.

'You will talk of it for the rest of your life,' Stefan assured him.

In spite of an almost incredibly luxurious evening in a

city of widespread shortages and controls, Palfrey could not rid himself of a feeling of insecurity. When they entered the flat he was on edge, and when each door opened he was prepared for trouble; but none came, and by twelve o'clock he was in bed and asleep.

His last waking thought was a fear that something would prevent them from leaving the next day, but when he was called by Stefan just after seven o'clock he was told that they would have to leave for the airfield by eight. Palfrey's mood quickly became buoyant. He bathed and shaved, had a light breakfast, feeling slightly under the weather after the excesses of the previous night. As he was driven to the airfield two other men followed them in a small car which kept pace with the Rolls with impudent ease.

He had seen nothing of Murray, and wondered whether the man would contrive to turn up again. He doubted whether he would evade Madame Crikov's long arm.

An aircraft was waiting for them.

'Have we been told how we are to go?' asked Palfrey.

'By air to Riga, then by boat,' said Stefan. 'I have the instructions. We shall sail as members of a ship's crew.'

'Oh,' said Palfrey. 'That's more like it!'

The feeling that there would be complications came back, although the flight went without a hitch, and, after some three hours, they landed at Riga. There were the usual formalities at the airport before they left for the centre of the town. They did not go to a hotel, but to a small lodging house, patronised mostly by sailors. Their luggage was put into a small room, which they shared. They had been driven to the hotel in a small closed car and they did not go out again that day.

They stayed in during the whole of the following day, too, but in the evening Palfrey was brought a set of rough clothes, a blue woollen jersey, trousers which were as stiff as boards, and a pair of heavy boots. Someone had obtained similar clothing large enough for Stefan. They changed, and regarded each other critically.

'This is more like it, Stefan!' Palfrey said mildly.

'I have just come from the manager of the house,' said Stefan. 'There is a small ship, a cargo steamer, leaving for Sven tonight. Arrangements will be made to take us off and we will be met and escorted at Sven. There we shall pick up the latest information.'

'Not forgetting Alex and Brian, I hope,' said Palfrey.

He could not rid himself of a feeling of disquiet. Had Stefan asked about it, he would have said that he felt that they would not get to Sven. He had no faith in premonitions, but this one persisted, even after they had gone through the dark streets of the town and walked along a wide gangplank on board a ship which smelt of tar and fish and dirty oil. Shadowy figures moved about him, and he heard whispered voices, all speaking Russian.

They were allotted a small cabin, in which Stefan could not stand upright. The bunks were clean, but the smell of oil and tar and fish was nauseating. Palfrey, stretched out on a bunk and lay still feeling very wideawake; he thought Stefan was asleep. He heard the strange, mysterious noises of a ship leaving port, the lapping of the water outside, the heavy footsteps of the men on deck. There seemed a hush over everything. He knew that there would be hazards in the crossing, and wondered whether he had been right—it would have been much simpler to have gone by air.

He dozed off eventually and was woken up abruptly. The engines of the ship were beating steadily, but he could hear nothing else. Light filtered through a darkened porthole, so it was morning. He yawned and stretched himself, then heard the sharp crack of a gun. The ship seemed to quiver and, as it did so, he heard the harsh note of an aeroplane engine and he knew that the ship was being attacked.

13: Attack at Sea

Palfrey swung his legs from the bunk and jumped down. Stefan was sitting up, wide-eyed. The *crack-crack-crack* of the ship's anti-aircraft gun was interspersed with the whine of the aircraft, which drew nearer and grew so loud that it seemed to fill the cabin. Would the pilot never come out of his dive?

Crump! The explosion was muffled, but a second later the ship began to rock. There was a clattering sound as water and perhaps pieces of shrapnel came hurtling aboard. Someone cried out, a man swore, the gun continued to bark like the yapping of an angry terrier. There were periods of tense quietness, punctuated only by the gun, then the distant whine of an aeroplane, probably a second bomber just peeling off. It came like the previous one, drawing nearer and nearer, making Palfrey stiff with a fear he always had when he could not fight back.

The ship rocked wildly.

'They are close,' Stefan said, calmly enough.

After another explosion, the ship rocked gently.

'That was further away,' said Stefan. 'Would you rather be on deck?'

'I think I would,' admitted Palfrey.

They pulled on their boots and staggered up the steps to the deck in a blast of cold wind. Men were standing about, most of them wearing sou'westers, and only three with steel helmets. They were the three by the gun, which was still barking defiance. Patches of mist hung about, but on the starboard was a clear stretch of sky; out of it they saw another plane approaching.

Palfrey tried to count the aircraft, but could not see them clearly enough—he thought there were two waiting to come down, and certainly there was one on the way, its engine roaring, its whining, nerve-racking note drawing nearer.

Yet the bombs fell further away, well to starboard, and one of the men on deck grinned and spat at the Stuka as it pulled out of its dive and flew south.

'We should have been escorted,' Stefan said, 'there has been an error.'

'Would they take such trouble?' Palfrey asked.

'If they haven't, I shall have something to say to Crikov,' growled Stefan. 'The truth is, of course, that she would not want to make it obvious that the vessel was escorted, that is one of the difficulties. I—ah!'

Two fighters came haring across the sky; he saw them before Palfrey, who knew that they could not hope to stop the next Stuka coming at them, although they might drive the rest off, or even bring some down. He waited eagerly. The whine and the crash were followed by three distinct explosions, still further away. The gun had stopped barking and the crew stood watching. They could hear the stutter of machine-guns in the air. It continued, mingling with the faint droning of engines, for perhaps five minutes. Then the sounds faded and the ship ploughed onwards, bows cutting the green, swelling water in two, a greyish wake behind her.

'Have you any idea where we are?' asked Palfrey.

'We should not be far from Sven.'

'What do you mean by "far"?'

'An hour's journey, perhaps,' said Stefan. 'I think we can go downstairs again; if you're like me, you're hungry!'

He led the way. The crew returned to normal stations, and the gun was unmanned. They were served with fried herrings and eggs, a mixture which almost turned Palfrey's stomach, but which, when he began to eat, went down surprisingly well. The coffee was even worse than that served in Moscow.

Palfrey returned to the deck. He believed that he could see the outline of the Nordian coast as he stood straining his eyes. There were no aircraft overhead. The mist had gone, the sky was brighter, and there were few clouds; the spell of excellent weather looked likely to continue.

In the quarter of an hour that he was alone, the coastline grew much clearer and he believed that they were sailing towards the territorial waters, planning to creep along the coast in the hope of being insured against further attack. A vain hope, he thought, for if the Huns came after them territorial waters would be no protection. Yet he no longer felt keyed-up, believing that the one effort was all the enemy could manage. His dislike of supervision was partly offset by the arrival of the Russian fighters, although he was eager to be at work on his own responsibility.

Stefan's shadow loomed over him.

'We are all right now,' he said, 'and we have only half an hour's more sailing. You see that promontory?' He pronounced the word very carefully.

'Yes.'

'It is the extremity of Sven fjord. Beyond it is the town. We are going to berth at a little quay near the end of the promontory, not in the main docks. I think that is wise.'

'Yes,' said Palfrey, idly. He lit a cigarette and hugged his coat more tightly about him, for it was surprisingly cold. They watched the coastline gradually emerge. The rising slopes and rocky hills of the promontory which projected the fjord seemed barren and there was no sign of life except, on the shores of a tiny inlet, he was able to pick out a few whitewashed cottages.

No one was speaking, but a man was singing in a deep, musical voice. Two stocky men stood on the grey, drab bridge. The A.A. gun was covered with tarpaulins, steel helmets were hanging on rails near it. The contentment of relief after the sharp encounter possessed all of them.

Then, quite suddenly, the ship quivered.

Palfrey felt it, stared, saw Stefan turn abruptly—and there was a dull roar, an explosion which sent up a great cloud of smoke shot with flame. It came from the bows, Palfrey and Stefan were in the stern, but the percussion sent them heavily to the deck and hardly a man kept his feet.

Too surprised to be afraid, Palfrey got unsteadily to his feet. The ship hove to, someone shouted hoarsely. Stefan looked over the side, and Palfrey, following his gaze, saw a torpedo coming towards them. Had the ship been moving it would have crashed into the side, but instead it sped past, leaving a furry, sinister wake. Palfrey watched it, fascinated, but conscious of no fear. It disappeared from sight, but still he watched, hearing the explosion as the torpedo hit the shore, and seeing the rising cloud of smoke with a mingling of yellow flame.

'Come on, Sap!' Stefan cried.

The ship was listing heavily, there was no hope of it keeping afloat. The land, which had seemed so near only seconds before, now seemed an infinite distance away, quite out of reach.

Palfrey said: 'U-boat?'

'It must be,' said Stefan. 'We're leaving the ship.'

The crew had jumped to action at a shout from the bridge. The two men there seemed to be almost at right angles to the water, obviously finding it hard to keep a foothold. Palfrey and Stefan moved unsteadily towards one of the boats in the davits, where men were busy, and winches were turning. Palfrey kept looking seawards, searching for the periscope of the U-boat which had caught them. He could not see it, but he saw another torpedo coming; it went far astern. It was bad shooting at a sitting bird.

'Hurry!' Stefan urged.

'Yes,' said Palfrey. He was surprised to see his case clutched in the hand of one of the sailors. Stefan was donning a lifebelt, and Palfrey wondered why he had been fool enough not to bring his up on deck. The man carrying his case had it; he put it on.

Water was already lapping over the bows.

They climbed into the lifeboat, two dozen men in all, and another dozen clambered into a smaller boat near the stern. The gun crew remained at its post, tight-lipped. Palfrey, still searching those calm waters, which seemed too innocent to harbour death, suddenly exclaimed:

'There she is!'

Slowly, almost majestically, the bows of the U-boat rose out of the sea, water spilling from it in a smooth torrent. Men appeared as soon as it was afloat, and the hatches came off guns and machine-guns. The lifeboat was between the submarine and the ship itself, and although the men bent to the oars, all scowling and grim, there was no protection from fire. But the ship's gun began to fire steadily, and scored a hit, scattering the crew of a machine-gun. The larger guns of the U-boat opened fire, not at the ship but at the lifeboat. Shells fell short, hitting the water with an ominous *plop-plop-plop*.

'We'll have to swim for it,' Palfrey said. It did not occur to him that he had been far more worried by the aircraft, although the chances of being hit by bombs had been much smaller.

'Yes,' said Stefan. 'Be ready, Sap.'

'I'm ready,' said Palfrey.

Instinctively, he ducked when a shell screeched over their heads, and a second and a third followed. The cargo vessel lurched, they felt the pull as it began to settle down and then submerge, stern uppermost. He saw the gun-crew sliding off the decks into the water; the two men on the bridge did not jump. Needless sacrifice, thought Palfrey, they shouldn't stay; but stay they did. The ship turned turtle, its red bottom heaved itself out of the water like a grotesque sea monster. Two or three heads bobbed about, then disappeared in the vortex created by the sinking ship.

A shell fell only a foot or two ahead of the lifeboat.

The U-boat's machine-guns opened fire again and bullets sent a spray of water into Palfrey's face. He heard a splintering sound, and saw holes appear in the side of the boat. He was surprisingly detached, as if it did not affect him personally. The stutter of the machine-guns continued, another series of holes appeared in the boat, close to the water line.

Palfrey grew conscious of a strange emotion—*anger*. It was nothing else, just cold anger that the men on the U-boat could do this thing. It did not matter that it had happened a hundred times before, his anger now was fierce and personal. He could see the faces of the men who were shooting, and he wondered dispassionately how long the boat would stay afloat; there was water in it already.

Stefan said: 'We would be better off if we swam.'

'We'll have to,' said Palfrey.

The first mate, in the boat, spoke sharply.

'Abandon ship,' Stefan said, slowly.

'Yes,' said Palfrey, 'it's high time.'

If he stood up, he would make a better mark for the machine-gunners—the big gun had stopped, since the lifeboat was obviously sinking. Then he saw with some surprise that a small boat—a rubber dinghy—was being sent off from the submarine, with three men aboard. They pulled steadily as man after man dived overboard from the lifeboat. Palfrey took a last, lingering glance, was aware of another small craft, a motor-boat, coming out from the shore. An aircraft flew overhead, and he heard another, fiercer roar of shooting. The submarine's guns turned towards the sky; the immediate danger for him was over, but the dinghy came on.

The boat was sinking rapidly, rising out of the water every time a man jumped overboard, then settling deeper. Palfrey tensed his muscles and jumped, head first. The icy water closed over him, sending a shock through his whole body. He kept eyes closed tightly and did not allow himself to strike out too soon. He felt something scrape over his back and felt a moment of panic; then he found himself above water, and took in a great gulp of air before he went down again. He had seen nothing of what was going on.

The coldness increased; it had a burning effect, and the pressure of the water all about him seemed unbearable. He struck out, making himself move steadily, then broke water again and, by striking out more vigorously, kept himself afloat.

After a while, he was able to look about him and see more clearly. He was in the middle of a sea of heads, there were twenty or more men swimming. The smaller lifeboat was already halfway to the shore; it did not turn back. Palfrey wondered why, for he had expected it to do so; then he realised that it was far better for twelve men to get safely ashore than for all of them to perish. Perish? Odd word.

He was swimming strongly, but his heavy boots made progress difficult. He doubted whether he would have kept afloat but for the lifebelt. Stefan was by his side—Stefan would stay although he was a much more powerful swimmer.

The little dinghy was coming from their right—Palfrey saw it clearly. The men were in German naval uniforms. He saw a young fellow, an officer, staring at the men amongst whom the boat was now sailing.

There was a wild discord of gunfire as the U-boat, the

motor-boat from the shore, and the aircraft engaged in a fierce battle. That fight seemed something alien to Palfrey, not part of his show. He swam mechanically, his mind engaged wholly in thinking of the three men in the little German boat—*why* had it come? Had it not, the submarine could have submerged by now. The purpose of the attack had been served, since the vessel was now on the bottom. So: why, why, why?

The men in the dinghy were *looking* for someone.

The realisation dawned slowly upon him. He saw the officer leaning forward in the bows, passing several men, and speaking sharply. The word reached Palfrey's ear.

'Nein—nein—nein.'

'No, no, no,' echoed Palfrey. 'They haven't found who they're looking for.'

The shore was no more than a mile off, but appeared much further away. The water seemed to get colder. A shivering fit shook him, his teeth hurt as they chattered, and for a while he forgot everything but his own agony. When it had passed, a touch of cramp shot through his right leg, but faded as quickly as it had come; it left him gasping. Vaguely, he heard:

'Nein—nein—nein.'

The gunfire was stronger, perhaps closer, but the little boat with its three occupants nosed among the swimming men, examining each in turn, sometimes drawing a man near with a boathook before the officer said: '*Nein.*' Palfrey, on the fringe of the swimming party, suddenly realised who they were looking for.

He exclaimed: 'Stefan, they're——'

He was about to say, 'looking for us', but the words trailed off, for there was no sign of Stefan, although a minute before he had been swimming strongly by Palfrey's side. In a panic caused by the joint discoveries, Palfrey swam in a a small circle, but could find no trace of the Russian. Perhaps he had been wounded, and been unable to keep up the pace; perhaps he had gone under. 'Damn them!' thought Palfrey, fiercely, 'damn them!'

He tried to swim more swiftly, but the weight of his clothes prevented him. That little boat, easily collapsible, looked very frail, with the officer leaning over the side, staring into the face of the survivors.

'Nein, nein, nein!' he intoned.

Palfrey wanted to turn his back on him, and even tried, before realising the folly of it. He saw one man half-lifted out of the water, stared at, then dropped back. '*Nein.*' He splashed out more vigorously. The dinghy was near enough for him to see the officer's eyes and the gun in his hand. Another man was allowed to fall back. The dinghy drew to within ten feet of Palfrey, he was to be the next victim. He drew a deep breath, and tried to dive, but the effort was too much for him. The dinghy drew nearer, remorselessly. Now he saw that they were using the boathook to drag the men up for inspection, and it groped out towards him. It missed him as, with a sudden violent movement, he sheered away. The officer swore, and raised his gun, the boathook came out again.

Then the dinghy was pushed out of the water.

Palfrey saw it rise, stern first. The officer slipped, and fell overboard with a great splash, the man with the boathook followed him. Palfrey caught a sudden glimpse of the dinghy, almost in mid-air, only its bows touching the water. The man at the paddle had lost control of it, and was sliding down and shouting. The dinghy capsized, now all three of the Germans were in the water. Palfrey grew aware of a strange quiet, not real silence, for there was the gurgle of water, a hissing sound, and the splashing as men swam patiently towards the shore and, further away, the stutter of the motor-boat.

The U-boat was no longer firing.

Palfrey looked over his shoulder, and he thought it was submerging. Then the quiet was broken as depth-charges went up, sank, and exploded.

He turned his head.

With a sudden rush of excitement he saw Stefan swimming near the upturned dinghy, to which two men were clinging, including the Nazi officer. Stefan had swum under water, to upset the little craft!

'Stefan!' croaked Palfrey.

Stefan might have heard him; he smiled and then turned towards the dinghy. The officer had lost his gun and most of his arrogance, and was clutching the little ship with both hands. As Stefan reached him, the dull boom of the depth-charges seemed further away.

Keeping afloat without trouble, Stefan used one hand to prise the officer's fingers from the dinghy. There was a short, sharp struggle. The man swallowed water, released his hold, then bobbed up again on the swell. Stefan, using his other hand, struck him beneath the jaw; what the devil *was* he doing? It was not like Stefan to take revenge, even on such a man. Yet the officer was unconscious, and sank helplessly into the water.

Stefan did not let him go, but gradually manœuvred until he was swimming on his back, towards the shore, still supporting the German. It was an incredible business, and Palfrey could see no sense in it. He was amazed at the speed with which Stefan moved, the Russian seemed to be overtaking even those who had obtained a good start.

They were much nearer the shore, for the tide was taking them in. Palfrey made a great effort but just then a wave swamped him, and he swallowed a mouthful of icy salt water. He retched, bringing it up, and felt momentarily exhausted. He grew aware of the motor-boat, coming towards him, and the others. It hove to, and began to pick up some of the survivors, but Stefan ignored its approach and continued to swim, powerfully and rhythmically, towards the shore. Palfrey tried to follow but could not make such speed; Stefan rapidly out-distanced him.

Another twinge of cramp made Palfrey cry aloud.

He gave up all idea of getting to the shore under his own power, the main question was whether he could keep afloat long enough to be hauled aboard the Nordian patrol vessel. Cramp gripped his leg and his arm, and he stiffened with the pain; then something tugged at him. He felt himself being dragged to the side of a boat. He was lifted aboard, not gently but with rough certainty, and his knees doubled under him. He heard rough voices, someone helped him to sit down, and he was propped against the sides of the cabin. He retched, feeling abominably sick, but above it all the thought of Stefan persisted.

Why had he headed for the shore?

Why had he taken the German officer with him?

Waves of nausea came over Palfrey. He tried to retain consciousness, but he slumped forward, with everything blotted from his mind.

      *   •   •   •   •

In a house in Sven, the man with one arm talked to Antonio Gagliani, whose full face was pale and who was bundled up in furs, although the temperature was high for Nordia at that season. Gagliani was frowning, and the one-armed man was staring at him with the blank look characteristic of so many Nazis.

'I have a right to know,' Gagliani said, 'I helped to make it possible, it is not right that——'

'I am only passing on my instructions,' said the one-armed man, 'I will also pass on your protest, but I do not wish to be worried by this matter at the moment.' He stood up from a desk and paced the room, restlessly. 'Word should soon come,' he said, 'they are a long time.'

'You have nothing to worry about,' Gagliani told him, 'we heard the explosion, and the ship was seen to sink.'

'Palfrey and Andromovitch were not seen to die,' said the one-armed man, sharply. 'I shall not be satisfied until all of them are dead.' He snapped his fingers sharply. 'They have the luck of the devil! I cannot understand how they have got so far, they should never have been allowed to leave Moscow.'

The telephone rang and the one-armed man swung round to it, as Gagliani stared at him, his eyes smouldering.

'Yes, yes!' he said. 'What . . . you are *sure*?' He drew in his breath, then spoke with a harsh, menacing voice, rating his caller and impressing even Gagliani with the variety of his epithets. He delivered a final obscenity, then hung up and turned to the Italian. 'Palfrey is being brought ashore—so much for your assurances! Send Gregarov here at once!'

Gagliani went out, slamming the door. The German stared at the wall, without moving, until a well-built, well-dressed man entered the room and smiled into his face.

'What is funny?' rasped the one-armed man. 'Listen to me! Palfrey is coming ashore, he must be made harmless. See that it is done.'

'I will handle Dr. Palfrey,' said Gregarov, confidently.

'If you do, you will succeed where many have failed,' said the one-armed man. 'Have him killed——'

'But my friend,' said Gregarov, 'why is that necessary? I can take him to my home, he will have every confidence in me and I shall be able to find out whether he knows anything worthwhile. Surely that will serve our purpose best?'

'If it can be done, yes, but take no chances.' The German waved dismissal, but as Gregarov reached the door, spoke again. 'Wait!'

The door opened and Gagliani came in, but the one-armed man ignored him.

'There is a woman just arrived, they say, from France,' he told Gregarov. 'She is an actress, and is appearing with the Repertory Company. The Company is suspected of harbouring English agents. This woman must be interrogated.'

'Her name?' asked Gregarov.

'She calls herself Madame de Casson. In appearance, she is not unlike Palfrey's fiancée, an Englishwoman named Blair. Blair was in England until two days ago, so it is not likely to be her, but you will make sure.' His thin lips twisted in a sardonic smile. 'It will suit you, Gregarov, she is very beautiful.'

'I shall do my duty,' Gregarov said, formally.

'Do what you will with her, but first make sure she is not one of Palfrey's people,' said the one-armed man.

Gregarov bowed and went out; there was an ugly glint in his eyes, like that in Gagliani's, who stared at the German without speaking.

'Well?' snapped the one-armed man, 'I thought I told you that you were not wanted.'

'I thought I would remind you that I will not be fooled with,' said Gagliani, harshly. 'Remember that I know a great deal, a *very* great deal. This is not Nazi Germany, you cannot——'

The other looked as if he would fly into a rage, but after a tense moment he relaxed, rounded the desk, and rested his hand on Gagliani's shoulder.

'My friend, I am rude to you too often— I apologise! It is a trying time, and I am haunted by this Palfrey and his friends. But you have no need to worry, Gagliani, your services are greatly appreciated. I cannot tell you what you want to know until I have permission, but it will soon be forthcoming. As for what you know—only those who can be trusted know so much, my friend! You have our full trust! You know——' he paused, his expression altered, became malignant, and when he went on it was in an evil voice. 'You know, my friend, what will happen if Palfrey should find us, don't you? You know what revenge we shall take. There are moments when I hope he does find us, when I hope that he will let loose the flood of——'

He stopped abruptly, and turned away.

'He will not find us! You and all the others will be loyal. We are planning a great triumph here, in Nordia, you know all about that. It will make the fools laugh on the other side of their faces. It was I who first thought of Nordia, I who saw how the country could be made to work with us. You are in the presence of a great man, Gagliani, a very great man! Now, be good enough to leave me, I have work to do.'

14: Palfrey Arrives in Nordia

The boat bumped against a quayside. Palfrey saw some motor-ambulances waiting near a crowd of people, mostly fishermen. Stretchers were carried to the edge of the quay, and as most of the men in the boat were unconscious, they were lifted on to them. There was a mobile canteen nearby, where a woman was serving something hot. '*Hot*,' thought Palfrey, and shivered.

Palfrey swayed, but was able to put his feet forward. He was helped to the quayside, where the woman proffered him a cup. The smell was delicious—it was meat soup of some kind. He took it gratefully, smiled, and sipped.

A horse-and-cart clattered up.

Palfrey watched it as the little woman told him that it would take him to the hospital. Palfrey stared, caught the word 'hospital,' and shook his head. She laughed, and gave him a friendly shove.

'To hospital in a horse-and-cart,' thought Palfrey, 'at least it's a new experience.'

It was cold, and the Russians huddled together; one man's teeth began to chatter.

They looked sturdy, and he wondered why they did not talk among themselves, until he realised that they were keeping silent out of respect for their privileged passenger. He forced a smile, and spoke in English. They shook their heads, but there was an easing of the tension. The cart jogged along to the rhythmic 'clip-clip-clip' of the horse's hooves.

The cart reached a narrow road on the outskirts of Sven, and the horse dragged up a hill, until they came to a standstill outside a long, low building. The grounds were tidy, shrubs and conifers and very bright grass were tended like a child's garden. Two ambulances were still outside the front door—presumably the authorities could only spare petrol for the more urgent causes.

They were helped down, and walked into the hospital, where smiling nurses greeted them. The marked friendliness towards the Russians was significant, for Nordia had leaned towards America and England but, in pre-war days, had acted more like the Finns towards the Soviet.

They were taken to a rest-room, not a ward, and offered chairs and camp-beds. There was a roaring log-fire, cigarettes and tobacco and more soup. Palfrey was pleasantly surprised at the comfort and the consideration given to rescued seamen.

In some queer way he enjoyed the quiet hour that followed.

The door opened, making the fire roar. Two men entered, the first a thick-set fellow in a white smock; the second had a familiar face which made Palfrey stiffen.

It was the unprepossessing Laski, whom Palfrey remembered as one of his 'shadows' in Moscow.

'This is the man I wish to take,' he said.

'If you insist,' said the doctor, distantly; apparently he had no liking for Laski. 'He would be better off here for the rest of the day and night.'

'He will be well-cared for,' Laski said. There seemed to be a Satyric quality about his grin, although Palfrey told himself not to be a fool.

'You will be glad to come?' Laski asked him, in broken English.

'Yes, of course,' Palfrey said. He could not put much feeling into his words, but he must have sounded convincing, for the doctor shrugged, Laski grinned again and, after Palfrey had smiled and waved farewell to the Russians, he followed the doctor and Laski out of the room. They went to a small office, where the doctor, grave-faced, looked into Palfrey's eyes and said, also in broken English:

'You understand, please, that you do not haff to go. If you prefer to stay here, not go to Russia—you are at liberty. Please understand that.'

'I am grateful,' Palfrey said, 'but I shall be with friends.'

'You are a very lucky man,' the doctor said, 'that was a bad business.'

'Lucky in more ways than one,' Palfrey said, 'I wish I could find a better way of saying "thank you," but——'

'Nonsense! We are always glad to do what we can to help, it is humane, that is all. The English are not unknown for their kindness!'

The doctor shook hands with him, then pressed a bell-push.

An orderly came and led them from the office, along the white, clean-smelling passages of the hospital, out into the drive. There to Palfrey's surprise, was a small car; it had the badge of the Russian Embassy on the bumper. Laski opened a door, waited for Palfrey to get in, then got in himself on the other side and let in the clutch.

He drove for a while without speaking. Then:
'You understand my English?'
'Very well,' said Palfrey, mechanically.
'Thank you. Where is Andromovitch?'
'I last saw him swimming.'
'He was not dead.'
'He was not!' Palfrey said, warmly.
'It would take much to kill Andromovitch! So, the Nazis' —he pronounced the word 'Nazzis'—'failed once more. It is very good.'
'Not for some of the crew,' Palfrey said.

The man ignored the remark and took the road which led up hill, and Palfrey could see Sven spreading out in front of him. It was a city of nearly half a million inhabitants, housing almost a third of the population of Nordia. The buildings were mostly white, although there were some coloured roofs and some of the walls seemed to be yellow. It lay on either side of the fjord which, now that the sun was high, looked blue and friendly; the choppy water had become a gentle, sparkling swell. He could see the port, congested with shipping, but everything appeared to be in miniature. He noticed one large spire, much higher than any of the others.

They drove through squalid streets lined by wooden houses, where the sight of the car was so unusual that people stood and stared and children ran out into the road to gaze.

At last they left the mean streets and reached a district where there were large houses, standing in their own grounds. Shrubs, trees and grass, with some colourful poppies, many of them already fading, were on all sides.

Laski slowed down and turned into the drive-way of a house with blue tiles, a square building which had a certain prim charm, the appeal of clear line, white walls and blue paintwork.

The door was opened by a maidservant.

Laski waited in the hall, as if for instructions. A man came hurrying forward, a large, well-built fellow who wore his dark clothes well. He was black-haired and his cheeks were reddish, the bones high—he looked more Slav than Stefan, although there was a vague similarity between the two men.

In excellent English, he said:

'I am delighted to see you, Dr. Palfrey!' When he shook hands, his grip was powerful. 'When I heard that the ship had been sunk, I was afraid that you would be drowned.'

'Thanks to Andromovitch, I'm alive,' said Palfrey.

'And he?'

'I think he is,' said Palfrey, and told the man where he had last seen Stefan.

'Now you have come, you must have some decent clothes,' his host said, 'and food—you will require it! There is not much that you can do this evening, you will be well advised to relax, my friend.'

'Ye-es,' said Palfrey. 'May I know who you are?'

'Of course, how foolish of me! I am Maxim Gregarov, and I am known here as a Russian merchant!' He laughed. 'Only for special occasions do I open my house to friends like you, Dr. Palfrey, but the emergency was obviously great.' He talked as he led Palfrey up the stairs to a small bedroom.

'You would like to bath?' he asked.

'I don't think so,' said Palfrey.

'You have had plenty of water! Doctor, I will have clothes sent to you, and a razor—you will, I am sure, wish to shave. Meanwhile, I will have inquiries made for Andromovitch, I hope very much that he will have arrived. I am waiting to hear from him exactly what you want me to do. Unless you would care to tell me——' he broke off, hopefully.

'He knew the instructions, I didn't,' Palfrey said, truthfully.

'Of course, he would have them. I will have to go into the town to make inquiries,' Gregarov said, 'and I will take Laski with me, but my wife will entertain you.'

Palfrey smiled. 'Please don't put anyone out.'

'It will be her pleasure! I, then, must leave you,' went on Gregarov, 'I will be no longer than I can help.'

Palfrey watched the door close, then looked at himself in a mirror on a white-wood dressing-table. His forehead was wrinkled, as if expressing the vague uncertainty in his mind. The roundabout drive, Laski's half-successful effort to be genial and the bluff friendliness of Gregarov, should have struck a note of confidence, yet he disliked the smiling Russian just as he disliked Laski. Relief at seeing a familiar face had quite gone. 'Dislike' was right, 'distrust' was too ominous.

A servant brought him a suit of clothes, of heavy blue serge. With it were good quality woollen underclothes, socks, a shirt—white with a collar attached—and a packet of English cigarettes and a box of matches. Palfrey lit a cigarette gratefully, donned the underclothes and was glad of their warmth, then shaved and washed before dressing. The suit was a reasonable fit.

The house was very quiet, and he had just finished when he saw the handle of the door turning.

He had heard nothing to warn him that anyone was approaching. He stood tense, staring at the handle. It continued to turn, very furtively, and there was a faint click before the door began to open. A foot came through—slim and narrow, a woman's foot, quite bare and very white. The hem of a long white dress showed—a night-dress. Who the devil was there?

'Stop!' He heard a man's voice, in Nordian. It was pitched on a high note, almost one of fear. 'Stop!'

The foot was withdrawn. Palfrey heard a gasp, followed by heavy footsteps and rough voices; the door was closed sharply.

No more than five minutes had elapsed before there was a tap at the door.

'Come in!' he called, forcing a smile.

The door opened at once, and a woman appeared. She was tall, almost statuesque, a lovely creature, prepossessing enough to impress Palfrey. She was fair-haired, not beautiful, perhaps, but with a superb complexion, and blue eyes which were smiling a welcome; about her neck was a single rope of pearls.

She smiled more widely; there was a glowing vitality about her, a marked contrast to the brittle geniality of Gregarov. He smiled in turn, and she held out her hand, taking his; the pressure of her fingers lingered.

'I am Ingrid Gregarov, doctor,' she said. 'I have been so impatient to meet you that I could wait no longer.'

She closed the door and leaned against it.

15: The Lovely Wife of Maxim Gregarov

Palfrey regarded her steadily, smiling faintly and smoothing the wispy hair at the sides of his head. *Why* was Gregarov's wife standing with her back to the door and smiling like that? *Was* it a seductive smile? Palfrey was inclined to think that it held a hint of mockery, as if she were amused at what she was doing, and found in him a source of malicious entertainment.

'Well,' thought Palfrey, briskly, 'it's something to be entertaining!'

He became more troubled about this house and Gregarov and Laski. Whatever game the woman wished to play, he would join in wholeheartedly—with reservations! He smiled more widely.

'You do not look like a man who has been rescued from the sea,' said Ingrid Gregarov.

'What do men look like when they've been rescued?' asked Palfrey, amiably. 'Especially when they've fallen on their feet——' he paused, but she looked as if she understood the colloquialism, it was a help that her English was good.

'Madame Gregarov, I was really startled just now!' He smiled.

'Were you?' she asked.

'Yes.' Palfrey laughed. 'I saw the handle of my door turning, and someone started to come in—a bare-footed woman, I think! I almost thought I was suffering from hallucinations!'

'I can relieve your mind, Doctor, it was not a delusion. My sister has been ill; she *does* suffer from hallucinations.'

'Oh,' said Palfrey, and mumbled: 'I'm sorry.'

'She is recovering,' said Ingrid Gregarov, 'but her nurse was foolish enough to leave her untended, and we are told that she must have absolute rest and quiet for another week or more. He called to her—perhaps you heard him?'

'Oh, yes,' said Palfrey.

'If you stay long, you will have the pleasure of meeting her,' said the woman, lightly, 'she is very beautiful.'

'Like her sister,' said Palfrey.

She smiled. 'That is kind of you.'

'I am so glad you have come,' she said, straightening up. 'But why am I talking to you here? You will be hungry, and dinner is ready—or nearly so. Let us go down,' she added, stretching out a hand.

Palfrey touched it, she slipped her arm through his, and he opened the door, and they went downstairs.

The story of her sister struck him as being particularly weak; on the other hand, she had told him it almost casually, making no effort to impress him. The promise that he should meet the sister had been a convincing touch.

The wide, richly-carpeted, wooden staircase, the panelled walls, hung with a few excellent water-colours, and the heavy furnishings, all created an impression of wealth. The hall was large, and it struck warm; it was obviously centrally heated. She led him to a room near the front door, and he entered a large drawing-room, exquisitely appointed in modern style; the carpet was cream-coloured, the colour *motif* of the room red and cream, with red predominating. Often, the effect would have been a failure, but here it was brilliantly successful. The room was warm, and a log fire burned brightly in the wide fireplace at one end, shining on warm red tiles.

A settee was drawn up on one side of the fire, and there was a single standard lamp burning behind the settee.

'What would you like?' she asked.

'*Is* there sherry?'

'Of course,' she said. She picked up a bottle of *Amontillado,* and two glasses.

Palfrey took the bottle, and their hands touched; hers were cool, long, and slim. They touched again when he took the glasses. He handed her a glass, and raised his own. 'To the success of my visit,' he said.

'Success!' echoed the woman. 'Have you been to Nordia before?' she asked.

'I've looked in,' Palfrey said, 'obviously I didn't stay long enough!'

'It is a pity that you are going to be so fully occupied,' she said. 'I would have liked to show you Sven, it is a wonderful city and too many people think of it only as a fishing port. Absurd! Doctor—do *you* think Bruckner is in Nordia?'

The question absolutely took him by surprise. He stared at her blankly, his heart beating a trifle faster, and then mumbled:

'There has been talk of it, hasn't there?'

'Oh, talk!'

'Just as well to make sure that that's all it is,' said Palfrey. 'I don't know much about it. I wouldn't be surprised to learn that it's only rumour, but even if he were here, I think the search for him is rather extravagant.'

'*Extravagant!*'

'Yes. Oh, don't misunderstand me, I know we must find the fellow, but it's hardly worth bringing Andromovitch and me to Nordia.' He sounded gloomy.

'What of the others?' she asked more sharply.

'Others?' queried Palfrey.

'Zukmayer and Schlessing?'

'*If* all three of them are together, it would make a difference,' conceded Palfrey, 'but three men supposed to be dead and suddenly turning up—doesn't it strike you as being rather fantastic?'

'Does Andromovitch think like you?'

'Stefan? No,' said Palfrey, 'oh no, he's very keen! Perhaps he feels more deeply than I do. Don't misunderstand me,' he repeated, hastily, 'I shall do everything I can to see the thing through, and if we catch Bruckner——'

'It will be difficult to get him out of Nordia,' she said, 'especially if the Nordian authorities know that he's here.'

Palfrey stared: 'What's that?'

'Especially if his presence is known to the Nordian authorities,' repeated Ingrid Gregarov, deliberately. 'You did not think the Nordian Government might be concerned?'

'I didn't think the Stething would play false,' said Palfrey.

'Although the Stething is based on your House of Commons, Doctor, that does not mean that the system operates as well as it does in England,' she said. 'Three or four men control this country. I am glad that I am a Russian!'

Palfrey looked surprised. 'Are you Russian?'

'Oh, I was born Nordian,' she said, 'but when I married Maxim Gregarov I took on Russian nationality, which has been approved in Moscow, so I am a good comrade! You understand?' She laughed, reminding him of Madame Crikov with her ironical use of 'comrade'. 'The politics of Nordia are not what they might be, it is the result of being so powerless, squeezed between strong neighbours, but—' she shrugged. 'It is worrying.'

'Whom do you suspect in the Government?' asked Palfrey, lightly.

'The Premier, perhaps; the Foreign Minister, certainly.' She spoke with feeling, but did not mention their names. Palfrey knew that Gunda Erikson was the Prime Minister of Nordia, and Gustav Horst the Foreign Minister; he had always thought them to be men of integrity and knew that they were respected in London. Was London wrong?

He was glad when the maid entered and announced dinner.

It was served in a small room across the hall. Wall-lighting gave a soft, seductive glow to the oak-panelled room. The long table was set for two, with small lace mats, so that the light reflected from the polished table, which stood on a cream, star-shaped carpet.

After an excellent dinner they returned to the lounge and sat together on the settee. The fire had been piled high with logs, which were just catching alight, and the heat made Palfrey move back a little. It also made Ingrid's nose a little shiny, an oddly human touch. She said little; he felt that she was on the alert for something outside.

In another room, a clock struck nine.

She did not revive the subject of Bruckner or the possibility of Nordian complicity in Bruckner's plans. Something he had said, or some thought that had struck her, seemed to have made her jumpy. She pretended to be enjoying the warmth of the fire, but now and again he saw her glancing towards the door. Once, she caught her breath. The tension increased, and Palfrey found it difficult to pretend that he was enjoying the relaxation.

He was so much on edge that when a telephone rang it made him jump. He could not see the instrument, but Ingrid rose quickly, as if this were what she had expected. She spoke in Nordian, giving her name, and listened intently, looking at the door all the time. Then she said quickly:

'Yes, I will come.' She replaced the receiver and looked at Palfrey, trying to pretend that she was regretful, but obviously relieved. 'I must leave you for a little while,' she said, 'my sister is asking for me. I will not be long, I hope. You will not mind?' She pointed to a table on which were several magazines. 'They will amuse you.'

'I shall be perfectly all right,' Palfrey stood up and stepped across the room, opening the door.

He could not resist standing and watching her walk up the stairs before returning to the settee.

He heard a faint sound by the door when Ingrid had been gone for half an hour, but the door did not open. He jumped up, looking at it; the noise continued, and he was reminded of the scratching of Amata's cot.

Then he saw an envelope being pushed beneath the door.

He saw it sliding over the carpet; there was hardly room for it, because the carpet was flush against the bottom of the door. He resisted the temptation to find out who was there, and waited until the envelope stopped moving. There was a faint sound, perhaps a footstep. Only then did he turn the handle.

The door was locked!

His heart began to beat fast; there was no doubt it had been locked on the outside, accounting for the sound.

He smiled wryly, quite certain that Ingrid's summons to her 'sister' had been an excuse to get away. The door was locked as a precaution, to prevent him from trying to follow her.

He bent down and picked up the envelope, which was plain and sealed. He slit it open with his forefinger, and unfolded a single sheet of note-paper. The lettering was carefully done, almost like a child's hand. The words were in Nordian, a single sentence which read: '*Do not trust anyone in this house, least of all the Gregarovs.*'

After examining it more closely, Palfrey screwed up the note with the envelope, and tossed it on the fire. The flames were so fierce that the paper uncurled at once, and then began to swell and blacken. Sparks flew from it up the chimney.

The note purported to confirm all that he had suspected; one of the servants might have slipped it beneath the door, one who knew something of the treachery, but was afraid to come into the open. The brooding atmosphere of suspicion and danger thickened.

The last trace of dark paper ash disappeared.

The woman had been away for nearly an hour when he tried the door again, to find it still locked.

After a while, he heard the sound of a car-engine.

It came from near at hand, and he thought the car passed the window. He stepped to the window quickly, and pulled aside the curtains; the rear light of a car was disappearing down the drive.

'Enough!' he said, aloud. 'I'm getting out!'

He stepped to the door, but hesitated; he could not force the lock back without an instrument. Before searching for something that would serve, he tried the handle again.

The door opened.

He drew back, then smiled wryly; they were not fools. He wasted no time, but hurried towards the stairs.

He reached the door of a room, and it opened at a touch; it was as if he had suddenly come upon the *open sesame*. He pushed the door open a couple of inches; the room was in darkness. He widened the opening and groped for a light-switch, found it—and looked into the empty room.

It was larger than his own, charmingly furnished, with a divan bed against one wall. There was a faint perfume in the room, but no other sign that it had been occupied. Then, on the floor, he saw something white; he retrieved it, to find a handkerchief, damp, but not otherwise soiled.

Worked in white in one corner was a monogram which he

could not make out at first; it was small, the needlework exquisite, and the design puzzling. He took it nearer to the light. '"M",' he murmured. 'What's the other letter? "M"—"M.G."! My oath! It's Madalena's!'

He smoothed down his hair, looking about the room, alert for any sound. The bare foot was explained, and much of the mystery with it. Madalena Gagliani had been in the room, a captive—a 'sister' to Ingrid! He did not seriously consider the possibility that the 'G' might stand for a 'Gregarov'.

He turned hastily and switched off the light, closed the door softly, and stepped across to his own bedroom. No one appeared to be about. He went in, locked the door and examined the handkerchief again; there was no possible doubt about the initials. The sooner it was destroyed, the better.

'More for the fire,' he murmured.

He screwed it up and thrust it into his pocket before going downstairs. Although all the lights were on, he saw no one. He was fingering the handkerchief in his pocket, ready to toss it into the fire. As he entered the lounge he was about to take it out, but he stopped abruptly—for standing with his back to the fire was an unknown little man.

With a questioning smile, Palfrey went forward.

'Good evening,' said the little man, in fair English. 'Have I the pleasure of meeting Dr. Palfrey?'

'I am Palfrey,' Palfrey said.

'I must apologise, sir, if I alarmed you.'

'Oh, not a bit,' said Palfrey, tucking the handkerchief deep into his pocket.

'I am Sylva,' the little man declared.

'Indeed,' said Palfrey.

'Ingrid Gregarov is my daughter. She perhaps mentioned me.'

'I believe she did,' said Palfrey, mendaciously.

This was such a strange little man, bearded and pale. He looked weary—no, dreary was the word—as if the life had been drained out of him, and the very effort of speech was excessive. He had not the slightest resemblance to Ingrid Gregarov.

'She asked me to apologise,' said Sylva.

'For what?' asked Palfrey, amiably.

'Her hurried departure and the fact that she left you alone for so long,' said Sylva, 'it was a most unfortunate necessity, my daughter has many worries.'

'I'm sorry about that,' said Palfrey, politely, wondering what this visit implied. Could such a faded little creature be a party to the activities of Gregarov? He seemed too tired, too worn out, to be capable of even the most mild deceptions. Even his voice was monotonous and tired.

'Gregarov!' cried Sylva suddenly. 'Twice married, twice divorced. And she married him! Now—look at what is happening! And she laughs at him. Laughs! But at heart she is troubled. She is the blood of my blood, the flesh of my flesh. Her heart is heavy, but she is very brave. Woman after woman! Always a new *amour*, it would break the heart of a saint! Only yesterday, another,' cried Sylva, 'she should be told.' He looked at Palfrey with a curiously hopeful yet cunning glance.

Palfrey kept silent.

'She will not listen to me,' went on Sylva. 'And yet there are times when I think, perhaps, she knows the truth. It should not be necessary for her to spend two hours at the hospital, with Bertha. Should it, sir?'

'Perhaps not,' conceded Palfrey.

'I am glad you agree.'

The man *was* unbalanced.

'Perhaps she has gone to the ballet,' Sylva said.

Palfrey's mind stopped groping, he straightened up, hoping that the man did not notice the sudden quickening of his interest.

'There is a ballerina,' Sylva said, his lips twisted in disgust, 'a scraggy creature, all bone and sinew! And, also, another *inamorata*, whom he met yesterday. The ballerina, only the day before. What would you do, sir?'

'Most difficult,' said Palfrey, reluctantly, but still intrigued. 'The ballet——'

'From Russia, of course.'

'Has it been here long?' asked Palfrey.

'The new one came but two days ago,' said Sylva. 'And that bony creature—of the other woman, I would not say so much. One can admire her. But a Russian ballerina, fifty years old at least.'

'Difficult,' repeated Palfrey.

'You are most understanding, sir,' said Sylva. He smiled for the first time, showing a set of even false teeth, a little too large, making his mouth look like a miniature piano. 'And I have been most rude—family matters to a stranger.'

'Perfectly all right,' said Palfrey.

'Thank you, sir.' Sylva looked at his watch, frowned, and murmured as if to himself: 'She should be back; she knows that I do not like being left long on my own. Another drink, sir?'

'No, thanks,' said Palfrey.

'In that case—will you excuse me? I will return shortly, and shall enjoy a further talk.' Sylva bowed and went out.

He walked erect, his shoulders very square; his suit fitted him perfectly. It was grey, and it was difficult to see any difference between its shade and that of his hair. As he disappeared and the door closed, Palfrey smiled meditatively, lit a cigarette, and dropped on to the settee.

The sad, dreary little man had acted the part of a worried father to perfection, but his abrupt conversation had been curious in itself. At first, his English had been stiff and formal, then it had grown much more colloquial, suggesting that he had lived in England for some time.

For the rest—had Sylva given voice to a genuine but repressed hatred of Gregarov, or had that been intended to arouse Palfrey's suspicions? Sylva might have written the note, but been afraid to say so.

It was easy to imagine the handsome Gregarov fancying himself as a Don Juan; yet surely the man had the sense to recognise that his wife was a woman in a thousand?

He stood up, flicked the ash from his cigarette into the fire, and frowned at the window. So much wanted doing, he felt imprisoned. Had Conroy reached Moscow? Was he even in Sven? What of Brian Debenham? And—Stefan?

If Stefan were alive, Laski and Gregarov might find him, but Palfrey had a reassuring belief that Stefan would come out on top.

'While I'm stuck here,' he mused, 'quite the star turn! And not even doing what I could! That handkerchief——'

He took it out of his pocket hastily, finding it still damp. He stepped to the fireplace where the wood had burned down to a fierce red glow, and dropped it in the middle.

'Doctor——'

Ingrid's voice came so suddenly from the door that he jumped. She was looking at the fire, and had certainly seen him drop the handkerchief. She was dressed in furs—a cloak, and a close-fitting hat, drawn over her ears. Her cheeks glowed, her eyes sparkled.

'Why, hallo!' exclaimed Palfrey. He stepped forward and took the cloak from her—it was mink, of fine quality.

'I am really sorry to have left you for so long, but Maxim will soon be back,' she said. 'He will probably have much to tell you.'

'Have you seen him?'

'Yes.'

She sat down, crossing her legs and folding her hands, leaned forward and looked into the glowing logs. The handkerchief had burned away. She sat motionless for several minutes, with Palfrey staring down at her. If their object was to confuse him, they had won hands down.

Footsteps outside and a bell ringing somewhere in the house disturbed her reverie.

'That will be Maxim,' she said. 'You will excuse me?'

'Of course,' said Palfrey.

'The servants leave after dinner,' she said. 'At night, there is usually only my sister's nurse, but my sister has been removed to hospital.'

Ingrid went out and opened the front door. The drawing-room door being ajar, a cold draught of wind swept in, telling Palfrey how bitterly cold it was outside. After a noticeable pause, Ingrid spoke.

'Maxim——'

'It is all right, my dear,' said Gregarov.

'Maxim, you dare to——' Her voice was thick with anger.

'Oh, my lord!' thought Palfrey, 'what is it now?'

'Do not address me like that!' snapped Gregarov. 'There are things I must do. Is Palfrey——' He broke off sharply, probably because he had noticed the other open door. 'Is Dr. Palfrey downstairs?'

'Yes.' Ingrid's voice was harsh, and Palfrey found it easier to believe Sylva's story.

'I will come down shortly,' said Gregarov.

Standing so that he could see into the hall but not be seen, Palfrey heard Gregarov say to someone with him:

'Come!'

Just that, before he moved into sight, with his hand on a woman's arm. She was tall, but not so tall as Ingrid, dark haired, and dressed in furs. Palfrey caught only a glimpse of her profile, but it was more than enough. He stood still, even when Ingrid moved towards the room, and when she pushed the door, it knocked against him.

He was thinking: *'Drusilla! Here!'*

16: Night at the Home of the Gregarovs

When Palfrey retired for the night he half expected to find Drusilla waiting for him, laughed at himself, but still felt buoyed up. He went out, going along the passages in the hope of meeting her and on the pretence of looking for the bathroom, but he had no luck. The fine edge of his excitement began to wear off; Gregarov might have discovered who she was, and have outwitted her—not a nice thought.

He was outside his room when a door slammed.

He turned, hearing a woman's cry, and there was a thud, as if someone had fallen. He hurried towards the sound, which came from another passage, and he had to cross the landing. From it, he saw Ingrid at the foot of the stairs.

The woman called out again; he knew that it was Drusilla.

Ingrid came running up, holding up her dress for greater freedom of movement. Palfrey reached the door of the room from whence the sound was coming. Gregarov's voice was pitched on a low, angry key; Drusilla's—she was talking in French—was higher-pitched and angry.

The voices stopped abruptly, and there was silence until Drusilla called out in fluent French, her voice quivering.

'Who is there? I wish to leave this house at once!'

Gregarov said something in Nordian. The key scraped in the lock, the door opened violently, and Gregarov stood in front of them, glaring. He ignored Ingrid, but rasped at Palfrey:

'What are you doing here?'

'I thought——' began Palfrey.

'You thought! Understand that this is no way to abuse my hospitality!' Gregarov's gaze switched to his wife, whose expression was freezing; if this were acting, it was superb!

'How important your *business* is,' Ingrid said, 'how reliable are——'

'That is enough!' Gregarov pushed past Palfrey and gripped his wife's forearm. 'You will go immediately to your room.' They stared at each other, oblivious of the others. Palfrey tried to see Drusilla, but, as he was pushed against the wall, he could only see a narrow strip of the room.

'Go to your room!' Gregarov repeated, harshly.

'When that woman has left my house, I will go,' said Ingrid.

'You will do as you are told!'

Movements were audible, Drusilla was walking about. The tension increased. With an oath, Gregarov gripped his wife's wrist and led her away; she made no attempt to hang back.

As they turned a corner, Palfrey slipped into the small room.

Drusilla was standing by the foot of the bed, fastening the side of her dress and looking into the mirror, as if she had no idea of Palfrey's presence. Her dark hair was dishevelled, but her reflection in the mirror was a smiling one. Palfrey went nearer, forgetting that his footsteps were inaudible on the carpet. When she saw his reflection she gasped, and swung round.

'Sap!' she cried, incredulously.

'Hush!' exclaimed Palfrey. He put his arms about her in a bear hug which made her gasp. 'This is strictly off the record!' He kissed her and stood back, his eyes shining. 'You've got too much powder on your nose, and——'

'Don't fool!' she said, 'it *is* you!'

'In the flesh, and on the warpath,' Palfrey said, 'but this is no time for private quarrels. I love you!' He kissed her again. 'Are you after Gregarov, or is he after you? Forgive the crudeness, but——'

'Of course I'm after him,' said Drusilla. 'What a situation! I'd no idea that you had got here.'

'I always knew we were working too many angles,' said Palfrey. 'When it comes to playing hide-and-seek among ourselves, it's time to stop. Gregarov thinks you're a scarlet woman?'

'Undoubtedly!' Drusilla said.

'So he mixes his business with pleasure. Poor Ingrid!' Palfrey considered the situation, his ears strained. There was no sound outside. 'Darling, don't go if you can hold on at all, we must have a pow-wow. If the worst comes to the worst, demand retribution! Have you seen Stefan?'

'No.'

'Conroy?'

'He arrived by air this morning. Brian's outside in the grounds, convinced that I've met my match in Gregarov. And I have! But I *can't* stay——'

'Wait for a bit,' Palfrey said, firmly. He kissed her again, eyed her with his head on one side, and added: 'Dr. Palfrey is about to work one of his world-famous miracles! I mean it—stay put, my sweet.'

He hurried out.

There remained the possibility that it was an elaborate trap, but he did not seriously think so. There was grim earnestness about the Gregarovs' mutual animosity. He hurried to his room, hearing voices coming from a room further along his passage. A door was ajar, and Gregarov was saying: 'If you don't get out, I——'

'Never, never!' It was Sylva, his voice much firmer. Palfrey could imagine him standing like a little bantam cock and defying the Russian. 'I will not allow you to mistreat my daughter!'

'Oh, I say! said Palfrey, distressed.

Ingrid was standing by the dressing-table, a statue in blue stone; one of her cheeks was red and angry.

'I'm dreadfully sorry,' Palfrey said, 'but you ought to know. The lady in the other room——'

'Well?' barked Gregarov.

'She isn't well,' said Palfrey. 'As a doctor——' he brushed his hand over his hair, a picture of embarrassment. 'No business of mine, I know, but I think she should stay the night. She wishes to leave, but I have persuaded her not to go yet. It—it might be dangerous.'

'What nonsense is this?' demanded Gregarov.

'Your guest,' said Palfrey. 'As a doctor, I should insist——'

'There is nothing the matter with her!'

'Well, I found her unconscious,' Palfrey said defensively.

Gregarov swung round on Ingrid. 'You——' he began.

'I know that this is extremely embarrassing,' said Palfrey, more firmly, 'I do hope you realise that I dislike intruding, but—she mustn't go. I mean it. Gregarov, do *you* feel all right?'

'*I?*' gasped Gregarov.

Palfrey advanced and the man was so taken aback that he allowed his wrist to be held. Palfrey looked anxious, clucked his tongue and touched the man's eyelid, raising it and peering intently. Gregarov wrenched himself away.

'What the——'

Palfrey looked distressed. 'This is disturbing. I would not have thought—Gregarov, *do* you feel all right?'

'I am perfectly well!'

'I hesitate to give a firm opinion yet,' Palfrey said, distantly, 'there is no reason to cause alarm, but—that sudden faint—the low pulse—the swelling under the armpit. Your pulse is very much below normal. I *strongly* advise you to go to bed immediately, with hot-water bottles. And hot milk—have you any milk?'

'I will have nothing to do with this nonsense!'

'I can only advise,' said Palfrey, still coldly, 'although in fairness to yourself—this excitement doesn't help. I must inform the authorities at once if anyone leaves this house tonight. If I am right, they will have to be told soon anyway. Madame Gregarov, will you permit me?' He stepped forward, felt her pulse, looked at her eyes. '*You* don't seem affected,' he said.

'Affected with what?' screamed Gregarov.

Palfrey said: 'As you insist, I will tell you. At the hospital this afternoon I was told of a case of smallpox in Sven. It is unusual as far north as this, but——'

If they knew the first thing about smallpox they would see through the ruse, but few people did, and it seemed safe. If he could frighten Gregarov into staying in his room for a few hours, he could call it a triumph.

Sylva breathed: 'Smallpox!'

'Mind you, this might be deceptive,' Palfrey said quickly, 'but the swelling under your guest's arm—come, Gregarov, be sensible!'

'Do you *mean* this?' Gregarov demanded in a strangled voice.

'What's got into you?' demanded Palfrey. 'Of course I mean it, you ought to be in bed—I shall be able to tell in a few hours whether I'm right. The symptoms suggest that the incubation period is nearly over, but your appearance later will make it conclusive. Have you any pain beneath either arm-pit?'

Gregarov felt beneath each, gingerly.

'No-o.' He sounded doubtful.

'Good!' said Palfrey. 'A good sign. But there are limits to what I can do; if it is smallpox, I mustn't allow anyone out of the house, it could spread through Sven like a plague. I understand that your guest arrived recently from France, where there has been an outbreak.' When Gregarov did not answer, but stared at him aghast, he went on: 'If your guest leaves, I shall have to make a report in any case, my conscience wouldn't permit me to wait even until I am sure.'

'She must go at once!' The cry came from Sylva, who stepped forward, his lips working. 'Do you understand, she must go at once!'

Palfrey said, coldly: 'If you insist, we must send for an

ambulance. Personally, I recommend that she stays in that room until the morning. By then, we shall know the truth. Vaccination will make all of us immune, we are in no danger. If I am wrong, we'll have done no harm. Get to bed, and I'll look after your guest.'

'The woman——' Sylva began.

'I will look after her,' Palfrey said, brusquely. 'Good man, Gregarov! Madame Gregarov, the hot-water bottles—will you get them?'

She nodded and went out and Sylva followed her. Palfrey hesitated as Gregarov began to untie his tie and loosen his collar. He was pale and frightened, and twice touched his armpits.

Palfrey said: 'Do you know your guest well?'

'No,' growled Gregarov. 'I had to meet her. I was told that she might be an enemy agent.'

'And is she?' Palfrey demanded, sharply.

'No. After half an hour, I knew that it was a mistake, but——' he scowled, 'I had no idea that she might be——'

'How could you guess!' asked Palfrey. 'Now, a friendly warning—don't let yourself get excited tonight. I'll come and give you a run-over when you've been in bed for an hour,' he promised. 'Oh, those arms.' He peered at the armpits, frowning. 'I *think* they're all right.'

He left the room, closing the door, and hurried along to Drusilla's room. Sylva was standing at the foot of the stairs, and called out to him.

'In a moment,' Palfrey said. He hurried to Drusilla, making her rise quickly from a chair. 'Get your clothes off and into bed!' snapped Palfrey. 'You've had fainting fits, you're running a temperature, you've a swelling under your right arm, and you're suspected of suffering from smallpox.' He grinned at her. 'If any one comes in, feign a stupor.'

'Sap——' she began. 'Oh, it doesn't matter, I'll behave!'

'Bless you!' said Palfrey. He stepped to the door and removed the key from the inside, went out and locked the door, slipping the key into his pocket.

After a couple of minutes Ingrid came to tell him that her husband was in bed. She inquired, coldly, about the other patient. Palfrey looked serious, but spoke as reassuringly as he felt he dared. After a while she said good night, and left him, and he waited for half an hour before going up to see Gregarov.

The radiator in the room had been switched on to its full

heat, a small electric fire was burning, and there were four hot-water bottles in the man's bed. He looked as red as a turkey-cock and was perspiring freely.

He sent a long-suffering look at Palfrey.

'How do you feel?' Palfrey asked, formally.

'I—I *am* ill,' said Gregarov. 'I did not realise it, but I *am* ill! Palfrey——'

'I will give you a draft which will help,' said Palfrey, 'there is everything I need in the bathroon. I saw it earlier. I think, if you keep warm, you will be all right.' He smiled, reassuringly. 'It might be only chickenpox, which is quite bad enough in an adult.'

'Spots?' said Gregarov, hoarsely.

'They will come,' Palfrey assured him. 'Let's see your arms.'

He examined them and nodded without speaking; then he went to the bathroom, looked through the medical cabinet, which was well-furbished, and mixed bicarbonate of soda with some mouth-wash and water from the hot tap.

Smiling happily, he went back to Gregarov's room and stood over the man while he drank the noxious mixture down. Gregarov was disinclined to talk, and Palfrey went more leisurely to Drusilla's room, fingering the key in his pocket.

17: A Meeting with Friends

Drusilla's story was simple.

Brett had been fully acquainted with the situation as the Russians saw it, and had received corroborative information from English agents in Nordia. The latter had reported that although Gregarov appeared to be in Moscow's confidence, they suspected him of double-dealing. As Moscow put a lot of trust in the man—Gregarov was the leading Russian resident in Nordia—Brett had sent Drusilla to get in touch with him.

'There is a small repertory theatre in Sven, and several of the actors and officials work for us,' said Drusilla. 'They're not very active—but friends in need and an excellent blind. Ostensibly, I'm a French actress. Gregarov's reputation with the Company is low, and Brett knew that.'

'I'll deal with Brett!' said Palfrey.

'I hadn't been there for three hours before Gregarov was sending me flowers!' said Drusilla.

'How did you get him to bring you here?'

'I was *so* sympathetic,' said Drusilla, 'and he was *so* helpful! Sven is overcrowded. I complained of my lodgings—he told me that his wife would be only too glad to offer me a room. I pretended not to understand Nordian, and his French isn't so good. He had been drinking heavily, and I thought he might be drunk enough to talk. He wasn't, but he's all we think he is.'

Palfrey said: 'You've been snooping?'

'Yes, I took his keys while we were in the taxi—that's why he had to ring. When he went downstairs, I explored and looked in the only locked room I could find,' said Drusilla. She might have been saying that she had gone for a walk. 'It was a study, where there were papers worth a fortune. He's in touch with Berlin—*and* Bruckner!'

Palfrey said: 'This is certainly your day out. Where are they?'

'I left them where I'd found them, after I'd made sure what they were. There was one box I couldn't open.'

'You've still got the keys?'

'No, I left them in the study. I thought——'

'You were right,' Palfrey said, 'you'd done your job. Is the door locked?'

'No. I hoped he'd think he'd left them and forgotten to lock the study,' said Drusilla.

Palfrey moved quickly, glad of the thick carpets. The study door was open; it was a large, barely-furnished room, and very cold. He shivered as he picked up the bunch of keys on the desk.

The desk was of steel; without the keys its three locks would have defied an expert cracksman. Palfrey unlocked it swiftly, pulled out the right-hand drawer and saw a small steel box, next to a file of papers. Apparently Gregarov had no fear of being robbed. In another drawer was an automatic pistol and a clasp knife. Palfrey opened the drum, saw that it was loaded, and slipped both into his pocket. He relocked the desk, left the keys on it, and went out with the booty.

Drusilla was fully dressed, and wearing her furs, when he returned. He led the way to the door, peering carefully into the passage, but the house might have been deserted for all the indications of occupants. He led the way downstairs and to the front door, which was locked, bolted and chained. He unfastened it carefully, opened it—and saw the shadowy figure of a man in the porch.

He stopped, making Drusilla bump into him.

'Stay where you are, Dr. Palfrey,' the man said, in heavily accented English. 'Do not move.'

Palfrey did not, but looked hard at the man; in the light from the hall he saw that it was Laski, and in his hand was an automatic.

Drusilla half turned.

'Stay!' snapped Laski. He stepped forward, making Palfrey back away. Drusilla, ignoring him and moving quickly, exclaimed aloud. At the far end of the hall, standing by the stairs, was Gregarov, who also had a gun.

'How very convenient,' sneered Gregarov, 'and how convincing, Palfrey! Put that case down.'

Palfrey stared at him, heavy-hearted.

'Put it down, I tell you!'

Palfrey dropped the box and papers, and Drusilla moved back to his side.

Gregarov said: 'How unfortunate for you, Doctor! My good friend Laski was in the room next to your lady friend, and heard your conversation.'

'The forgotten risk,' thought Palfrey, dully.

'It is an intriguing situation,' said Gregarov. 'I shall be interested to see how you react now, Doctor! Go upstairs, passing the study which you so thoughtfully left open.'

Palfrey did not move.

'Go upstairs,' repeated Gregarov, but he was smiling widely as he looked first at Palfrey, then at Drusilla. He laughed. 'You have a poor opinion of me, my beautiful, but you will change it, and you will learn that I do not like being disappointed.'

'I——' began Palfrey, but he broke off.

There was no point in talking, and nothing he could do. The only hope was Brian, but when Laski closed the door, he seemed to cut that off.

Palfrey began to move, and, looking up, he saw Ingrid.

She was walking to the head of the stairs, along the landing. Laski saw her and pointed his gun upwards. She started down, and Gregarov spoke sharply, his expression less smug.

'Ingrid, go to your room! Palfrey, I told you——'

'There are three cars coming up the hill,' Ingrid said, coldly, 'and I think they are coming here.'

'Be quiet!' snapped Gregarov. 'Take them upstairs, Laski.'

'Go quickly,' Laski ordered.

As there was no sensible alternative, Palfrey lengthened his stride, walking beside Drusilla. Ingrid returned to the landing, moved aside for them to pass, but paid attention only to her husband. She probably knew who was coming, the air of expectancy touched her as well as the men. They were not fearful, but keyed up with excitement.

'Go to the next staircase,' Laski said, as they passed Ingrid.

Outside, a car stopped, and the whining note of the others ceased. Doors began to slam and footsteps echoed near the house. Obviously, it was a large party.

'Quicker!' Laski snapped.

Palfrey measured the chances of a quick rush to a corner. The main obstacle was Drusilla—he had no way of warning her. His gun felt heavy against his side, tempting him to rashness.

At the foot of a flight of narrow, wooden stairs, the urge to act strengthened. Men's voices floated up, and he thought Laski was trying to hear what they said. He heard the word 'Excellency' several times. A glimpse of the visitors, then escape, would be a triumph; he must try.

'*Sap!*' Drusilla whispered, 'be careful!'

So his expression had betrayed his thoughts. He saw a man at the head of the staircase, a shadowy figure holding a gun; obviously, Drusilla had seen him, too, and he had taken away the last hope of escape. He smiled reassuringly, and with his hand on her arm, they went up steadily, with Laski following behind. There was no stair carpet, and their heels rang out loudly.

The man at the head of the stairs backed away from an open door.

'Go in there, Palfrey,' Laski said.

As Palfrey obeyed, Laski stopped him and with swift efficiency tapped his pockets. He took the gun and the knife. With the same impersonal thoroughness, he searched Drusilla, then looked in her handbag. Satisfied, he pushed them into the room. The door slammed and the key turned in the lock.

Drusilla drew her furs more tightly about her; the small, barely-furnished room struck bitterly cold. There was no window, only two small ventilation holes with iron grills.

The walls were of yellow wood, varnished and speckled with dark knots. There were several upright chairs with rush seats, a long, narrow table and some benches. The walls were bare, and the only thing in keeping with the other rooms of the house was the luxurious cream-coloured carpet.

Palfrey buttoned up his coat.

'If Gregarov were murderously inclined, we would be corpses.'

'Nonsense! He wants——'

'To know what we know, of course,' said Palfrey, 'which means that he prefers us alive and talkative than dead and dumb. Hence, the reprieve. There's an old saying——'

'If you say "while there's life there's hope" I'll scream!' declared Drusilla, half-laughing.

'No scream due,' said Palfrey, 'you said it yourself. About Brian—just what did you arrange between you?'

'He came here ahead of me,' Drusilla said, 'he was at the theatre, and I had a word with him. He was to wait outside until I came out, or until an obvious emergency.'

The handle of the door was turning. He remembered how loud his footsteps had been on the uncarpeted staircase and passage; this surely meant a stealthy approach. Had Ingrid

The door opened and he saw Laski at the side of a tall, well-built, fair-haired man whose eyes looked angry and whose cheeks were red. There was a nasty scratch on his forehead, and the shoulder of his heavy tweed overcoat was torn.

'Oh, Brian!' said Drusilla, in a choky voice.

Laski pushed Brian Debenham into the room and closed the door swiftly. Brian half turned, a hand clenched; he glared at the door, then turned and faced Palfrey and Drusilla.

Then he stepped to an upright chair, pulled it round and sat astraddle, resting his arms on the back, a picture of despair. 'I thought I was sitting pretty. I saw you at the door, Sap, and knew things weren't desperate then. When that little tyke pushed you inside again, I was in two minds whether to go down to the town for Alex and try to get a crowd, but I thought I'd have a stab at it myself. Then the cars arrived.'

'Yes?' said Palfrey.

'I thought I was bright,' said Brian, bitterly. 'It looked a god-sent chance of sneaking in—there were three chauffeurs and several other men, apart from the main party. They went round to the back and I joined up with them, thinking one more in a crowd wouldn't be noticed. I thought I'd got away with it, but they came at me by the back door.'

'Too bad,' said Palfrey, lightly.

'I was crazy!' Brian said. 'I was so darned anxious to get to you that I——' he broke off, in disgust.

'We've been worse off. You don't know who's downstairs, I suppose?' Palfrey asked.

'Men of standing, I gathered,' said Brian. 'There was much kowtowing, and an "Excellency" or two.'

'No names mentioned?'

Brian said: 'No, Sap, except——' he drew his brows together and stared at Palfrey.

'Except what?' asked Palfrey.

'I heard them talking,' Brian said, 'they're Nordian.'

'Or talking in Nordian?'

'Oh, they're natives,' Brian said, confidently, 'and the name of one of them is Gunda. Christian name, I gathered. A short fellow was talking to a lanky one, it looked so odd, even in the darkness, that I couldn't miss it. Colonel Up and Mr. Down,' Brian added, brightening a little.

Palfrey said, thoughtfully:

'Gunda Erikson, I wonder? You've got something, Bry.'

'I don't see——'

'Gunda Erikson is the Prime Minister of Nordia, a tall, thin man. Gustav Horst, the Foreign Minister, short and fat,' Palfrey said. 'I'd been told that they might be involved. The "Excellencies" place these two as men who matter.' He did not say that Ingrid had told him this, it was no time for trying to understand her motives. 'If they're in it, small wonder that Moscow is fidgety!' He coiled hair about his forefinger and went on, as if talking to himself. 'Would the Kremlin get so worked up about a few Nazis who were on the run? There are more important things today, and there will be for a long time to come. The majority will be caught, the others can be hunted down more or less at leisure. Or am I wrong?'

'No,' said Drusilla.

Palfrey said: 'It hasn't rung the bell from the beginning. I've been more intrigued by what I haven't known than by what Brett and others have told me. I mean,' he added, 'if we'd been told to find Bruckner, and left to work it out ourselves, it would have been easy to understand, but it's not been so simple. Individuals mean one thing, a neutral Government still hand-in-glove with the Nazis—or even members of it—is another. Our job is to send news of the two politicians, without relying on unknown quantities. So one of us must get out.'

'I'll open the door,' said Brian, sarcastically.

'One, I said,' said Palfrey, sharply. 'The three of us should be able to kick up enough din to cover the escape of one. If we can pull that off, we ought to be satisfied. Bry, did you make any fuss coming upstairs?'

'I pushed one fellow down,' Brian said, with a faint smile, 'He yelled as if he were going over a cliff. Why?'

'We didn't hear a sound in here,' said Palfrey, 'which is odd.' He tapped the wall by his side; it gave off a sharp sound, and a similar one came when he rapped on the table. Then he approached the door and tried there; the note was duller as was that from the wall on either side of the door.

'We could yell our heads off and not be heard. They're good.'

'How does that help?' asked Brian.

Palfrey laughed, without humour. 'It's not your night out, Bry——' he broke off, peering at the door.

He stopped abruptly.

He had heard no sound, but the handle of the door began to turn again. Brian jumped to his feet, and Drusilla sat rigid.

18: The Broken Conference at Sven

When Brian had come, the door had been thrust open. Now it opened slowly. After what seemed a long time, a hand appeared, followed by the top of a man's head.

Sylva!

The opening widened, and the little man slipped through and closed it, furtively. Much of his dreariness had gone, he looked younger, and there was a gleam of excitement in his watery eyes. When he spoke, it was in a hushed, urgent voice.

'Do not say too much, please. I have come to help you. There is a guard, but he has left for a few minutes. He will be back shortly. Here is a key——' Sylva held one out to Palfrey, who took it but watched the little man warily. 'You must not allow it to be known that I have helped,' Sylva went on, 'but now you can escape. Turn right to the end of this passage, Doctor. There you will find another staircase. Do not go to the foot, but use the window at the first landing. Is that clear?'

'Yes,' said Palfrey, but he was looking for the catch.

Sylva patted his forearm.

'You are a man after my own heart!' he declared. 'I owe you this, Doctor, but I charge you with one thing. If I am killed because of what I am doing, let it be known that I have one purpose, one purpose only—to injure Russia!'

'Come on!' snapped Brian, striding to the door, 'we'll never have another chance like this!'

'Stop!' cried Sylva. There was terror in his eyes as he ran to Brian and clutched at his coat. 'If I should be seen going out with you, they would kill me. I have given you a chance, give me one, also!'

'Hold it, Bry,' said Palfrey.

Sylva shot him a grateful glance as Brian moved back, then he went out swiftly; as the door closed, sound was cut off.

Perhaps five minutes passed before the handle turned, this time going back without a sound.

'The guard's there now,' Brian said, restlessly.

'Maybe,' Palfrey said. 'But there is only one guard. If there's serious trouble we'll meet it later. Are you ready?'

Brian said: 'Yes, the quicker the better.' This was his moment. 'You stand to the right of the door, Drusilla to the left, and keep out of sight of the fellow outside. I'll open the door and duck as I go—no, we can do better! I'll be at knees bend, *you* open the door. As it opens, I'll jump; he won't know what hit him!' There was a new note in his voice.

'It ought to work,' Palfrey said, tensely, and Drusilla and he took up their positions.

Brian squatted on his haunches, hands touching the carpet, as if at the start of a sprint. Palfrey inserted the key and turned the handle cautiously.

He pulled the door open.

Brian launched himself forward. There was a tense second of silence as Palfrey stepped swiftly after him, Drusilla moving at the same time. They heard a gasp, the thud of two bodies meeting, another gasp and a softer thud.

Brian reeled back into the room!

Palfrey stepped hastily to one side, Brian rushed against his legs and fell heavily. A shadow darkened the doorway and a man appeared, bending his head beneath the lintel and rubbing gingerly at his stomach.

After what seemed an age, Palfrey spoke in a faint voice.

'Well, well, so you can swim!'

'Stefan!' cried Drusilla.

The massive figure of Stefan filled the doorway, and the sight of his wide smile put new life into Palfrey.

'I did not expect such a welcome,' he said, soberly, 'and I hope I have not hurt Brian too much.'

'I—*I'm* all right,' gasped Brian, from the floor.

.   .   ,   .   .

A flood of relief surged through Palfrey as he recognised the Russian. Yet at heart, he was not surprised; he had been sure that Stefan had escaped and would turn up again. Since Stefan had presumably been intent on finding how the leakage about their presence on the ship had come about, it was natural that he should discover that Gregarov and Laski were traitors, and so reach this house.

Stefan made no attempt to conceal their presence, obviously he did not mind being seen.

'Shall we explain afterwards, Sap?' he asked.

'You can't explain a miracle,' Palfrey said, 'but you can try to later. Are you on your own?'

'You need not worry at all,' Stefan assured him, 'my men are with me. This floor and the next are occupied by us, only the downstairs is still held by Gregarov. You see——' He pointed towards the door as a man stepped past, a burly fellow who did not even trouble to look into the room. 'A trick for Moscow, Sap!'

'Do you know who's downstairs?'

'I do,' said Stefan, grimly. 'His Excellency the Prime Minister of Nordia and His Excellency the Foreign Minister! That is a disadvantage. We shall have to act carefully, for the Government must not be annoyed.'

'It's still that way?'

'For the time being, yes. They will probably give Gregarov protection——'

Palfrey said: 'Downstairs there are some papers that will prove a bad case against Gregarov, and a tin box which might do more. Don't worry too much.' He smiled. 'But this is your show—just what are you after?'

'What I think we shall find,' said Stefan; 'that is—proof

that high personalities in Nordia are conspiring with Bruckner, Schlessing and Zukmayer, but until that proof has been sent to Moscow and London, until we know whether Horst and Erikson are acting for their own or their country's ends, we must be cautious. The problem is at least as grave as we feared.'

'Should we stay up here?' asked Drusilla.

'We shall be told when things begin to move downstairs,' Stefan said. He thrust his hands into his pockets and stepped into the passage. They followed, and saw the huddled figure of the guard on the floor, with one of Stefan's men standing near him. Farther along the passage, presumably at the head of the secondary staircase, stood a second man. At the foot of the stairs up which Palfrey and Drusilla had walked, there were two armed men.

Stefan held a brief exchange in Russian.

'There is a frightened old man in one bedroom, but otherwise the floor below this one is empty,' he said. 'The study has been searched, and a box was found on the desk—one of steel, the one you mentioned, I expect.'

'It sounds like it. Have you seen Laski?'

'He was the first to fall,' Stefan told him, 'and he has been taken away, for we shall went to talk to him!' There was a bleak smile in his eyes. 'Only residents and guests are downstairs, then; there are no other household servants on duty.'

There was eeriness about the walk downstairs to the hall. Armed men stood at all the corners and outside all the doors, and their footsteps were muffled by the thick carpet.

On the floor by the door was a large suit-case, opened like a large hollow book. A small black cylinder and a mass of intricate wires—it looked like a portable radio transmitter—gave Palfrey some idea of its significance. A wire lead ran up to the key hole of the door. The cylinder was turning slowly, and the machine gave off a faint humming noise.

It was a dictaphone.

One of the guards pressed a switch on the side of the case; a second cylinder began to revolve, obviously there was no more room on the other. The guard took the first off and stored it in a small case, then fitted another in its place. So there was another reason for their secretiveness down here, Palfrey realised; they wanted the conference to go on, so that *everything* said could be recorded! The voices of Horst and Erikson, as well as Gregarov, would be preserved and put to good use.

Palfrey began to smile.

'How long shall we stay here?' Drusilla whispered.

'Until it is over,' said Stefan. 'I hope that we shall be warned in time to make off before they come out of the room. They will know that something is wrong, but they will not know exactly what has happened. Would you prefer to go now?'

'I would not!' said Palfrey.

'Are you just going to pack up and leave?' asked Brian incredulously. 'Why, that mob——'

'We can hardly make a physical attack on their Excellencies!' Stefan said, sardonically. 'We shall take care of Gregarov and his wife afterwards.' There was a bleak note in his voice, and Palfrey felt uneasy, less for Gregarov than for Ingrid. He felt Drusilla's gaze and glanced at her. She smiled, as if she understood his feelings.

An odd situation, Palfrey thought, made stranger by this stealthy raiding party, by the silence from the room, and the perpetual revolving of the cylinders as they collected and stored details, perhaps of a plot which would overthrow a Government.

This was Stefan's show, there was really no point in his staying. Drusilla looked on edge, and he thought she would prefer to leave the whole affair to Stefan's men. Brian was probably feeling a strong sense of anti-climax.

He said: 'You've plenty of men, haven't you?'

'More than enough,' said Stefan, and smiled engagingly, 'but stay if you prefer it, although when the crisis comes we shall have to move very quickly, and you will have to do exactly as you are told.'

'We'll go, I think,' said Palfrey, 'we might just do the wrong thing.'

'I will give you a guide,' Stefan said, with surprising alacrity. 'There is a car further along the road, and you will be driven to the *Hôtel Haaka,* where I will join you later.'

Palfrey smiled. 'Why didn't you say, "get off with you"?'

He turned away, Drusilla followed suit, and although Brian seemed reluctant, he appeared to realise that it was the wise course. At a signal from Stefan, a man joined them at the front door, which Stefan opened.

'I will not be long,' he promised, 'I hope——'

His words were interrupted by a sharp cry from the far end of the hall, near the door they had just left. A *crack* followed, like a pistol shot; a door banged. Stefan swung round and ran towards the sounds, without a word, but with alarm in his expression. It had come so quickly that Palfrey had no time to think.

One of the guards with the dictaphone was lying across the suit-case, and blood was coming from a wound in his head.

Palfrey reached the man as Brian passed him, and, with Stefan, launched himself against the conference room door.

The door did not yield.

A man opened a nearby door. Light streamed from the hall into the grounds, where torches were flashing—they were not only near the house, but also some distance off. Palfrey stood watching. Car headlights were on, revealing trees and shrubs and the hurrying figures of men, in a glaring light.

He thought he saw a tall man, next to another who was short and rotund. The conference had left by another door, or else the windows.

Much was easy to understand now. The suspicions of the people in the room had been aroused, and to distract attention one of them had opened the door, firing at the guard. He must have been a quick thinker, to have done so, and then slammed and locked the door again. The party had broken up in a hurry, and was getting out by another door or by the windows. Palfrey felt sure of Horst and Erikson, but—who had warned them? Where were Stefan's men, who had been patrolling the grounds? Who had switched on the car headlamps? Who held the powerful torches? There were thirty or forty of them, stabbing through the gloom.

A man came hurrying in, as a stab of light outside was followed by the bark of a pistol shot. Palfrey could not hear what the newcomer said, but as he finished, Stefan turned to them. His voice was calm, but it was clear that he was worried, and had been taken by surprise.

'The militia have come, Sap, someone must have got away, to summon them. My men, watching the main window, were attacked. I thought I had everything under control, but I have been outwitted, and the place is surrounded. You must do exactly as I say. We have a plan to meet the emergency.'

He bent down and took off the two cylinders, putting them in the case with the others, while the wounded man was carried out.

Brian picked up the second case.

'We are to keep together,' Stefan said, 'with closed ranks. I cannot insist too strongly on that.'

Brian snapped: 'If they start shooting in earnest——'

'If we split up, some of us will be caught. We must try to force a way through without loss,' said Stefan, simply. 'Drusilla, stand between Brian and Sap, please.' He called out, giving orders; the hall light was switched out, and only a dim glow shone upon the men gradually forming up; most of the headlamps and torches appeared to be at the rear of the house. Stefan went ahead, out of sight.

At a word from Stefan, the line of men started to move forward.

Palfrey tucked Drusilla's arm beneath his. He saw that the militia was now moving towards the front of the house.

The party went faster, with an increasing rhythm; Palfrey could discern Stefan's tall figure outlined against the light from torches and cars, still some distance off. Only the fact that the main opposition had been massed at the wrong side, saved them. There was some sporadic shooting, but no steady fire.

Palfrey saw Stefan turn right, as if into the street, and a moment later he reached the gate. He was running as fast as he could, with Drusilla keeping pace by his side. Brian linked up on the other side and put a hand on her elbow. The shooting grew fiercer, but it was now clear that Stefan had shown good judgment.

Stefan loomed out of the darkness.

'We are all right,' he said, 'the tyres of the cars were punctured, so they cannot follow. This way, Sap, we have the car near.' He led the way across the road, carrying the case with its all-important cylinders, Brian holding on to the dictaphone. They stepped into a side-street, which was little more than an alley.

There were no sounds of pursuit, although lights appeared in the windows of houses on either side.

Stefan slowed down to walking pace as they neared the car.

'I hope all of my men escaped,' he said, gravely, 'but it will be morning before I can be sure. I shall not be happy until I know.'

'We might get an unpleasant surprise when we hear those records,' said Palfrey, 'because that show was very well arranged.'

An uneasy silence followed his words, broken by Stefan telling them what plans he had made for the night.

· · · ·

Just before noon on the following day, Stefan stood at the foot of a double bed in a large room at the *Hôtel Haaka*. On the previous night he had told them only that the hotel was in the centre of the town and that rooms had been reserved for them.

Now Stefan, smiling with evident satisfaction, clean-shaven and wearing a brown suit of excellent cut, stood at the foot of the bed in Palfrey's room and regarded them amiably.

'Yes, every one of my men escaped,' he said, 'there will be no repercussions.'

'Does that mean maybe?' Conroy demanded. He had been restless all the morning, slightly resentful because he had not been with them.

'No, it is certain,' Stefan told him.

'Do they know about the cylinders?' said Palfrey, soberly. 'They were seen at the doorway, I suppose?'

'Yes. When the door opened when you were on the point of leaving, Gregarov saw the case and the guard. There are many very worried men in Sven today.'

'Including us!' said Conroy.

Stefan laughed. 'What is it you say? Doubtful Thomas? No, Alex, we are all right, for now at least. The men whose voices are on those records have to worry. The police and the militia have instructions to search for the cylinders, so we will not keep them here much longer.'

Palfrey asked: 'Is there time to explain?'

'Oh, yes,' said Stefan, 'briefly, at all events. The story of the night's adventure is really very simple—and, of course, it started much earlier than last night. You saw that I had a prisoner with me when I left you after the ship went down?' His eyes were gleaming.

'So you got the U-boat officer ashore?'

'Yes. It was clear that he was looking for certain individuals, and it could only have been for you and me, Sap, so I knew that the U-boat's crew was aware that we were on board.'

'I'd got that far,' admitted Palfrey.

'There had been, then, a grievous leakage of information. I thought that the U-boat officer could name the traitor. Under pressure, the man talked freely and described his informant well enough for me to recognise him at once— Laski, of course. Laski had been working on this assignment for some time, and was in regular communication with Gregarov, our most influential agent here. So inquiries were made about Gregarov's treachery, and reasonable proof was obtained.'

After Stefan had explained his campaign of the previous night. Palfrey asked, 'Dare we venture a walk?' He was looking out of the window, at a fountain playing in a charming little park at the back of the hotel.

'Go out with Drusilla if you must!' Stefan said, laughing, 'there is no need for you to stay indoors. Gregarov knows you are in Sven, so there is, perhaps, some danger, but'—his smile was positively Machiavellian—'I will send someone to watch you, have no fear! Where will you go?'

'There *are* English agents in Sven!' Palfrey said.

He took Drusilla's arm and hurried her across a wide road, then along several of the main boulevards, slipping into shops which had entrances in two streets, walking through department stores which still had a fair variety of goods on display. After twenty minutes, they reached the big square in the centre of the city, where Palfrey said:

'I don't think our shadow feels so good, my sweet! He hasn't been in sight for a quarter of an hour.'

'It would be a help if you were to tell me what you hope to learn from Cardyce,' Drusilla said, dryly.

'If nothing else, he can send word to Brett for us,' said Palfrey.

When he had last been in Nordia, he had visited Cardyce at his exclusive dress shop in the heart of the Sven West End. Palfrey remembered him as a tall, unctuous individual, with a dozen counterparts in Paris, but also a shewd, reliable fellow.

There were three models in the front window of the shop and seven assistants inside. The room was narrow, but had a high ceiling, and its hushed atmosphere was like that of a church. The carpet was pure white, the walls a duck-egg blue. A statuesque woman approached them, smiling at Drusilla; her expression looked strained, Palfrey thought.

'How can I help *Mam'selle*?'

Palfrey smiled. 'M. Cardyce was in London recently, and discussed a new model with my wife. Is he in?'

The words were pre-arranged, a simple key to gain access to Cardyce himself; Palfrey had used it before, and there had been no hesitation. Now, the woman looked hesitant.

'I am afraid it is impossible, *m'sieu*.' She paused before adding: 'I have been expecting him all the morning, I am puzzled by——' she stopped, as if afraid of saying too much, and Palfrey spoke more decisively.

'Is he unwell?'

'Not to my knowledge, *m'sieu*.'

'He hasn't telephoned you?'

'No.' The woman frowned, then grew dignified. '*M'sieu* will forgive me if I am unable to say more. M. Cardyce would not wish me to exaggerate a trifling thing.'

'Is it so trifling?' Palfrey asked. 'Do you even think it is?' He stared into the woman's troubled eyes, knowing that she was afraid, but reluctant to admit it. He went on more softly: 'I am a good friend of *m'sieu's*, and it is extremely important for me to see him, or to find out where he is.'

After a moment of indecision, she raised her hands resignedly, and turned and led them to a small office. It was modern and in good taste, with three walls fitted with long mirrors. She pushed aside a white-enamelled telephone and spoke in a low-pitched voice:

'You are right, *m'sieu*, I am anxious about M. Cardyce. I have never known such a thing happen before. If he is not coming to the *salon*, he always tells me, or sends word. I have telephoned his house three times, and obtained no reply.' She drew a deep breath. 'Last night, I understood, he had important work, and last night there was much trouble in Sven.'

They found a horse-drawn cab, driven by a venerable gentleman who seemed reluctant to put his horse to a trot, and the journey to the Svenborg residential suburb where Cardyce lived took nearly half an hour. When they reached the corner a dozen people were hurrying along and, a hundred yards away, a crowd was congregated about two cars and an ambulance.

'I don't think we need go much further,' Palfrey said, slowly. 'You stay here.' He swung himself down from the cab, and hurried along to the White House, where the curious crowd was laughing and talking.

Palfrey spent five minutes making casual inquiries before being told that the Englishman, Cardyce, had been murdered.

Palfrey returned leisurely to the cab, told the driver to start up slowly, and sat back. Drusilla did not break the silence which lasted until he looked at her.

'He was found murdered when the police went to see him,' he said. 'They thought he might have been concerned in last night's show. Someone got wise to Cardyce.'

They went back to the *salon*, where Palfrey prepared for

a painful interview with the manageress, but she took the news more calmly than he expected.

He turned to go, but the manageress stepped forward, looked about to speak, but stopped herself. Palfrey said:

'What is it, madame?'

She hesitated, then said in a low-pitched voice:

'I do not know who you are, God forgive me if I tell the wrong man! But I must tell someone, it is so horrible.' She caught her breath. 'When last I saw M'sieu Cardyce, he was in great trouble, he was worried almost to death. He—he had been working on some secret business, I do not know what——'

Palfrey interrupted, quietly:

'I am a colleague of those for whom he worked, madame.'

'I will have to believe you,' she said, 'but I am greatly afraid. He did not say what it was, but the look in his eyes—it was one of great horror, as if he had set eyes upon something too terrible for words! He talked little of it, all he said was that he must make quite sure before he sent word away. I—I believe that someone knew what he had discovered, and that he was killed because of it.'

'You were right to tell me,' Palfrey said. 'You've no idea at all what he discovered?'

'I know nothing, *m'sieu*, only the look in his eyes warned me, and I questioned him. He was a sick man, he——' she broke off and turned away, her eyes filled with tears.

She had recovered her composure when they left, soon afterwards. The effect of her story subdued them as they walked back towards the centre of the city, until Drusilla said:

'Have you any idea what it could be?'

'No,' said Palfrey, 'but I've heard outbursts like that before, I believe every word she said.'

They were misdirected, and lost their way back to the *Hôtel Haaka*. When they were enquiring again, they were startled by an explosion which seemed to come from the hills behind the town. The people passing by ignored it, and a man who was directing them carefully—they were half a mile from the hotel, he said—paid no heed to the explosion, and Palfrey took it to be a regular occurrence. Nordia seemed to be normal, the people were going about their customary daily tasks, the country had not known the stresses and strains of war. Again, Palfrey remembered that the

Germans had not pillaged the small state; again, there seemed a sinister significance behind that fact.

They reached the corner of Haakastrasse, in which the hotel was situated. Many people were turning into the street, and three cars were threading their way through the throng. It was like the scene in Cardyce's street, but on a major scale. Policemen were about, some of them on horseback, and in the distance a fire-alarm clattered.

And there was a smell of burning.

They hurried along the street, which turned almost at right angles a hundred yards from the main road. At the corner was a cordon of militia and police, pushing the crowd back. Smoke was billowing from a building further along.

Someone asked a policeman where 'it' was.

'The *Hôtel Haaka*,' said the policeman, gruffly, 'it is almost destroyed.'

Palfrey looked steadily at Drusilla, who said sharply:

'*Our* place. And the others——'

'Come on!' cried Palfrey and, taking her arm, he pushed his way past the policeman and ignored the indignant shouts which followed them.

19: Palfrey on a Fearful Quest

One of the policemen, a tall, youthful, blond man, grabbed Palfrey's arm and forced him to a standstill; without trying to get away, Palfrey said, quickly:

'Some of my friends are at the *Haaka,* as well as my belongings.'

His Nordian was good enough to make the policeman understand; the man's scowl faded, he released Palfrey, and said: 'I am sorry—yes, you can go.' He left them, and they hurried on.

Smuts were falling thickly, and the smell of burning had grown stronger; twice a rumbling, roaring sound made Palfrey think of crashing walls. Knowing that the explosion they had heard had really been at the hotel, he felt a deep fear for his friends. A fire which gained hold so quickly surely meant that it had been carefully prepared.

Firemen were already dealing with escapes and hoses on

the road outside the hotel and the adjacent buildings. Palfrey took in the scene swiftly, seeing that no attempt was being made to save the *Haaka*, all efforts being concentrated on confining the fire. Already the street was covered with a film of soot, while the roar of flames, going straight upwards, was like distant thunder in his ears. The heat seared his breath. It seemed impossible that anyone was still alive inside that inferno.

There was no opportunity to ask questions, as everyone about was busy. Nor was there any chance of getting through an alleyway which led to the grounds at the back of the hotel. The front had already caved in; the remaining walls were like jagged edges of rock and brick, from which smoke billowed to a great height. Palfrey was hardly aware of that, but was obsessed by his fears for Stefan, Brian and Conroy.

Since they had been at the rear of the hotel, in a room overlooking the small park and the playing water fountain, there was a chance that they were safe.

Still holding Drusilla's arm, he led the way past the building, keeping close against the shops on the other side of the road. All the windows were broken, the street was strewn with goods, hats and dresses and boots and shoes, a chaos over which they picked their way while the heat bore down on them.

No one tried to stop them.

Fifty yards from the hotel, where it was cooler and where fewer people were gathered, was another side street. A barricade had been erected across it, and four armed members of the militia were keeping back the crowd on the other side.

Palfrey reached the barricade, and asked quietly:

'Have any people escaped from the hotel?'

An oldish man, with broad features, gazed upon him in a kindly fashion.

'Some, yes. You have friends there?'

'Yes,' said Palfrey.

'Those who escaped are in the gardens at the back,' the man told him. 'Come, I will clear a way for you.'

At last they reached the little park.

The first thing Palfrey saw was the playing fountain, shooting water several feet into the air. Further away was a fire-engine, with men swarming about it. A turn-table nearly reached the top of the hotel, from which men and women were being lifted. Escape ladders swayed as men came down, carrying others. Three ambulances were standing by, and doctors and nurses were already at work.

Palfrey was appalled, although he should have expected the sight.

He wondered whether there were enough doctors on the spot, and saw a row of wounded people on the ground by a beech hedge, already seared. Few were burned, and they appeared to be victims of the explosion. The line was so long that he calculated there must be a hundred people or more, but only a few were getting any attention. Obviously, the doctors had not yet been mobilised.

He turned to Drusilla.

'I'm going to offer to help,' he said. 'Will you look for——'

'Yes,' said Drusilla, not letting him finish.

She went to the far end of that grim line, where no one was attending to the victims, while Palfrey approached a little group of doctors and nurses, who were bending over what he assumed to be the most urgent cases.

One by one the victims were removed, as more and more ambulances and attendants arrived.

Palfrey drew a deep breath.

A mobile canteen came into the square, and the nurse brought him tea and sandwiches; he was more grateful for the tea than the food. Vaguely he wondered what time it was. Then he laughed sombrely at himself, and glanced at his watch.

'Half past *four*!' he exclaimed aloud.

He had been working for four hours—and still Drusilla had not come back.

He remembered hearing several falls of masonry, and imagined her trapped beneath one.

Palfrey went first to the line of dead, fearful of what he might find. At the sight of a dark-haired woman—only the top of her head was uncovered—his heart began to beat fast, and he felt a wave of nausea. He forced himself to turn down the blanket; it was not Drusilla.

'I must get a hold on myself!' he said, aloud.

The grim search continued, with Palfrey afraid of finding Brian or Conroy, as well as Drusilla, although he knew that Stefan was not there; no one as tall as the Russian was on the ground. He reached the last half-dozen bodies, and looked at each one. The suspense—real physical agony—grew unbearable; but there was no one whom he knew.

He straightened up and lit a cigarette. It made him regain

control of himself, and helped to clear his head; but that was no consolation, for it made him realise that there were many wounded whom he had not seen; probably, too, there were many bodies already at the mortuaries.

Had he found one of the others safe, he would have had something to grasp upon, but the sense of being quite alone, allied to the continued absence of Drusilla, became a heavier burden with every passing minute.

To ease the strain, he began to ask questions, and found everyone ready to talk. He saw the manager of the hotel, burned slightly, but not badly wounded, surveying the scene of the disaster. Palfrey approached, and the manager, whom he had only seen at a distance, recognised him at once.

'I am glad you are safe, sir,' he said. 'You have been a great help. I have seen you working.'

'I did what I could,' Palfrey said. 'Do you——' he hesitated, almost afraid to ask the question for fear of the answer —'know where it started?'

'On the first floor,' he was told, 'but there were other explosions on the ground floor.'

Palfrey said: 'I was in Room—87.'

'It began in that passage,' the manager told him, slowly.

Palfrey said: 'My friends were there when I left.' His voice seemed that of a stranger.

'Among them, a very big man?' asked the manager.

'Yes.'

'I have since seen him,' said the other. 'He had come downstairs to the back hall, and was thrown out, but he was not hurt.'

Palfrey said, fervently: 'Thank God for that! You saw none of the others?'

'No, but the reception clerk escaped—it was a miracle, but he escaped,' said the manager. He raised his voice. 'Olaf! Here, please!' A short, broad-shouldered man whose face was vaguely familiar to Palfrey, and whose right hand was heavily bandaged, approached at once. 'Olaf, you remember the friends of this gentleman?'

'Yes, sir,' said Olaf, eyeing Palfrey steadily. 'They left the hotel a short while before the explosion.'

Palfrey stared, almost giddy with the relief, coming on top of his fatigue.

'They were not seen to return,' Olaf went on, 'they will be safe, I am sure.'

'You haven't seen them since?'

'No, sir, I have not.' Olaf's eyes, red-rimmed and dull, were fixed on Palfrey's. 'You left a little while before, with a lady, I believe.'

'Yes,' said Palfrey, and forced himself to wait.

'I saw her removed in an ambulance,' Olaf told him.

Palfrey said, sharply: 'You're sure?' Then he wished he had not asked the question, and was glad that the man only nodded in reply. He asked whether anyone had seen how she had been hurt, but Olaf could only tell him that she had been taken off in the ambulance.

'Did you see the attendants?' Palfrey asked.

'There were two. I remember only that one was dark, and had but one arm.'

Palfrey stared at him, his heart beginning to thump.

'Can you be sure of that?'

'I am quite sure,' said Olaf, quietly.

He forced himself to face up to the next few hours, and began a nightmare tour. The wounded had been taken to five different hospitals, all within easy reach of the hotel, and Palfrey visited each in turn.

He finished the last ward without finding a trace of Drusilla.

Nearby, a man was asking:

'Are there *no* others?' The anguish in his voice matched that of Palfrey's.

'Only those who have died,' a nurse told him, quietly.

'Died,' echoed Palfrey. 'Died?'

At the door of the morgue, a large room in the basement of the hospital, he stopped abruptly.

'What——' began the nurse, only to break off, for Palfrey's expression was less strained, and there was a glow in his eyes.

Five dead people were there, and bending over one of them was Stefan! He straightened up, shaking his head, as an attendant replaced the sheet.

'*Stefan!*' exclaimed Palfrey. His cry sounded loud in that hushed chamber, but no one looked round to reprove him, only Stefan turned. The relief in his eyes matched that in Palfrey's as he gripped Palfrey's forearm.

'Sap, how good to see you!'

'Yes,' said Palfrey, and added quickly: 'Have you seen Drusilla?'

'I am looking for her, she was brought away in an ambulance.' Stefan kept his voice low.

Palfrey said: 'Who were you looking for here?'

Stefan said, slowly: 'I have been to all the hospitals and seen no trace of her. I thought perhaps I should seek here.'

'Where have you been?' Palfrey asked. 'Which morgues?' His voice was sharp.

'Only this and the Kirche Hospital.'

'She wasn't at the Kirche?'

'No, Sap, why——'

'I've been to the others, both wards and morgues,' Palfrey said. 'If she isn't here or at the Kirche——' he stopped.

Palfrey knew what it meant, but shied from admitting it. Without speaking, they went out into a wide tree-lined boulevard, with tall shops on either side, and a ceaseless flow of traffic and people.

Palfrey said abruptly: 'One of the attendants was a one-armed man.'

Stefan said: 'Brian and Conroy went out soon after you. But did not return. They hired a taxi, a hansom cab, and my men lost them. All three have gone, Sap.'

Palfrey stared at him, turned over some coins in his pocket, then lit a cigarette. After a long time, his lips curved wryly and there was a calmer expression in his eyes.

'So Moscow was out-trumped,' he said, 'we'd better have a new deal.'

20: Palfrey Faces the Facts

By evening, certain facts were established beyond doubt.

Stefan's agents had been very active all day. Conroy and Brian had climbed, unsuspectingly, into a cab which had been served by Gregarov's men. The existence of the one-armed man from Rome was also acknowledged. That neither Palfrey nor Stefan was safe, by night or day, was so obvious that they did not speak of it.

They had interviewed half-a-dozen servants who had escaped from the hotel. Two others besides Olaf had noticed Drusilla when she had returned after the explosion to make inquiries. They had seen her being led towards an ambulance, but had not seen what had happened after that. One thought that her head had been bound, another swore that her face had been swathed in bandages. All agreed that she had been the only one in the ambulance, a small one, more like a tradesman's van.

Stefan's men began their probing. Within two hours—it was then eight o'clock—they were assured that no such ambulance had been sent from any of the hospitals, or other organisations which had sent help.

'She might not even be injured, Sap,' Stefan said.

Palfrey looked at him thoughtfully.

'No, a blow over the head, perhaps, and then—but confound it, *why* did they leave me?'

'You were busy and too many people were near you, no attack on you would have succeeded,' Stefan said, 'but in the confusion it would have been easy for one of them to attack Drusilla. There is one good thing.'

Palfrey said: 'Yes. Had they wanted to kill her, they would have done so then.'

'That is what I was thinking,' said Stefan. 'It is safe to say that she is alive.'

Palfrey frowned. 'Why should they trouble about a hostage?'

'It would be characteristic of the Nazis.'

'Ye-es. Does the same apply to Brian and Alex?'

'I imagine so,' said Stefan.

Palfrey said: 'We're going to have a pleasant day or two!'

He had washed, although he still wanted a bath, and his clothes had been brushed and cleaned. He was at a small hotel, an annex of the *Haaka*, further along the Haakastrasse. He had already been there for some hours with Stefan, had had dinner, and was smoking an American cigarette.

'How many men have you got here?' he asked.

'Enough,' said Stefan, quietly. 'In all, perhaps, fifty—we have been concentrating on Nordia for some time.'

Palfrey smiled. 'I know that that job is in hand. Meanwhile, there's another. I should have told you about this before.'

He went into detail about Madalena Gagliani's presence at Gregarov's house. Now that he could look back on the incident, he realised that the evidence was flimsy; yet coupled with the appearance of the dark-haired, one-armed man, he thought it was conclusive, although Stefan would be justified in disagreeing.

Stefan spoke thoughtfully.

'You think that the so-called sister of Ingrid is actually Madalena? There is a chance that you are right, Sap. The evidence of the handkerchief is important. I cannot imagine that anyone would conceive so tortuous an idea as to leave one there with her initials, so as to trick you. Anyway, the initials are surely not coincidental. I will find out what is known about this woman,' Stefan promised. 'You see what your discovery might mean, of course?'

'That Gagliani is still here,' said Palfrey.

'Yes. That this is a funk-hole—don't you say—for both Fascists and Nazis. We will go to make inquiries at once, Sap.'

Palfrey began to toy with his hair.

'There's another thing on my mind. Since Cardyce was murdered, I haven't been anxious to go direct to English agents.'

'Go on,' said Stefan.

'The theatre where Drusilla went is a rendezvous for English agents,' Palfrey said, 'and by now Gregarov will have realised it. He'll probably expect me to try to make contact.'

'Of course!' Stefan snapped his fingers, 'I had not seen that.'

'It's probable, anyhow,' Palfrey said, smiling darkly. 'We want a prisoner, above everything else. We're in the dark and all we can hope for is a slice of luck. We won't get it if we wait for it. So if I go to the theatre, and it's watched——'

Stefan said: 'You think they will probably try to kill you?'

'Kill, or kidnap are equally on the cards,' Palfrey said. 'No, if you played your favourite game of double-watch, and had half-a-dozen men at hand when I went to the theatre, we might make progress.'

'We will do it,' Stefan said, 'well thought, Sap! But you realise that they may just shoot at you from a corner?'

'They'll probably have a go at getting me alive,' Palfrey said, 'they still want information. For instance—who knows just what we suspect?' He went on, in a harsher voice: 'We've got to get them, if only for the Haaka massacre.'

'We will, or someone else will after us,' Stefan said, confidently.

'Speed might count,' Palfrey reminded him, tartly.

'Oh, we will lose no time. I misjudged their cunning and their thoroughness,' Stefan admitted, 'yet at least we know how important it is to them. The destruction of the records, at such a price, makes it probable that Horst and Erikson are not working for the Government. Even a Government dealing in shady diplomacy would not permit such a crime as that.'

They left together, Palfrey wearing a fur-lined overcoat borrowed from the hotel. To offset the chaos during the emergency, the *Haaka* had performed miracles, housing in its annex, or in smaller hotels, all of its guests who had been stranded, and providing emergency clothes for those who had lost their luggage. Palfrey was glad of the coat as he stepped into the street—not blacked-out, but darkened—for a chill wind coming from the hills made him shiver.

He was more cheerful now that the first shock had passed, and had admitted the probability that Drusilla and the others had been kidnapped to try to dissuade him and Stefan from continuing the hunt. His knowledge of the thoroughness of Stefan's organisation—or, more correctly, Moscow's—gave further grounds for restrained optimism.

But there was no escaping the fact that he and Stefan were completely on the defensive. They had no idea where to find Gregarov, his wife, Madalena, or any of the others.

They walked swiftly through the darkened streets. Few people were about, although twice they passed crowds coming out of theatres or picture houses. Stefan led the way towards the harbour quarters, seeming to be as familiar with Sven's side-streets as Palfrey was with London's.

He stopped at a small house near the docks.

'We shall not be long here,' he said, quietly.

'Up to you,' said Palfrey, as Stefan opened the door with a key. They went in and, when the door was closed, Stefan switched on a light. A tall thin man, dressed in rough fisherman's clothes; came out of the room on the right. He smiled when he saw Stefan, who spoke in Nordian for Palfrey's benefit. The other spoke the language as fluently.

'Are there any fresh reports?' Stefan asked.

'None of importance, no.'

'There is no word of Gregarov or his wife?'

'No.'

'Of the man, Sylva?'

'He remains at the Gregarov house.'

'Alone?'

'Yes. The house is being watched.'

'It should be. What is known of Sylva?'

'You have been told everything we know,' the other said.

'How many daughters has he?'

'Two,' said the rough-dressed man, and Palfrey's interest quickened. 'Gregarov's wife, and another, named Bertha.'

'An invalid?'

'Yes—she has been away to a sanatorium for a long time, it is not known from what she suffers, but tuberculosis is suspected.' The man repeated the information like a parrot, and yet Palfrey was greatly impressed. 'She returned to the house of Gregarov three days ago, in an ambulance, and as reported, was taken away again some hours before your visit.'

'Was she followed?'

'No, she was not.' There was a slight hesitancy about the answer, as if the man feared a rebuke.

'Is it known where she was taken?'

'It was said, to the Kirche Hospital.'

'No inquiries have been made?'

'No.'

'Is her appearance known?'

'She was seen to arrive by Orlov.'

'Is Orlov here?'

'He is asleep, but I will have him called.'

'Do so,' said Stefan.

The first man returned with a sleepy-eyed fellow, rotund and jolly in appearance, dressed in a thick woollen jersey and knee-breeches. He was barefooted, and made hardly a sound as he approached. His eyes beamed at Stefan.

'Greetings, Comrade Andromovitch!'

Stefan smiled. 'I am sorry to have to awaken you,' he said, in Nordian, 'but I am anxious to learn what the daughter of the man Sylva looks like. You saw her return from the sanatorium, I am told.'

'I did,' said the little fellow, cheerfully.

'Can you describe her?'

The man's eyes widened, his expression was droll.

'Can any man describe perfection? She was of a beauty which is given to few!' He winked, roguishly. 'How I would like to know her better! But I am delaying you, I apologise! Tall?—she was, yes, taller than I, not so tall as your good friend.' He looked at Palfrey. 'Dark, very pale—yes, I thought she was ill, there was no doubt of that, she had no colour at all.'

Palfrey said: 'What colour were her eyes?'

'Brown,' said Orlov, promptly.

'You were as near to her as that?' Stefan asked.

'There were plenty of bushes in the garden, and I was quite close. Such eyes!' Orlov rolled his own.

Palfrey said, slowly: 'Did she look like a Nordian woman?'

'She was dark,' said Orlov, 'there are not many dark Nordians. I cannot say more than that.'

'Did anyone else see her?' asked Stefan.

'None of us,' he was assured.

Palfrey asked: 'Did she speak?'

The rotund little man looked at him owlishly.

'Very little.'

'Did she speak at all?' Stefan demanded, sharply.

'I am trying to remember,' said Orlov, frowning. 'Ye-es, perhaps—yes! She spoke a little. I did not understand what she said. The nurse with her—an old crow, that nurse!—told her she must not speak.'

'You would have understood Nordian?' Stefan said.

'As I would Russian,' admitted Orlov, and reproachfully:] 'As I speak it, *m'sieu.*'

'Stir your memory,' said Stefan. 'Repeat her words.'

Palfrey thought: 'He'll think up something.'

Yet, as the little man stared back at Stefan, his drollery quite gone, Palfrey doubted it. He like the fellow, and believed that in the house there was genuine liking for, and trust of, Stefan. If Orlov could not remember, he would say so. The system of reporting minor mistakes irritated Palfrey, yet Stefan's own attitude relieved him.

Stefan waited, patiently.

Palfrey got the impression that Orlov's mind was working with complete detachment. The man was probably picturing 'Bertha' lifted from the ambulance——

The ambulance! He started to speak, but stopped himself.

Orlov said, slowly:

'I do not recall what she said, the words were confused. They were perhaps in a foreign tongue. I recall only one word—it was repeated several times. It had a strange sound.' Orlov drew a deep breath, then went on slowly: '*Ar-mar-ta.* Yes, I am sure of it.' He repeated the word more quickly. '*Ar-mar-tar,*' keeping each syllable distinct.

Palfrey snapped: 'Amata?' He uttered the name as an Italian would, with more smoothness. Orlov's eyes lighted up.

'That is so—it is exact!'

'Amata?' Stefan asked, quickly.

'Madalena's daughter, the child I told you about,' said

Palfrey, 'there isn't any further doubt. "Bertha" and Madalena are one and the same!'

Stefan said: 'Good! Orlov, I shall report this feat of memory. Now, you have another task—the woman must be traced, we must find out where she was taken. It is as important as the discovery of Gregarov and his wife. You understand?'

'Yes, comrade!' Orlov's spirits were brighter, and his eyes shone.

Palfrey said: 'Stefan, an ambulance crops up again! It might be the same one.'

Stefan said: 'A thought! Orlov, was it a large ambulance?'

'No, a very small one.'

'More like a tradesman's van?'

'So I thought, yes.'

'Trace that van,' said Stefan, quickly, 'it must be found; it was probably the one which was reported at the *Hôtel Haaka.*'

Not only did the others know what he meant, but they were quick to appreciate its importance. There was a swift exchange of orders and questions in Russian, before Orlov led the three men out.

The tall fellow stood regarding Stefan, smiling faintly.

'Is there anything else?'

'Yes,' said Stefan, 'and we shall need another six men to do it, at least. You know of the Repertory Theatre?'

'Yes, it is well known.' The Russian shot a quick, humorous glance at Palfrey, and Palfrey grinned, ruefully. 'It is the place of our good allies,' the man went on.

'Is it watched?'

'No,' said the other, quickly, 'I have had no orders——'

'That is all right,' said Stefan, 'but six men are to go to it, at once—they will approach quietly, and will take up positions in convenient hiding-places, where they can have the main entrance under their eyes all the time, and get to it quickly.'

'I will arrange it at once,' the Russian said.

'They must be there within half an hour,' said Stefan, 'and soon afterwards, Dr. Palfrey and I will arrive. We may be shot at, or else be attacked in some other way—and your men will prevent the attack succeeding. If you are able to find out beforehand whether men are watching, so much the better, for each watcher can be covered. You understand exactly what is wanted?'

'Yes, Andromovitch, it is all very clear.'

'There is another thing. If there is an attack, at all costs we must capture one of the assailants. That is more important than anything else—even more important than foiling the attack on us, do you understand? Should it be impossible for me to give instructions immediately afterwards, you will work with Dr. Palfrey as if he were myself.'

The man inclined his head.

'Good!' Stefan smiled, as if he knew these precautions would not be necessary. 'If both Dr. Palfrey and I should be hurt, take the prisoner to the *rendezvous* on Linnstrasse, and question him. You want to find out where his leaders are living.' He gave detailed instructions.

When the men had gone, they sat in the warm room, Palfrey smoking. They heard men leaving the house, their footsteps fading in the quiet of the night.

Palfrey said: 'There's another thing, Stefan—the new ballet. It could be the one that has disappeared from Moscow.'

Stefan smiled. 'Filov's, yes. It has been visited, Sap. Although the people have different names, they are those who came from Moscow. The problem is how to get them back to Russia without upsetting the Nordian authorities. This I can say—only one, or two at most, are playing any active part in affairs in Sven. Gregarov has not been there, and the one-armed man has not been seen. The company will be watched very closely, of course, but I do not think they will cause us any great concern here.'

Palfrey said, thoughtfully: 'They probably realise that we've spotted them, so Gregarov won't go near them while we're alive.'

'What gloom!' exclaimed Stefan. He glanced at his watch. 'I think it will be safe to go.'

Palfrey wrapped his coat more tightly about him when they reached the street. It was much colder, although, after walking briskly for ten minutes, his body glowed. Stefan seemed to walk leisurely, taking one stride for two of Palfrey's.

After twenty minutes, they turned into a wide street where several cafes were open and, further along, a row of red lamps shone dully.

'That is the theatre,' Stefan said.

Music was coming from the building, but the street near it seemed to be deserted. The red lamps shed a poor light, and each street lamp spread a glow for a radius of about ten feet; beyond that, there was shadow. They passed two or three side turnings, but saw no one. Two men were lurking in the doorway of a shop, and Palfrey hoped they were Stefan's agents.

They crossed the road towards the theatre.

Stepping beneath a street lamp which showed both of them in clear silhouette, Palfrey hesitated. If anything were to happen, it would be now. The pause seemed to last for a long time before he stepped forward. Anyone nearby had had a chance to recognise him.

Stefan was just ahead.

Palfrey stopped short, as a man ran out of a doorway, and another appeared behind him. Stefan turned sharply, but the nearest man evaded him and kicked at his shins, making him stagger. Palfrey struck at a man who reached him, hit him on the neck and heard him catch his breath. The other struck him on the side of the head, but the blow was not heavy and Palfrey grabbed at his shoulder. Stefan had recovered and was hurrying forward.

'It's worked!' thought Palfrey, exultantly.

On his words, a tommy-gun opened up. There was no mistaking the sharp, staccato note, nor the flashes of flame. A man near the theatre was using it, but his aim was bad and bullets sprayed the pavement a couple of yards in front of Palfrey, who released his assailant and flung himself down, cradling his head in his arms.

21 : *The Taking of a Prisoner of Importance*

Palfrey did not look up.

He heard something fall with a crash which nearly deafened him; then the firing ceased. He kept his head buried in his arms until he grew aware of a scuffling sound, and running feet. He heard a movement at his side, and looked round to see Stefan getting up. Just within the radius of the light lay a tommy-gun. The footsteps grew fainter, but the scuffling continued. As his eyes grew accustomed to the gloom outside the range of the lamp, he saw two men struggling.

A third loomed out of the darkness, and spoke to Stefan.

'Are you hurt?'

'No,' said Stefan.

'We were afraid we were too late,' the man said, speaking in Nordian. 'We have been watching, as ordered. We knocked the gun aside in time.'

'You did well,' said Stefan. 'Is there any sign of the police?'

'A watch is being kept.'

'Good!' Stefan stepped towards the struggling men as one of them sagged at the knees. The other drew away, breathing heavily, but made no attempt to run. They had their prisoner, the risk had been justified. Before Palfrey reached the man, another appeared out of the gloom and said urgently:

'The militia are coming, the police have summoned them.'

'Come on!' cried Palfrey.

Stefan bent down, lifted the semi-conscious victim, and slung him over his shoulder. They hurried to the other side of the street, hearing the clump of footsteps and an excited chattering. Turning down a side street, they ran for some seconds, only to hear footsteps ahead of them. A torch beam shot out, dazzling Palfrey and revealing the party clearly. A stentorian voice bellowed:

'Stop! Stop, or I shoot!'

'Would Stefan's men shoot as well?' Palfrey wondered. He felt an urgent desire to call out and halt them, but there was no need, for they stopped at once. Behind the light, Palfrey saw a uniformed man holding the torch in one hand and a gun in the other. The footsteps behind them drew nearer.

The man in front put the torch beneath his gun arm and raised a whistle to his lips. The shrill blast was ear-splitting.

Stefan said in a penetrating whisper:

'It will be all right.'

A man moved swiftly from the side of the street, a dark shape hurtling towards the policeman. They crashed down together as the footsteps of the pursuing militia drew nearer, hidden from them by the corner. Stefan hitched his prisoner up on his shoulder again and started forward, with the others; Palfrey dug his elbows into his sides and ran on.

A few yards along, he kicked against the kerb and pitched forward.

No one in the party noticed him fall; he heard them racing ahead, while the pursuers were drawing dangerously near. He drew a deep breath, staggered to his feet, and began to run again. The movement helped him to clear his head, although for a hundred yards he moved automatically, afraid that he would lose touch with Stefan. A shot rang out behind him, and he heard the bullet crack into a glass window. A street lamp at a corner shone on him, and three more shots followed; but when he reached the corner, he saw Stefan.

'Are you all right?' The Russian's voice was hoarse.

'I can make it,' Palfrey was gasping for breath, but with Stefan's hand on his elbow he went more swiftly; the prisoner seemed to make no difference to Stefan's speed. They ran across a small square, from which branched several streets, and then plunged into the shadows of a narrow lane, hoping it would confuse their pursuers. He heard them clatter into the square; the footsteps ceased and the sound of voices followed.

Stefan said reassuringly: 'We shall be all right, Sap.'

Palfrey glanced at him. 'Ye——' he began as he looked at the prisoner. His head and shoulders were behind Stefan and he was raising his hand; in it glittered a knife. 'Look out!' he cried, and lunged at Stefan, sending him lurching to one side and forcing him to lose his hold on the prisoner.

The man struck his head against the pavement, gasped, and released the knife.

Stefan straightened up, glanced once behind him, and then at Palfrey. 'Thank you,' he said, simply. 'I will have to be more careful.' He picked the man up again and slung him over his shoulder, but this time had an arm about his neck, so that the man would hardly be able to breathe.

There was no sound of pursuit.

Ten minutes' walking along narrow side-streets brought them to a broad highway, and they turned into a street leading off it.

'This is Linstrasse,' Stefan said, 'we shall not be long.'

The house at which he stopped was one of many in a long street, lighted by two dim street lamps. They were similar to Victorian houses in England and were approached by short flights of stone steps.

One of the men rang a bell, the door was opened promptly and they entered a narrow passage. A woman, who was shown in silhouette against the light from an open door at the end of the hall, led the way upstairs, asking no questions. All the men crowded into one small room, and the door was closed.

The garish light came from an unshaded lamp. The room was furnished comfortably with easy chairs and a settee, a threadbare carpet and two radiators which made the atmosphere pleasantly warm. Palfrey loosened his coat, while Stefan dropped his prisoner on the settee.

He was an ill-favoured specimen, whose thin lips were set tightly; he was obviously terrified. His eyes were narrowed; one was higher than the other and his thin nose was set on one side of his face, giving him a grotesque, unbalanced appearance.

The other Russians stood silently about the room, as Stefan looked down on the prisoner.

Stefan spoke in a voice so genial that Palfrey looked at him sharply.

'Well, my little friend! How would you like to talk to me? You are bursting to talk, are you not?'

'I—I do not understand——' the man began.

'I did not mean "how would you like to engage in idle conversation,"' said Stefan, with the same deceptive geniality, 'but how would you like to tell me who sent you, and where you came from? You know of me, of course?'

The man said: 'You are Andromovitch.'

'Ah! You are a man of knowledge! You know that I have a reputation for harshness?'

The prisoner said nothing, but looked away, as if to find help.

Stefan said: 'You are a fool, you are employed because you are prepared to risk your life for money. I do not know how well you are paid, but I will give you double what you now receive in one month and, after a week or two, I will allow you to go free, unhurt, if you talk freely now.'

The man kept silent, but his eyes widened, and his agitation grew noticeably less.

'On the other hand, if you refuse, I shall have to take you away from Sven,' said Stefan, softly. 'I shall, of course, take you with me to Russia. You know Russia? You have heard, perhaps, of Siberia? They say it is a very cold region! To live there, one has to work very hard.'

'I—I am a Nordian!' the prisoner gasped.

'If you were not, I should not bargain with you. The protection of your country is good, you see.'

'I—I know little——'

Stefan said: 'I cannot believe it! Tell me exactly when you began work for these people and for Gregarov. Give me all the information you can. If I find them, I will keep my promise. I have not asked your name, and no one will know my informant.'

'It will work,' Palfrey thought, but he was surprised that so little persuasion was needed.

The man talked, quickly and anxiously. He had been employed by Gregarov for some weeks. He did not know for whom Gregarov worked, but believed he was a criminal of some notoriety. He had been given a number of jobs, always guarding people whom, he said, were understood to be in some danger. He had followed Palfrey from the *Haaka* that morning, and had seen Gregarov just before——

'So Gregarov's still in Sven,' Palfrey thought. 'We'll get him yet.'

The prisoner had seen Gregarov in a house on the outskirts of Sven, where he was staying with several others. Gregarov himself had told him to watch at the stage door of the theatre, and to try to kidnap Palfrey. He swore that he knew nothing of the plans to shoot them, and they were mistaken about the knife; it had fallen from his pocket!

'Naturally,' said Stefan sarcastically. 'Can you tell me the address of the house?'

'Yes. It is in Kelstrasse, at the far end.'

'The number?'

'Three hundred and eighty-one.'

'Three hundred and eighty-one, Kelstrasse,' Stefan repeated.

'Whom do you know by name of the people at Kelstrasse?'

The little eyes narrowed. The prisoner sat up on the settee and stretched out a trembling hand, as if to ward off disaster.

'I do not know them by name! There is a sick woman and an Italian, an old man. Sometimes there are Germans. They are going north, that I can tell you, they are preparing to winter in the north.'

Palfrey leaned forward, as Stefan asked sharply: 'How do you know that?'

'I have seen the clothes they are packing—furs, fur gloves, everything needed for a winter in the north.'

'When do they plan to leave?'

'I do not know!' the prisoner gasped; whenever there was a question he could not answer his fear revived.

'We can hardly expect you to know everything,' Stefan said, and turned to his men. 'You heard the address—two of you go there at once, one of you hurry to fetch more men there. The house must be closely guarded, all who leave it must be followed, all seen to enter, described. Off with you, it is urgent!'

They went out quickly, and the door closed sharply.

Alone with the prisoner and Stefan, Palfrey stood up, while Stefan stared down at the man, his expression no longer genial. That alone was enough to frighten the fellow, who obviously thought that he had been deceived. He could not stop his limbs from trembling, and turned his eyes piteously towards Palfrey, whose heart was beating uncomfortably fast. He had forced the personal issues to the background, while the more important task was being done. Now——

'Your turn for questioning, I think,' Stefan said.

Palfrey said: 'Who else has been to the house on Kelstrasse?'

The prisoner gulped. 'There have been visitors. I have told you who stays there, but——'

'Who were the visitors?' Palfrey asked, his voice low. 'We want no lies.'

'Your—your woman was there, but I did not attack her! I knew nothing of it, but she was brought in the ambulance while I was there.'

Palfrey said: 'Was she badly hurt?'

'No, no, she was only bruised. She was conscious when I saw her, and I do not think they intended to injure her, she was sent away with—with your other friends. They stayed only a short while,' the man declared, now looking at Stefan imploringly, 'there was nothing I could do.'

Palfrey snapped: 'Were any of them hurt?'

'The—the Englishman tried to scape. He—he was shot.'

Palfrey said: 'How seriously?'

'I do not think he will live,' the prisoner gasped. 'I did not shoot him, it was one of the others!' He looked so terrified that Palfrey thought it likely that he had fired the shot; and also, Brian might now be dead. How like Brian to be shot trying to escape!

Stefan said quietly:

'How was he when you last saw him?'

'He was alive, I swear it!'

'Was there a doctor?'

'I did not see one, they were in a great hurry to send your friends away. They had been to the hotel for—for madame, and the others were brought in a cab. I swear that I knew nothing of it; I did not know that I was one of a gang of murderers. But what was I to do? If I had tried to escape, they would have killed me or betrayed me to the police. I swear that I could do nothing, although I tried to help. I have told you everything, everything!'

Palfrey said: 'Were you at the house on Kirche Hill during the trouble?'

'I was in the grounds.'

'Did you know who was there?'

'No, no, I had no idea. I have since heard rumours, but I do not know for certain. You would not want me to tell you of rumours. I have told only the truth.'

Palfrey said: 'Did you kill Cardyce?'

The man stared, blankly; it was not pretence, the question puzzled him, making him momentarily forgetful of his fears.

'Cardyce—I do not know the name.'

'He lived at the White House, Strenberg.'

'*That* one! No, I did not go there, but I was told that others did. He was an Englishman, he had been too interested in what Gregarov was doing, and was making inquiries. I heard that he was to be killed, to make sure that he could not talk of what was happening. There was a fear, also, that you would see him. It was done hurriedly.'

'Who told you all this?' Palfrey demanded.

'There are others of the party and we have always talked of what has happened. Like me, they wished to leave Gregarov, but that man has made it impossible—we had to obey him or else be killed. Even if we had escaped, he would have betrayed us. I told you that before—we were trapped, we had to obey!'

Palfrey eyed him with disgust.

'It paid you well enough, I gather. But never mind that. Do you know of any others working with Gregarov?' When the man did not answer, he went on: 'A one-armed man, perhaps an Italian——'

'There was a man with one arm, yes! He was with us at the hotel when we took your woman away in the ambulance. But he is not Italian, he is a German, or perhaps a Czech, I cannot be sure.'

'Was he often with Gregarov?'

'I saw little of him. I believe he came with the Italians a few days ago. I cannot tell you more than I know, *m'sieu*! I heard his name—it is Kloeb.'

Palfrey said sharply:

'Is that the truth?'

'I swear it,' said the prisoner. 'Kloeb, Hans Kloeb.'

'*Kloeb*,' said Stefan, 'the name is familiar, Sap. Bruckner's private secretary is named Kloeb, and the name is not usual. Kloeb was seen with Bruckner several times in the Baltic States, but it was not recorded that he had only one arm.'

'I could not make such a mistake!' the prisoner gasped.

Palfrey said: 'All right, we believe you. When did you last see him?'

'Today. He went with your friends.'

Palfrey said slowly: 'All roads lead to the North.'

'There are few roads leading north,' said Stefan, taking him literally. 'The main route is by the fjord and then up the River Sven. I think this man is speaking the truth.' He spoke in English, while the prisoner looked at them open-mouthed.

'Oh, he's not lying,' Palfrey said.

'A triumph for London!' said Stefan. 'But we need nothing else from him, do we?'

'No-o. Will you let him go?'

'Later—if it seems wise.' Stefan shrugged his shoulders. 'The promise is hardly binding, but I will keep it if it will do no harm. Now, we must be moving.'

'To Kelstrasse,' said Palfrey, 'where we might have more luck.'

They opened the door and Stefan gripped the prisoner's arm, and led him up another flight of stairs to an attic room. It was empty, but warm. The door was heavy and the only window was a narrow one, near the roof. They left the man there after going through his pockets and removing anything he might have used to try to escape. Stefan locked the door and put the key in his pocket, until, downstairs, he left it with the woman who had admitted them. She was a faded, middle-aged soul, with a weak smile, but with eyes which lighted up when she looked at Stefan.

Then they went out into the cold streets.

    .   ,   ,   .   ,

The house in Kelstrasse was in darkness, not a crack of light showed at the windows or the doors. It stood in its own grounds, next to one where light blazed at every window and from which came the bellow of a radio tuned too loudly, harsh voices, and occasional high-pitched, probably drunken, laughter.

As they approached the house, a figure materialised out of the gloom and addressed Stefan.

There followed a brief colloquy in Russian, before Stefan turned to Palfrey.

'No one has left here since our men arrived.'

'And your fellows are here in strength?'

'I have ceased saying "yours" and "mine", they are "ours"; the sooner we realise it the better,' said Stefan. 'Yes, they are in good numbers. You and I will go first.'

'To force entry?'

'We might knock at the door,' said Stefan, 'sometimes that is successful!'

They reached a narrow porch. There was an outer door —all Nordian houses had double doors, to help keep out the bitter winter cold—which was not locked. Palfrey wished it were, it would then indicate that someone was in. The inner door was locked, and Stefan shone a torch, revealing white woodwork and polished brass. He pressed the bell-push. The strident ring of the bell, which was a battery-set on the inside of the door, startled them.

No other sound came, except the cacophony from next door.

'I am afraid they have gone,' said Stefan. 'We shall have to break in.'

He bent his arm and cracked his elbow against a glass panel. The glass broke with a sharp report and pieces fell about their feet and inside the hall.

A man's voice came from the path; Stefan called out to reassure him.

Obviously, they were too late, and Palfrey's buoyancy, which had come after the interview with the prisoner, ebbed away.

Stefan shone the torch into the gaping hole.

Its beam shone along a furnished hall, but no one appeared. Stefan put a gloved hand through the hole and pulled back the bolt of the door, then turned the handle; the door squeaked as it opened.

They stepped through.

The eerie glow of his torch revealed a carpeted staircase, heavy-looking furniture and heavy curtains hanging at doors as well as windows. Their footsteps were muffled on the carpet, making hardly a sound. Stefan signalled for one of his men to come up.

'Is the back door closely guarded?'

'The place is surrounded, have no fear'
'Send two men to us,' said Stefan.

Two silent moving fellows came at once, but did not speak. Their presence was reassuring, for Palfrey had come to regard them as super-efficient. Yet he felt convinced that the house was deserted and began the search without much hope.

There were a dozen well-furnished rooms, mostly small, with evidence that several people had been living there recently. The radiators were all warm and the atmosphere in the rooms was comfortable.

A sense of anti-climax made Palfrey's spirits sink lower.

'They probably guessed the prisoner would talk,' he said.

'At least we have driven them away,' said Stefan, 'and as Drusilla had been gone some time we have not missed a chance of finding her. I——'

They were standing near the foot of the stairs, and he broke off at a tap on the front door. One of his men switched off the light before opening the door. Another hurried in and waited until the door was closed and the light was on again, before saying urgently:

'Someone is coming here.'

'Is it a band of men?' asked Stefan, quickly.

'No, a woman, on her own. She inquired of one of our men in the street, wishing to know which was Number 381. He misdirected her, but she will not be long. I have told the others to allow her to come here, unmolested.'

'Quite right,' murmured Palfrey.

Footsteps sounded on the path, drew near, and stopped; there was a sharp ring at the bell. Stefan motioned to a man to open the door, while he and Palfrey hugged one wall, so as to be out of sight when the door was first opened. The light was left on.

The man opened the door, and a woman spoke sharply, breathing as if she had been hurrying.

'Is this Kelstrasse 381?'

'It is,' the Russian said.

The visitor stepped into the hall quickly, as if afraid she might be refused admittance. 'I must see——' she began, but broke off when she saw Palfrey, who was staring at her fixedly. It was Ingrid, dressed in furs, flushed and lovely, and obviously in the grip of deep emotion.

Stefan moved forward and smiled disarmingly.

22: *The Party which Travelled North*

The other Russians had slipped away, and Palfrey could not see them in the doorways. The front door was closed, but Stefan, Palfrey and Ingrid stood together, Ingrid looking at Palfrey and ignoring Stefan.

She began: 'What are you——' but broke off.

She was more than startled at sight of him, while he was assimilating the fact that she had not known where to find her husband's house. The curious, bewildered expression in her eyes and her air of tension suggested an answer. He looked at Stefan, finding the Russian's manner puzzling. It was as if they knew each other, and Stefan was taken aback; but he certainly did not know her as Ingrid Gregarov.

Stefan said: 'Good evening, madame.'

'Good evening.' Ingrid's voice was sharp, and she looked towards Palfrey as if wondering why he kept silent. 'What are you doing here?'

'I was about to ask that of you,' said Stefan.

'I do not understand you.' She wrapped her furs more tightly about her, as if she needed their protection now that the first shock had gone; she was preparing to fight.

'We are not getting along very well, are we?' asked Stefan, in a curiously gentle voice. 'Whom did you expect to find, madame?'

'Some friends,' she said.

'I can assure you that the house is empty, but for ourselves.'

'What are you doing here?' she demanded again, now obviously playing for time. Palfrey saw the change in her expression, and knew that she realised the danger in which she had placed herself. She sent him a quick, almost appealing glance, as if imploring him to keep silent.

'You know Dr. Palfrey?' asked Stefan. 'Sap, do you——'

'Yes, I know her,' said Palfrey. 'She——'

She turned on him with such a blaze of anger in her eyes that he did not finish.

'Be quiet!' she cried. 'Be quiet!'

'Who is she, Sap?' Stefan asked.

'Gregarov's wife,' said Palfrey.

'As if you did not know!' she said, coldly.

Stefan backed a pace, and frowned at her. He found the news unpalatable, Palfrey was sure of that. The Russian took himself in hand, his smile was no longer gentle, but antagonistic. Ingrid's expression was equally hostile.

Stefan's face grew bleak. 'You are a citizen of Soviet Russia, I trust you remember that.'

'I am in Nordia, where I am not responsible to any individual, and I warn you that——'

'You are foolish,' said Stefan, 'your warnings are ineffective, and you should know that the authority of the Soviet over its citizens is as great here as in Russia. My name——'

'I know who you are,' she said.

'Indeed. Then you should acknowledge my authority to ask questions. Where is your husband?'

After a long pause, she said thinly:

'I expected to find him here.'

'He did not tell you that he had gone on a journey?'

'No,' she said. 'With whom has he gone?'

'Enemies of our country,' said Stefan. The words themselves were stilted, but his expression made them impressive.

'Your country is not mine,' she said. 'I am a Nordian, and I refuse to acknowledge any duty to Russia. Have that clear in your mind—I am responsible only to Nordia.' When Stefan did not answer, she went on fiercely: 'Are you trying to pretend that you do not know where to find him? Who else would know, since you and he work for the same authority? Oh, you need not look at me like that, I am not afraid of you, nor will I allow your dastardly plot to succeed.' She turned to Palfrey, her expression freezing, and her words scathing. 'And you, an Englishman, a party to such a betrayal! I will never take the word of an Englishman again!'

Stefan said: 'All this may have a meaning, madame, but I have yet to see it. If you think you are gaining time, put it out of your mind. Your husband works neither for Nordia nor Russia, and you know it.'

'He works for Russia!' She looked as if she would have murdered Gregarov, had he been within reach.

'He works for Berlin,' said Stefan.

She stared at him, her lips beginning to form words, then drawing together in a straight line.

Palfrey stepped forward, smiling faintly and looking a little diffident. They stared at him, as if at an umpire, expecting some decisive comment. His smile widened.

'Couldn't we all sit down?' he asked.

'This is no moment for joking,' Stefan said, unusually formal.

'Oh, we may as well be comfortable,' Palfrey said, easily, 'and we aren't getting very far like this.' He took the woman's arm, and she allowed him to lead her to a lounge. Stefan followed, after a moment of indecision.

Palfrey waited for Ingrid to sit down. She accepted a cigarette mechanically, but Stefan declined. Palfrey took out his lighter, bent down and lit her cigarette, but she did not thank him, although his action had given her time to regain her poise.

The room was warm, and she loosed her furs. Beneath them, she wore a dark green, close-fitting woollen dress, showing her statuesque beauty. She was heavily made-up, but nothing could hide the redness of her eyelids, nor the glassiness caused by lack of sleep or else some deep emotion.

Stefan looked at Palfrey, reproachfully.

Palfrey said: 'That's much better, for we'll probably be some time. Stefan's right, you know, Gregarov works for Berlin. I discovered it when I was at your house. Are you really so surprised?'

She looked as if she were facing an unpalatable fact which she had been trying to evade. Palfrey thought he knew the reason. He had known that she put a cause above her happiness and had doubted whether it was Russia's. If she worked for Nordia, it explained so much—especially her faithfulness to Gregarov, being convinced that he, too, was working for her country, although a traitor to his own. Her talk of betrayal confirmed it, and he believed that Stefan would soon acknowledge the truth.

'You'll have to acknowledge it sooner or later, so why not now? He's worked for Berlin for many years, while pretending to serve Russia. He's been building up for the present situation, and he's done it very well. Almost too well, I think, he's tried to keep too many fires burning at the same time. He is certainly no fool,' he added, 'to be able to convince you that he was working for Nordia, Moscow that he was working for Russia, and Berlin——' he shrugged. 'It's not good to hear, is it?'

She did not answer, but her expression told him enough. She looked away at Stefan, who was frowning but looked less hostile.

'Not good at all,' Palfrey said, 'and the probable truth is that he was working for himself—setting one country against the other for the highest reward.' He drew at his cigarette, thrust one hand into his pocket, and said lightly: 'If we're wise, we three will work together.'

'I am not so easily fooled,' said Ingrid.

'Oh, come!' said Palfrey, 'we won't get anywhere by fencing with each other, and the stakes are high. You do work for the Nordian Secret Service, don't you? That's your one concern, your only loyalty?'

She said: 'I—I have helped my husband.'

'Thinking that he worked for them?'

'Yes.' The word seemed dragged from her.

'Why do you lie to me?' she continued in a low-pitched voice. 'Why don't you admit the truth? Oh, I know that I can do nothing, you would rather kill me than allow me to leave here and spoil your plot. And I know that Russia is to annex my country and England is complaisant, she——'

'Stefan—has there been any talk at all of annexing Nordia, to the best of your knowledge?' asked Palfrey.

'None whatsoever,' said Stefan, emphatically. 'This is the first time such an idea has been voiced.'

'You may not know everything,' said Ingrid, coldly.

'I certainly do not,' said Stefan, 'but I have had very precise instructions to do nothing to antagonise the Nordian Government, and my orders came from a high authority. You see, I am very frank. We are anxious to remain friendly with Nordia, but that attitude would change if Nordia plotted with Germany.'

'My country is interested only in maintaining its independence,' Ingrid said. Stefan made no comment. 'According to my husband, Brett knows of the plot to annex Nordia, and is the intermediary working between Moscow and London, to try to make the action more palatable to the English.'

'The devil he is!' Palfrey gave a short laugh and went on: 'It's dangerously clever, Stefan, they've covered everything. Because both Governments are suspected of being complaisant, Nordia has made no direct approach to London or Washington. Now we know why the militia was ready! A sudden emergency, talk of interference by "hostile" agents, Horst and Erikson at the party for secret discussions before reporting to the Cabinet. I suppose Gregarov has also worked out a way in which the so-called plot can be defeated?' His voice was harsh as he went on: 'Oh, he's brilliant! And it's going to take some adjusting. He's doubtless convinced Horst and Erikson?'

'He has done that,' said Ingrid in a strained voice. 'And he has suggested a way of outwitting the Russians, by a plan which he explained to Horst and Erikson. I know that, but I was not in the room when that matter was discussed.'

Her voice was strained. She looked at Palfrey all the time, as if trying to probe his thoughts, and to make sure of his sincertity. His manner reassured her, although her knowledge of her husband's treachery—how she had discovered that he was working against the Nordians could be learned later—was going to help. And Stefan, now that he had recovered from the shock, was exerting himself to win her confidence.

Palfrey said, thoughtfully:

'We couldn't have made many more bad guesses. We thought that Erikson and Horst were working with the Nazis——'

'*Those* two men?' exclaimed Ingrid. 'There are no greater patriots in Nordia! They have not yet placed their information before the Stething, as they are anxious to obtain all the facts. There was great confusion when you were discovered in the house the other night. Orders were given for the dictaphone record—which my husband saw—to be destroyed at all costs, but'—her eyes closed as if to shut out a scene of horror—'the cost was too high. It was never intended that the *Haaka* should be wrecked.'

'How did you learn of this address?'

'A maid had heard him mention it on the telephone. As soon as I was told, I hurried here.'

'Good enough!' said Palfrey. 'Now, among other things, what about your sister Bertha?'

'She is not my sister, of course.'

'I'd realised that. Why did you pretend that she was?'

'As you were believed to be working with Moscow to connive at the annexation, it was necessary to confuse you. It was Maxim's idea; you were to be told of "Bertha", if you appeared to suspect another woman's presence.'

'So I asked for that one,' said Palfrey. 'Your father helped you, too, but he isn't exactly well-disposed towards Russia.'

'He is a Nordian,' she said, simply.

'Ye-es,' admitted Palfrey, 'fair enough.'

'It is the simple truth,' she said, swiftly, 'he hates Maxim, but——'

'Did you know that your father gave me a key to help me escape?'

'To help you to die,' she corrected, after a long pause.

Palfrey stared, uncertainly.

'To help you to die,' she repeated. 'Oh, I can hardly believe that it all happened! Had Andromovitch and his men not arrived, you would have left the house by a first-floor window. Two men were waiting below. As each of you came down, you would have been killed.'

'But why not kill us in the house?' Palfrey objected.

She looked startled. 'Is that all you can say to such information?'

'Well, what's the answer?' asked Palfrey, practically.

'It was to be said that you were shot when burgling the house,' she told him. 'As you are English, no incident was to be provoked.'

'Well, well!' said Palfrey. 'A family full of ideas! Concerning "Bertha"——'

'Please do not joke about it!'

'It's no joke,' Palfrey assured her, 'I am in dead earnest. Do you know who she was?'

'An Italian woman.'

'What was she doing in Sven?'

'Gregarov said that he first heard of the plot from an Italian secret service agent, a man named Gagliani,' said Ingrid. 'He stayed for a day, working with Maxim from early morning until late at night. He said that Gagliani had brought his daughter-in-law because she knew what was happening and he could not rely on her loyalty. That he did not want to kill her seemed natural.' She shrugged her shoulders. 'You can understand that?'

'Yes,' said Palfrey, briskly, 'but you forgot to ask yourself one question. Who brought Gagliani and his daughter-in-law to Nordia? Four days ago he was in Rome. Except through Russia, where such a man would certainly be stopped, there is only one route, which is across——'

'Central Europe!' she exclaimed.

'Germany,' said Palfrey bluntly. 'The fact that he and his daughter-in-law had safe conduct through Germany should convince you, if you have any lingering doubts. And to help to disperse any we might have—why did you talk to me so plausibly about Bruckner?'

'Maxim had told me that your excuse for coming to Nordia was to search for him.'

'Do you know anything of Bruckner?'

'I do not.'

'Nor of Schlessing, nor Zukmayer?'

'No,' she said, 'they were the names on which you hung your excuse, that is all.'

'Comprehensive,' admitted Palfrey, 'but they *are* in Nordia, and Gregarov *is* plotting for Berlin—but we don't know yet exactly what the plot is—except that it concerns Nordia.' He lit a cigarette. 'We also know that most of the party has gone north, up the fjord.' He spoke casually, wanting to get her reaction accurately. She looked astonished.

'Are you sure?'

'Reasonably sure,' said Palfrey.

'How far north?' asked Ingrid.

'I don't know,' said Palfrey. 'Does it matter?' He was disappointed because she obviously had no idea of their rendezvous.

'For perhaps a hundred miles it is comparatively mild,' Ingrid said, 'beyond that it is arctic—even now, it is thick with snow and ice. What could they do as far north as that?'

'That's our problem,' said Palfrey, 'and we've got to get on with it. You've never heard your husband speak of any particular northern region?'

'Not to remember,' she said, 'he is not a man for hunting or trapping, and only in the summer is there any fishing in the north. Even then, it is much better further south. Could you be mistaken?'

'There is a possibility,' said Palfrey, with an uneasy thought that the prisoner who had been so informative might have lied.

'Well, Stefan?' he said.

'I must make my report,' said Stefan, 'you will want to, also. Until we have convinced the Nordian Government of our real intentions, we will get no help in a search for the vessel going north. How will you report?'

'Through the Embassy, it's the only way,' said Palfrey.

'I would not like to have my story garbled by the staff,' said Stefan. 'Sap, I'm sorry, but I shall have to report to Moscow in person. I can go by air. It can only be handled by high authorities, and since the situation is so delicate, I must not allow the Kremlin to get the wrong idea.'

'Then you get off,' said Palfrey, promptly.

Stefan said: 'I must. But—' he looked at Ingrid, and for the first time touched on the earlier differences. 'Madame

Gregarov, I have to remind you that you *are* a Russian subject. What you have said is of vital importance to Russia as well as to Nordia. You owe it to Russia to give evidence.'

Palfrey stared. 'Why——'

'Please!' said Stefan, and added to the woman. 'I want you to come with me.'

'Into Russia!'

'You need not fear that you will be ill-treated,' Stefan said, 'your motives will be understood, but——'

He broke of, expectantly.

Palfrey realised that if she were prepared to travel with Stefan to Moscow, it would be evidence of her good faith, and few would doubt her story. Her agreement would settle any doubts in Stefan's mind, while the Kremlin would be more impressed. The issue was between them, and Palfrey waited with growing impatience.

At last: 'I will come,' she said, slowly.

'Well done!' exclaimed Stefan. 'And now that we have left it so late, we must hurry!'

There was no opportunity for a word with him out of earshot, and Palfrey had to draw his own conclusions. He was surprised by the expression in Stefan's eyes when Ingrid had agreed to go with him. She knew that she was taking a risk, Stefan knew that only if she were wholly sincere would she accept it. And each seemed pleased at the prospect of the journey.

'Odd show,' said Palfrey, *sotto voce*.

A week before, he would have thought Stefan was going to absurd lengths in flying to Moscow, but now he knew that for the Russian there was no other really satisfactory way.

Stefan left the house to the care of his men, and the three of them hurried off, reaching the centre of the town in twenty minutes. Stefan and Ingrid went on to the *Haaka* hotel annex, and Palfrey succeeded in obtaining a horse-drawn cab and was driven to the British Embassy.

It was then nearly twelve o'clock.

He expected a cold reception, but the young secretary who received him after surprisingly few formalities was genial enough. He hoped Dr. Palfrey would tell him his business, for the Ambassador was extremely busy and did not want to be disturbed. On the other hand—the young man smiled—there were instructions that if Palfrey insisted on a personal interview, it would be granted.

Palfrey said, slowly:

'Are they recent instructions?'

'I had 'em yesterday,' said the bright young man, 'but I don't know when Sir William received them. Months ago, probably. Will I do?' he added, hopefully.

'I'm afraid not,' said Palfrey, apologetically.

'I thought not,' said the young man, sadly. 'You may have to wait for a while, he's expecting another visitor—no, he's not in bed!' The man's cheerful laugh did Palfrey good. 'Some mysterious envoy arrived in Sven late tonight.'

'Ask him not to make it longer than he can help,' said Palfrey, 'it's really important.'

'I'll see what I can do for you,' promised the young man, and disappeared, leaving Palfrey in an imposing high-ceilinged room. It was warm, and Palfrey, sitting in a comfortable hide armchair, realised how tired he was.

'Hallo, there!' A cheerful voice disturbed him. He opened his eyes quickly and blinked at the bright young man, who said: 'Tired? Well, you won't be long, he'll be ready in ten minutes. Would you like a wash?'

'I would!' said Palfrey, gratefully.

Precisely ten minutes later, feeling much fresher and prepared to battle against ambassadorial scepticism, he was led to the Ambassador's study, convinced that the Embassy in Sven was a model one.

As he stepped into a warm, comfortably-furnished room in which a log fire was blazing and about which hung the blue haze and pleasing aroma of cigar smoke, his musings were cut short. There were two men in the room, the Ambassador, whom he knew slightly, and the Marquis of Brett, who was smiling at him.

23: The Problem that Remained

Palfrey schooled himself not to show too great a surprise, and Brett presented him to the Ambassador. The latter was a youngish man, tall but inclined to stoop, and with a deceptively mild and apologetic smile.

The Ambassador pushed a chair up for him and asked him hospitably what he would like to drink.

'Nothing now, thanks,' Palfrey said, 'this is no time for

pink elephants! Marquis, I've never been so glad to see you!'

'I thought you came to see me,' said the Ambassador, smiling.

Palfrey grinned. 'Oh, I did, but the Marquis will be able to present the case much more effectively. The truth is——' he accepted a cigar, absent-mindedly rolled it in his fingers, pierced and lit it. 'The truth is,' he repeated, 'that there's much dirty work on foot and preventative action is indicated at once, and on a large scale. Before I start, though—have you come about the same show, Marquis?'

'Probably,' said Brett.

'You know that Bruckner is in Nordia?'

'We received an up-to-date report from Moscow, and I came to find out whether there were rumours of trouble here,' said Brett, 'such as, any atmosphere in diplomatic circles which would make trouble for you.'

'Is there?' asked Palfrey, quizzing the Ambassador.

'One might call it an atmosphere of frigid courtesy,' said the Ambassador, soberly. 'I have been worried by it enough to send a report to London—the Marquis has answered both reports.'

'Do you know what the trouble is?'

'I have no idea.'

'Or you, sir?' Palfrey asked the Marquis.

'Only that you've been getting yourself thoroughly disliked,' said Brett.

'Well, at least the ground is paved,' Palfrey said. 'The root of it is that Horst and Erikson have been panicked into thinking that the Soviet is going to annex Nordia, and that the Allies are going to stand aside. Quite enough to freeze the atmosphere, you'll agree.'

He judged from Brett's expression that the news was quite unexpected, and he had the satisfaction of seeing an Ambassador gape! In a far more favourable atmosphere than he had hoped for, he told them exactly what Ingrid had said and added everything which concerned the two most influential ministers in Nordia. He did not lay emphasis on any part of his story, although he knew that they would take little convincing. As he proceeded, he felt convinced that Ingrid had told the truth. Everything was explained naturally and logically and it could not be untrue. As he approached the end, he found his mind grappling with the problems that remained. Bruckner—and Drusilla; and freedom of action in Nordia was the first essential.

There was a short, heavy silence when he finished. He leaned forward and allowed the ash from his cigar to fall into an ash-tray, smiling faintly. The first response came from the Ambassador, and it was not what Palfrey expected. The man stretched out for the telephone, and said brusquely:

'Get me the Nordian Foreign Office.'

Palfrey smiled: 'Thanks,' he said.

'If the Marquis weren't here to vouch for you, I would want a lot of persuading,' said the Ambassador. 'How long have you known about this?'

'For about two hours. Will Horst be so helpful?'

'I think so,' said the Ambassador. 'What do you make of it, Brett? What's behind it all?'

'Isn't that obvious?' asked Palfrey.

'No,' said the Ambassador, 'I find it utterly confusing.'

'Oh, no!' protested Palfrey. 'Get Nordia hostile to the Allies and you will make its Government more ready to listen to whispers from Berlin. Berlin wants some concession, but just what it is, we don't yet know. The whole precious scheme is intended to pave the way for some Nazi proposition, probably—' he shrugged—'well, what about an agreement to give sanctuary to higher Nazi officials? Once such an agreement is reached, it doesn't exactly matter whether Russia annexes Nordia or not. I mean,' he added, realising the absurdity of speaking too quickly, 'if Russia holds off, as she will because she's never intended to do anything else, the Nordians will put it down to their great gifts in diplomacy. The Nazi proposition will undoubtedly include generous offers of payment. Nordia isn't a rich country—so clever, isn't it?'

Brett stared at him, narrow-eyed.

Palfrey stifled a yawn which caught him unawares. His mind was busy, but his eyes heavy and aching.

'You need some sleep,' went on Brett. 'How are the others?'

Palfrey said, with a revival of the cold ache within him: 'Brian's been hurt. Drusilla and Conroy have gone north, ahead of the enemy's main party, and not willingly. I've told you about Stefan.'

Brett's eyes were filled with concern as he said slowly: 'Where is Brian? Is he badly hurt?'

'According to my informant, yes,' he said. 'He was shot trying to escape, but he was alive. They shipped him north with the others. If we can get the Nordian militia to join in the hunt, we might find them.'

'We shall get some help from them,' Brett said, confidently.

Palfrey needed complete rest to be ready for the next move. He thought of returning to the hotel, but after Brett and the Ambassador had gone, he was taken to a spacious bedroom in the Embassy and provided with all he needed. After undressing slowly, he climbed into bed and stared into the darkness for a long time before going to sleep.

. . . . .

He felt more composed next morning.

Just after eleven o'clock, a footman came to tell him he was wanted downstairs. He was led to the Ambassador's study, going through the magnificent reception rooms, in which echoes of peace-time banquets seemed to hover.

Brett was waiting with the Ambassador and with them was a short, fat man, bald-headed, and with large quiet eyes which gazed steadily at Palfrey.

'Horst,' thought Palfrey.

The Ambassador presented him ahd Palfrey bowed. Horst stepped forward and extended a plump hand.

'Dr. Palfrey, Nordia will always be in your debt.'

Palfrey smiled awkwardly. 'Not mine!' he said. 'I was only the messenger. Others, who——'

Horst smiled. 'I would expect you to say so, of course, but, believe me, I understand what has happened.'

Brett said: 'Maxim Gregarov was found this morning.'

Palfrey exclaimed: 'By George, quick work! Has he told you where——'

'He told us little, but he was destroying papers which proved conclusively that the story of the Russian annexation was a bogey put up by Berlin to make Nordia amenable. For the rest, there's nothing.' The Marquis looked sombre.

'Give me an hour with him!' Palfrey snapped.

Horst said, gently: 'I understand your feelings, Dr. Palfrey, and I am extremely sorry about the situation, but you will not be able to obtain the information you want from Gregarov. When he realised that he had no chance of escape, when the papers were obtained and the whole story of his treachery revealed, he killed himself. I am sorry,' he repeated, 'and I shall make every effort to find out where your colleagues have gone.'

Horst left soon afterwards; the Ambassador fussed at his

desk for a few seconds before going out, and then the room was very quiet. Brett stood looking into Palfrey's face as if knowing that he was hardly aware of his presence.

'Sap,' he said quietly, 'it isn't the end, you know.'

'Eh?' asked Palfrey, looking up with a start. 'Sorry, Marquis, I didn't catch what you said.'

'We aren't through yet,' said Brett.

'No-o.' Palfrey began to toy with his hair, his lips curved in a faint smile. 'No, I'm not so good, am I? First things first, when all is said and done. What's been arranged?'

'There is to be no official break between Nordia and Berlin,' said the Marquis. 'In the search, we shall have the assistance of the police and the militia, but ostensibly the search is for those of Gregarov's organisation not yet caught. The whole country is being combed, especially the upper reaches of the Sven fjord and the river itself.'

Palfrey did not look forward to the next few days, with no one whom he knew well at hand, after Brett returned to London. However, the Embassy was helpful, and young Mitchell frequently accompanied him on trips about Sven. He saw Sylva several times, and knew that the house on Kirche Hill was searched comprehensively, without result.

Nothing was learned to throw light on the main problem—the place where Drusilla, Brian and Conroy were imprisoned.

• • • • •

It was bitterly cold in the small room where the prisoners were held. Brian lay on a bed, his face white, and his eyes closed. Now and again he gasped with pain from his wounds. Drusilla and Conroy were by the small window, looking at the white expanse of hills and the spiky trees, the small plain beyond the village and, farther on, the frowning heights of a range of mountains.

In the next room, they knew, were Madalena Gagliani and her father-in-law; the Italians had some freedom of movement, but there was no friendliness between them and the two German armed guards downstairs.

'Not a sign of a doctor,' Conroy said in a harsh voice; 'they don't give a damn whether he lives or dies.'

Drusilla did not answer. Conroy lit one of a few remaining cigarettes, and approached Brian, who winced again, without opening his eyes.

'There's nothing we can do,' Drusilla said.

'Isn't there?' growled Conroy. 'Isn't there, by heck! I'll get that doctor if they kill me for it!' He swung round and leapt at the door, crashing bodily into it. The walls quivered, and Brian opened his eyes and tried to speak.

'Don't——' Drusilla began, urgently.

Conroy ignored her, turned and picked up a hardwood chair, and raised it above his head. He brought it crashing down on the door and one leg caught in the splintered wood. The rest of the chair fell to pieces. A voice was raised below and footsteps thundered on the stairs. Conroy wrenched the leg away and struck the door again.

'Alex, don't!' cried Drusilla.

'Stand back!' roared a man in German, 'stand back, or I shoot!'

Conroy obeyed, but stood glaring at his jailers as they opened the door and stood on the threshold, both heavily-built, youthful men, one with a revolver and the other carrying a tommy-gun at his waist.

'I told you to get a doctor!' Conroy snapped, in German.

'*You* told! You!'

'Yes, *I* did,' Conroy shouted, 'and——'

The nearer man swept his hand round and caught the American on the side of the head. Conroy fell against the wall but kept his hold on the chair-leg. The guard kicked his hand, forcing him to relinquish it, and kicked him savagely in the ribs; then he bent down, hauled him to his feet and pushed him roughly outside and slammed the door. He shouted orders to the other guard, then cursed Conroy as he hustled him downstairs.

Drusilla stepped to Brian's side.

His eyes, wide open now, were bright with fever. He had a rising temperature and his wounds, bound with strips torn from Drusilla's slip, badly needed attention. The bandages used in Sven had become foul, and the wound in his left arm was already turning gangrenous. No doctor had seen him for three days, and, although Drusilla was a trained nurse, there was little she could do without drugs, equipment, and antiseptics.

The blankets of the camp bed—there were two other beds in the room—were dirty, and there were no sheets.

'He shouldn't have tried,' Brian whispered.

Drusilla rested her cold hand on his head, but said nothing. Soon, he fell into a troubled sleep. Drusilla shivered, and turned away.

There was no heating in the room, and what little warmth there was came from the room below.

Footsteps outside made Drusilla turn to the door, but she had no hope that it was a doctor—whoever was approaching came from the same floor. After a low-voiced altercation, the door opened to admit Madalena Gagliani and the second guard.

Madalena smiled briefly at Drusilla, then turned to the bed. She carried a small box, marked with a red cross. Drusilla joined her quickly.

'No talking!' growled the guard, 'no talking!'

· · · · ·

Later that day, when darkness covered the snow and ice, Conroy lay on the floor of a room near the main pass from the village into the mountains. He was conscious, but his clothes were torn and his face was badly bruised.

At the door, a man with one arm gave instructions to the guard who had brought him here.

Conroy heard every word.

He was to be taken outside, made to walk towards the foothills, shot, and thrown into a crevice. He gave no sign to indicate that he understood, and let them kick him several times before he stirred.

'Get up!' the guard growled, and kicked him again.

Conroy rose unsteadily to his feet and staggered to one side. The guard gripped his arm, held him upright, and pushed him towards the door. Outside, two other guards stood waiting. The night was pitch black and the wind was howling from the mountains. Conroy, clad in ordinary clothes, shivered uncontrollably.

The chief guard gave instructions. By the open door of the little building, the one-armed man stood watching until darkness swallowed the party.

Conroy walked between two guards, while the leader walked behind, gun in hand.

The further they went from the mouth of the pass, the softer and deeper was the snow. Once or twice Conroy stumbled, but his captors held him up.

There was no sound, except for the wind and the heavy breathing of the four men.

Conroy had no idea how far they intended to take him, but as soon as the ground began to rise he knew that it would be a matter of minutes only. One guard switched on a torch, which shone on the glittering snow, and showed up the uneven ground, on which rocks rose ten and twenty feet into the air. There was no reasonable hope of escape, but Conroy, stumbling along as if too dazed to know what was afoot, intended to try; it would be better to be shot on the run than while he was unable to move. When he had lost his footing the guards' grip had loosened momentarily, and had not tightened as much again.

Only the long beam of the torch showed the way, and in a few minutes snow began to fall. Conroy, holding his muscles slack to aid deception, felt an agonising suspense, fearful lest he should be shot in the back before he moved, and afraid to move too soon in case the men tightened their grip on him.

The guard behind him spoke harshly. The attention of the others was distracted and Conroy stumbled. One man lost his grip completely, and the other's fingers slipped. Conroy kicked at the latter's legs and then swung round and leapt at the chief. He dived low; the man fired, but the bullet went over Conroy's head. Then Conroy was on him and sent him sprawling backwards; a second shot went towards the sky.

The torch fell and went out.

Conroy staggered on for twenty yards, then started to run, praying for a stretch of even ground. Twice he kicked against a stone, but kept his balance. The snow was coming faster, feathery flakes against his cheeks, making him close his eyes. The walk had made him stiff with cold, but already that was wearing off. He heard shouts behind him and grew aware of a faint light. Looking over his shoulder, he saw that the torch was on again, but turned away from him.

Ahead, there was only darkness, hiding the terrain, and the snow seemed to be coming down faster. He ran on, his feet heavier at every step because of the snow clogging them. The shouting had stopped, but twice the quiet was broken by the shrill blast of a whistle. Gasping for breath, Conroy tried to quicken his pace, but he found it difficult to put one foot in front of the other.

He kicked against a mound and fell flat on his face.

He could not get up immediately, and lay there, gulping in deep breaths of air with his eyes closed. When he opened them, he winced, not with pain but with surprise and sudden fear. To his right, carving a great white beam out of the darkness, a searchlight moved steadily; it was coming towards him. He put his head down and buried his face in his hands, but peeped through his fingers. The light drew nearer; at last it covered him and the ground ahead. He could see the ugly rocks, some white, some dark with shadows cast by the beam. The snow was coming down thick and fast, making it difficult to pick out individual objects.

The light passed on!

Conroy waited until it was ten feet away from him, then got to his feet and moved on. Soon, he was scrambling over rocks. Once he fell and struck his head against a sharp edge; it made him dizzy, but his forehead was so cold that he could not tell whether the wound was bleeding. He struggled on, until the searchlight drew nearer again and he crouched behind a rock, fairly confident that he would not be seen.

He heard voices and the barked commands of officers, which travelled clearly.

Soon, he lost all sense of direction, all hope and all feeling. Numbed, dazed, and so cold that he seemed afire, he went on automatically. The thought of reaching Palfrey, or even getting out of the storm alive, had faded.

He was vaguely aware of lights, some distance off, but he did not think it strange that he had walked for so long over even ground; nor did he see the square shapes of huts and houses before him, nor the men who were only a few hundred yards ahead in the centre of the village, shining their torches.

He had no idea that from the door of a house on the outskirts of the village, a man saw him and watched with eyes so long accustomed to the long dark nights of winter that they could see him clearly. He did not hear the man call out nor, when he took no notice, hurry towards him.

He was just conscious of a hand on his arm, and swung round in a sudden rebirth of fear.

'Not there!' the man said, in Nordian, 'not there—the Germans.'

Conroy did not catch the words, but judged that there was no need for immediate alarm. He allowed himself to be led across the road and towards the river. Only the snow, falling thick and fast, saved him from being seen. He was only vaguely aware of being led into a hut near the river's edge, and falling, semi-conscious, on to some sacks in a corner. He did not know that his guard kept watch throughout the night. When he woke up he saw daylight coming through the small window, and, once he was able to focus his gaze properly, saw that snow was still falling. As he struggled up, his rescuer came from the door, a short fellow dressed in sealskins, and smiling grimly.

'They have not come,' he said.

'Are they still searching?' Conroy demanded, tensely.

'Yes—they have offered a great reward for you.' The man spat on the floor. 'You were fortunate, I have no use for money or Germans. You plan to go south?'

Conroy said: 'I must go south! Or else——'

It was only then that he realised that he dared not send a message. Palfrey might be a wanted man in Sven, might even be in hiding.

His rescuer said: 'I can give you food for a day, and directions. You can leave soon, but in an hour or two the snow will have ceased, and if you are near here then, you will have no chance. I cannot go with you. If I were to go, my wife and family would be shot.'

Conroy drew a hand across his forehead. He winced, but ignored the pain as he dwelt on the need for getting away, on the slender chance that remained. In ten minutes, he was drinking hot cocoa and eating dry bread ravenously. In twenty, with the Nordian's directions ringing in his ears, he was out in the snow and heading south.

.   .   .   .   .

It was on the fifth day after he had left Sven, that Stefan returned.

The Russian gave Palfrey a résumé of his journey, the welcome from the Kremlin, which had not hidden its pleasure at the progress made and which, since Ingrid Gregarov had been 'influenced' by her husband, had chosen to ignore her pro-Nordian sympathies. There had been several conferences, reports from the Nordian and British Embassies and some routine work, before they had been sent back to help finish the job.

Stefan saw the lines on his forehead and mouth, and knew the depth of his anxiety; Palfrey was glad that he did not speak of Drusilla.

They had been there for half-an-hour, when the telephone rang. Palfrey answered it, to hear a familiar voice—that of Mitchell at the Embassy.

'I will say you've got some queer friends,' Mitchell said, 'there's a little fellow here who professes to be a real old crony—only he doesn't know your address. He wants it——'

'Who is he?' Palfrey asked, sharply.

'By name, Sylva,' Mitchell said, 'a little old fellow with a grey beard. Do you know him?' When Palfrey did not answer immediately, he went on: 'I seem to have heard the name somewhere—*do* you know him?'

24: The Discovery Made by Sylva

Palfrey said quickly: 'Yes, I know him all right. Tell him we'll be at his house in a little over half an hour's time, will you?'

As they stepped into the hall, the heat met them like a blanket. Sylva rushed out.

'Dr. Palfrey! I am delighted!'

His dreariness had gone, he no longer sagged at the shoulders, and the grey of his hair did not seem so lifeless. His eyes sparkled and he walked on his toes, alternately clapping and rubbing his hands.

'Oh, I am a happy man tonight. I did not think that such days would return!' he went on. 'Also, I make a great triumph!' He beamed at Palfrey.

'How?' asked Palfrey, slightly more hopeful.

'Doctor, I tell you this. The police and the militia, they come and search this house, they look everywhere and they find nothing, nothing at all of interest. Also, before them, other men, who were rogues. I did not know them, but I allowed them to stay because I knew they were armed. The crimes of Gregarov are not my business, and those who worked against him had my support.' He had a slightly sheepish air, and he looked at Palfrey as if wondering whether he knew the truth about the incident of the key, but as no comment was forthcoming he clapped his hands again. 'Come! I will show you what I have discovered!'

He led the way to the door, stepping out importantly, while the others followed in single file, going up the stairs and along the passage to the room where Palfrey had treated Gregarov for 'small-pox'. Sylva strode in, went straight to a chest of drawers of satin walnut, and pulled out the middle drawer.

It looked like any other drawer, and was filled with linen. Sylva took a pen-knife from his pocket and pushed the blade into the upright at the back. The wood of the upright was stouter than in most drawers, nearly half an inch thick. Gradually, Sylva prised up a thin layer from the top, wheezing with excitement.

The layer fitted close, like a stopper, and came out. Palfrey watched with bated breath, while Sylva probed again with his knife, bringing up a piece of paper. Palfrey forced himself to hold back, and not to rob the man of his triumph, while Sylva drew the paper out slowly. It was not one piece, but a dozen or more, sheets which were folded over and over again.

'There!' cried Sylva. 'You see—plans! Plans, hidden by Gregarov!'

He smoothed them out and the others crowded about him, Palfrey peering down with a quickening excitement; he thought he knew what they were. Soon, he was quite sure; they were duplicates of the blue-prints which he had found in Amata's cot!

He looked at them one after the other. They looked like original drawings, done in drawing-ink; the blue-prints had been photographed on his memory, and he knew he was not mistaken.

Stefan looked at him. 'Do you recognise them, Sap?'

'Yes,' said Palfrey, 'they're the same as we found——'

Sylva cried, aghast: 'You have seen them before?'

'Yes, but not here,' Palfrey said quickly, for the little man's face had fallen ludicrously, and he looked almost ready to cry. 'We had no idea that they would be here. Your discovery is of great importance, Mr. Sylva.'

'Ah!' Sylva beamed again, and clapped his hands resonantly. 'I knew it would be of importance, I had no doubt! But, Doctor, there is another paper—one which I have kept in my pocket, because I thought it meant so much.' He thrust his hand into his pocket and drew out a wallet, taking an unconscionable time to extract another piece of folded flimsy paper. He smoothed it out with great care.

'A map!' exclaimed Ingrid.

'A map of northern Nordia, with indications which I believe will be of great importance,' declared Sylva, proudly.

Palfrey pushed his hand through his hair, his fingers unsteady; he had not dreamed of such a break as this. He tried to restrain the sudden flash of optimism as he peered at the map, which was drawn in great detail. It showed the fjords and rivers, the lakes and mountains of the northern provinces; but one portion was shaded.

Palfrey had eyes only for that.

He saw the tiny dot denoting a village; written next to it was the word 'Staar'. It was on the west bank of the Sven River, perhaps a hundred miles from Sven itself; the fjord ended seventy miles from the mouth. The shaded area seemed to cover a district some ten miles square.

'Is it not important?' demanded Sylva.

'It's probably the biggest find we've made in Sven,' said Palfrey, warmly. 'You couldn't have done better.'

Palfrey clapped him on the back. 'You have worked miracles, Mr. Sylva, and I'll make sure that the right people know it. As soon as there's time, I'll tell you all about it, but now we're off—if we lose an hour, we might lose lives.'

Stefan wanted Ingrid to accompany them on their journey North, and although Palfrey doubted the wisdom of this plan he realised that between the woman and Stefan there had arisen an understanding which brooked no interference from him. He realised it with only half of his mind; nothing really counted against the possibility that they would find Drusilla.

As he reached the hotel, his high spirits began to wane.

Sylva had completely deceived him once, and might have done so again. Stefan's men were so thorough that they must surely have tested all the furniture, and the failure of the police to find the papers was surely odd. He was about to enter the lift, when he caught the reception clerk's eye. He went over to him.

'I thought you should know, sir, that there has been a man asking for you.' The clerk—Olaf—said 'man' disparagingly.

'Did he give his name?' asked Palfrey.

'No, sir, he just asked for you. When I told him you were out, he said that he would wait in your room. I made that impossible, of course, by refusing to tell him the room number. He went out again immediately, sir.'

'What was he like?'

'A short man,' said Olaf, 'dressed in very old and soiled clothes. Certainly he was not the type whom I would have expected to come to see you, sir, and——' the Nordian lowered his voice—'he did not take off his cap, and he kept his collar of his coat turned up so I had no opportunity of seeing his face. I thought you should be warned, sir.'

'I'm glad you told me,' Palfrey said. 'Thanks.'

He went upstairs thoughtfully. The clerk had made a

sinister figure of the caller, but Palfrey questioned whether any man coming with ill-intent would make himself so obviously suspicious.

But he was wary when he reached his room.

He opened the door and stepped swiftly to one side; nothing happened. His frown deepened, but he stepped carefully into the room and pushed the door sharply back against the wall. There was no one behind it. He went in further—and stopped abruptly.

On the bed a man was lying face downwards, his hands clutching the pillows and his feet hanging over the side; he was not moving.

25: News of Great Moment

A cloth cap was on the floor by the side of the bed; the man's tousled hair was dark, with a thin patch in the middle. Palfrey stood staring, his heart beating faster; for he knew who it was. Then he went forward abruptly, bending over the bed.

'Alex, old chap!'

It was Conroy, but he made no move and gave no indication that he could hear. There was blood on the pillow, and his hands were swollen and blue with cold. He was the caller, of course, the clerk's 'sinister' suspect. He had not known of the new situation, and had not dared to give his name.

Palfrey turned him on his back.

There was an ugly gash in his forehead, still bleeding slightly, but otherwise he looked unhurt, except for his swollen hands and blue face. Palfrey felt his pulse; it was very slow. He pressed the bell for a maid, then untied Conroy's shoes; they were damp and badly out of shape, as if he had waded through water for a long time. Palfrey took them off, then began to undress him. The clothes were wet and frozen stiff, and his whole body was blue.

There was a knock at the door, and the maid opened it.

'Yes, sir?' she began, then saw Conroy and stopped short.

Palfrey glanced round at her.

'Get hot-water bottles, please, and some extra blankets.'

'Y-yes, sir!' She turned away, forgetting to close the door. Palfrey pushed it to, then stripped the bed, put Conroy between the blankets, and began to massage him. The American's nostrils were moving, but his swollen lips were compressed.

The maid came back, laden with blankets and bottles.

'Put them down,' said Palfrey, 'and get me some brandy or whisky. Ask the manager to come up here, but say nothing to anyone else, please.'

He spooned a little whisky between Conroy's lips, sorry that he had to, for the wound in the forehead might prove dangerous under the effect of the stimulant; but the first job was to get the American to talk. Conroy's lips moved, and the muscles of his throat stirred as he swallowed the whisky.

A tap at the door heralded the manager.

Obviously the maid had warned him what to expect, for he showed no sign of surprise.

'How can I help, Doctor?'

'I don't know that you can do much, but you ought to know he's here,' Palfrey said. 'I will have to leave him, and I want him well looked after—can the chamber-maid do that?'

'I will send another to the floor, and leave her free for the task,' the manager promised.

The man went out and Palfrey turned back to Conroy. His colour was better and the blue tinge lingered only at his nostrils and lips. There was nothing else to be done, and Palfrey was in a fever of impatience.

There was a tap at the door. It was Stefan, bending to enter the room. Palfrey straightened up and smiled. He saw, but did not pay any heed to, the tense expression on Stefan's face before the Russian set eyes on Conroy.

'Alex?' he asked.

Palfrey nodded. 'I think he'll come round soon, and we'll know what there is to know. How've you been doing?'

Stefan said: 'There is a great stir in Sven. My men have been prepared and have been given facilities to go to Staar, and they are already on their way. I went to the Foreign Office, with our Ambassador. Others are being rushed to Staar, and all the militia and armed forces in that and the adjoining provinces have been warned to watch for the party of Germans. They are taking no chances.'

'Alex will put us right,' Palfrey said, 'and I can't believe we've been foxed about the north, they're up there somewhere. The problem is, how many of 'em? Stefan—do you remember a curious story of well-fed civilians being sent north, to some unknown destination?'

'Ye-es,' said Stefan, slowly.

'It might have been Nordia,' Palfrey said. 'I——'

He broke off, at a gasp from Conroy, and they turned to look at him. His body heaved, then was still. Palfrey waited a moment, but the sick man's eyes did not open. He smiled slightly; Conroy was conscious but 'foxing' because he was not sure where he was.

'It's all right, Alex,' Palfrey said. 'I'm here, with Stefan.'

Conroy's lips moved and a croaking sound came from them. He opened his eyes, so swollen that they showed only as narrow slits.

'S-Sap——'

'Take it easy,' Palfrey said.

Conroy gasped: 'Sap—Fienne Province—the mountains! Fienne Province—the mountains!' He drew a deep breath, then added: 'Make things hum! It's colossal. *Colossal!*' He tried to raise himself on one elbow, but Stefan pressed him back. 'Don't lose time,' Conroy croaked, 'don't mind me. It's—so big——'

Conroy blinked in the sudden glare of light, and Palfrey took out a handkerchief and tied it about the shade, putting the room in shadow, then he moved to the wall and pressed the bell-push.

'All right, Alex, we're all set, all we want are the details. You're sure about Fienne?'

'Don't stand there asking questions!' Conroy croaked.

'It's not Staar?'

'Staar?' echoed Conroy. He tried to sit up again. 'What's got into you? Fienne Province, Fienne village, the——' He sat back, gasping. 'Sorry! I'm—all in. But—don't mind me.'

Palfrey said: 'You'll be all right.' He stepped to the telephone and asked for the Foreign Office, not wanting to waste time going through the Embassy. He was told that the call would take some time. He went on: 'Is Drusilla up there?'

'Yes. And Brian—Brian's hurt badly, but 'Silla was all right. Sap—you might cut them off in the village, that's where I left 'em. 'Silla and Brian and—and a mob. Not all of the Huns—it—it's colossal! Don't take a policeman, take——'

'The army,' Palfrey said. 'We will.'

'You'll—need it!' gasped Conroy. 'Didn't think I'd make it, had——'

'You've worked miracles,' Palfrey said, 'don't spoil them now.' Would the Foreign Office never come through?

The door opened and the maid looked in; he asked her to

bring some strong, sweet tea or coffee and some thin sandwiches, and as she went out the telephone rang.

In a few minutes, he had given the revised information to Horst himself, and he said: 'We shall need biggish forces, and——'

'Biggish!' gasped Conroy, 'listen——' He broke off, fighting for breath, and Palfrey went on hastily, 'If you'll just wait a moment, sir.' He put the receiver down. 'Just how much can you tell us, Alex.'

He hated the sight of the American fighting to tell his story, but at last, Conroy spoke more easily.

'Thousands of people, thousands of men! Huge underground factories, in the mountains. Well armed. Well guarded. Fortified! The village on the river, the entrance to the place a couple of miles on—three, maybe. 'Silla and Brian were in the village, so was Gagliani. But—what the hell are you waiting for, get going!'

Palfrey passed on the information; Horst made no lengthy comment, and rang off at once.

Stefan said: 'Don't get agitated, Alex. We are going off as soon as the men are ready, and someone will come to tell us.' He looked at Palfrey, smiling grimly. 'You were right, Sap, the slaves went there.'

'It looks like it, it all ties up.' Palfrey went to the wardrobe and took out a small suit-case, already packed with clothes bought in Sven. He tucked an automatic and a dozen spare rounds into his pocket, and put on a woollen undercoat. Conroy had stopped trying to speak and lay back, breathing stertorously.

Stefan looked more worried then the circumstances warranted, but before Palfrey could ask any questions, there was another tap at the door.

A stocky man, swathed in a fur coat and with a fur skullcap pulled down over his ears, entered and looked about him. Behind him, two others carried furs for Palfrey and Stefan. The leader spoke in a harsh, clipped voice. They would need these clothes, and he was at their service, he had instructions to do exactly what they ordered. His party was forty strong, all men trained in Alpine warfare.

'You know we're going to Fienne, not Staar?'

'A message has just reached me, yes.'

'Good!' said Palfrey, struggling into the clothes and smiling at Alex. 'We'll be bringing home the meat!' he said, and hurried out.

The party caused a stir in the hall as it hurried through, Stefan looking gigantic in his furs. All of them were glad of the furs, even in Sven; when the party reached the northern territories they would be essential.

They crowded into a car and were driven off.

Palfrey said to the leader: 'You know that stronger forces will soon be on the way?'

'Yes,' The man peered at him through the dim light from the street. 'You should know, Doctor, that my name is Ohlson, Captain Ohlson.'

'Thanks,' said Palfrey. 'Our job is to try to rescue a small party, in Fienne village.'

'I knew of the small party,' said Ohlson.

'Fine!' said Palfrey.

They reached the fjord in a little more than ten minutes. A motor-launch was drawn up at a lighted quayside, and two armed men were standing on the quay, muffled in furs. They all walked across a narrow companion-way which was drawn in quickly, and hardly had they reached the deck than the engine, already turning over, was revved up. They moved swiftly into the choppy water of the fjord.

For a short while, Palfrey and Stefan stayed on deck.

Suddenly, a man came out of the darkness and advised them to go below. They did so, finding the stifling heat of a tiny cabin almost overpowering. They were left on their own, and, after taking off their outer clothes, they sat down on either side of a small table, with a dim, automatically balanced lamp between them.

Palfrey said: 'So we're on the last lap.'

'Ye-es,' said Stefan, and rose suddenly to his feet. 'Sap——' He broke off, and stared down. The bleakness in his face disturbed Palfrey.

'What is it?' asked Palfrey, quietly.

'In the excitement, you haven't missed Ingrid, have you?' asked Stefan.

He told Palfrey that after seeing her father that evening, Ingrid had been struck down by two assailants and carried off in a car. Sylva had been in a terribly distressed condition when he had told Stefan. Palfrey listened to the story as the launch chugged its way up the fjord. Stefan's man had reported immediately; Stefan had picked up the report and gone to see Sylva, who seemed stricken, and to whom a doctor had been called. Stefan made no attempt to guess at the reason for the attack, nor any to minimise the effect of the news on him. Palfrey remembered the moment when the Russian and Ingrid had first met; it had been a strange preliminary to a deep emotion.

'Well?' Stefan asked, 'what do you think of it? How can you explain it?'

'This isn't going to be easy,' thought Palfrey.

26 : The Approach to Fienne

'I think it's a repetition of the old trick,' Palfrey said at last. 'They learned that Conroy reached Sven, and set to work. They don't want you and I—you in particular—careering north, and they tried this to detain you. They've tried to hobble us before, remember—in Rome, in Moscow——'

Stefan said: 'You are being kind, of course. Don't, Sap.'

'What gives you that odd idea?' Palfrey demanded.

'It is so obviously a plan that could have been done by clever arrangement,' Stefan said, 'Ingrid was willing to stay with her father, although she has little regard for him——'

'A kindly gesture to an old man,' Palfrey insisted.

'I wish I were sure of it,' said Stefan. 'I must admit that I am afraid she might have known that the attack was to be staged, so that our trust in her would not falter.'

Palfrey said: 'I think you're carrying suspicions too far, don't flay yourself. Did she even have a chance to escape?'

'My man reported that she did not appear to make a serious attempt to get away,' Stefan said, 'and she stopped at the corner, where she could be clearly seen. The car arrived at exactly the right moment.'

'What motive do you give her?' Palfrey asked.

'That is clear. She can warn them that we are on the move.'

'She's not one of them!' Palfrey snapped, 'I can't believe it. It's much more likely that they tried to draw you off.'

'Oh, she had the opportunity,' said Stefan. 'Why do you laugh like that?' He was abrupt.

Palfrey said: 'Come, old chap! She might have sent a general alarm, but she doesn't know that Conroy is back, she could only warn them that we're on our way to Staar. If she tried to send us there, that wouldn't add up.'

'You make one mistake,' Stefan said, 'because you don't know the country. Staar is half-way to Fienne, so we are not making any alteration in our route, it would obviously be northwards. We shall be at Staar about dawn, and at Fienne tomorrow night, about dusk. Then, perhaps, we'll know more. Now, I am going to get some rest!'

He lay down on the bottom bunk of two, with his knees bent, and Palfrey took the top one. Neither of them undressed. Palfrey was disturbed by Stefan's frame of mind as much as by the possibility that Ingrid had contrived a grand deception, but his thoughts turned to the prospect at Fienne.

Thousands of men, sent there either across Finland or northern Norway, where secrecy would have been easy during the long winter nights—local authorities could have been bribed. The district was mountainous, and the mountains had certainly been used to advantage—the need for Gagliani, specialist in tunnelling, at least grew apparent—as did the probable reason for Madalena's abduction. She had overheard something of what was being planned in Rome; Gagliani could not trust her and, being on the point of leaving for Nordia himself, had taken her with him.

Palfrey frowned in the darkness. The forty men on board could relax until they neared Fienne, but should be warned to be on the look-out at Staar.

He listened to Stefan's heavy breathing, then carefully got off his bunk and tiptoed to the door.

As he opened it, Stefan said:

'What is it, Sap?'

'Sorry,' exclaimed Palfrey, 'I didn't want to disturb you.'

'I shall not sleep much, but I shall relax,' Stefan said. 'Where are you going?'

'To warn them about the chance of fireworks at Staar,' said Palfrey.

He tapped, and the cabin door was opened promptly. Captain Ohlson saluted him.

Palfrey stepped inside, glad of the warmth after the bitter cold outside. He rubbed his hands together briskly as he passed on the warning.

'Because of the earlier information,' Ohlson said, 'we shall be prepared at Staar.' The man's hard face held a faint smile, but he stood rigidly to attention all the time. 'There are detachments of the militia and of the Army up there, ready to co-operate with us. I will contact them by radio and will arrange to have the banks of the fjord closely guarded, for added security.'

'Good!' said Palfrey. 'Good night!'

He was awakened, when daylight was coming through the porthole, by a man as rugged as Ohlson, who held a cup of steaming coffee. Stefan was sitting on the edge of his bunk, a cup in his hand, and Ohlson was by the door.

Stefan looked up with a wry grin.

'The man who couldn't sleep,' said Palfrey, struggling to a sitting position before reaching out for the cup. 'Ah, that's just what I wanted, thanks!' He sipped the hot coffee, hugging a blanket about his shoulders, for it was bitterly cold. The sailor went out, and Ohlson's face was brightened by a wide grin.

'You will know what cold is, in Fienne!'

'Go away!' said Palfrey, 'I want cheering up.' He thought: 'We're that much nearer, it won't last long, now.' Then he said sharply: 'What's that?'

A cracking noise came faintly to the cabin. Stefan stood up abruptly and banged his head on the low ceiling.

'Rifle fire?' Palfrey demanded.

'Breaking ice?' hazarded Stefan.

'There was an attack on us, the other side of Staar, which we have just passed,' Ohlson told them, 'but our forces on the banks kept the river clear for us. They are still fighting, but we are not likely to meet trouble this side of Fienne. Your warning was timely, Doctor. I came to reassure you, there is no need for you to come yet. Breakfast will not be ready for an hour.'

He went out, and Palfrey finished the coffee and jumped down, running his fingers over his chin.

'I don't think I'll shave,' he said.

Five minutes later, clad in their fur coats and gasping in the teeth of a stiff wind which blew from the mountains, they stood amid a scene of indescribable grandeur. The fjord was little more than a wide river, and on either side were white-topped hills. Farther inland, the earth was an unbroken expanse of white. There was thin ice on the water, which was whipped by the wind; and the ice, cracking from time to time, made a sound not unlike rifle-fire.

Looking down river, Palfrey saw a group of buildings surmounted by the tall spire of a church; it was Staar village, only two miles away. The boom of a heavy gun travelled faintly, for the wind carried the sound straight across the fjord, not up river.

They began to pace the deck, where a dozen armed men were standing, on the look-out for snipers.

Twice within an hour, they saw tiny villages on the banks of the river—they were out of the fjord now—with smoke rising from low chimneys.

Palfrey began to feel hungry, and was glad when they were called below to breakfast—a meal of soup and fish, in ample quantities, with strong, hot coffee to follow, and plenty of good, brown bread.

Ohlson came to the cabin soon afterwards.

'We have made excellent speed,' he said, 'and there have been no delays. I was afraid of ice, but we shall reach Fienne in a little more than two hours. Also, I have received word by radio. Action is being taken immediately, and forces are being moved towards Fienne by air as well as by the river. No matter how many men there might be, we shall overpower them.' He paused. 'What orders have you, Doctor?'

'We'll have to take it as it comes,' said Palfrey. 'I suppose you know that the district is fortified?'

'My men are trained Alpine troops,' Ohlson reminded him.

Stefan said, slowly: 'They will probably be prepared for us.'

'If it is agreeable to you, we shall go ashore a mile from the town, and approach from behind it,' the Nordian said.

'You're in command,' Palfrey said, 'and you know exactly what we want—in case there's any doubt, we're after a party of three—or more—one woman and two men, one of the latter injured. We know they were in the village, and we want to try to prevent them from being taken into the mountains.'

'I understand perfectly,' Ohlson said, and went off.

Palfrey and Stefan followed him on deck. The invigorating air gave Palfrey a feeling of elation, and his fears subsided; a sober estimate of the situation might have made him sure that directly trouble started near Fienne, the Nazis would take the prisoners out of the village, but actually he felt that there was a sound chance of arriving in time.

Looking at the great peaks which seemed to move past them, so smooth was their progress, his exhilaration increased. Stefan was infected by it, judging from the sober smile in his eyes. The majesty of the scene fascinated them, although there was no sun, and mists curled down from the mountains and filled some of the valleys, so that the only colours were black, dark green and white, and all were mysterious. It was unreal; the thought of Bruckner coming to such a place, of the Nazis building a fastness within the mountains, seemed fantastic. Yet there could have been few places more secure, and with Nordian co-operation, it could have become a stronghold, such as had never existed.

Stefan said: 'Not long now, Sap, before we know the best or the worst.'

'The best!' said Palfrey, 'I won't believe anything else!| Ohlson is about the most comforting mortal I know.'

'A good man, yes,' said Stefan and raised his head sharply. 'What is that?'

They stood silent, and Palfrey saw members of the crew looking along the river. At first, only the rippling of the water and the occasional cracking of thin ice broke the silence, but suddenly he heard a booming sound, a long way off.

Stefan said: 'It's started.'

Palfrey nodded, but did not speak.

They approached a bend in the river, and Ohlson came forward to tell them that Fienne was just ahead. The shooting grew much clearer, both the rumble of field artillery and the sharp cracks of rifle shots.

The launch rounded the bend slowly, and they came within sight of Fienne.

27: The Pass Through the Mountains

Palfrey stood rigid, peering towards the shore as the launch made her steady way onwards, with bows crunching through the thin ice. Snow had fallen recently, and he was near enough to the banks to see the high drifts against the rocky hillside. The cracking ice did not muffle the sound of gunfire, which was getting louder. The rocky ground, rising abruptly from the small plain on which the village was built, had a grim, forbidding look as the launch swung round the bend and Palfrey saw Fienne.

His first impression was of a collection of wooden huts, but it was quickly lost in the sight of the mountain range beyond. Dark tree-clad slopes, menacing and formidable, reached high towards the brooding sky, the top-most peaks swallowed by heavy mist. The trees, all pines, showed dark green where snow had fallen from their branches, on the south side; obviously the blizzard had blown from the north.

Palfrey was oblivious to the biting wind and the icy coldness, and even to the shooting. The mountains of Fienne seemed to present an insuperable barrier; if the Huns were behind them, they would be able to defy any attack for months.

The ambush at Staar and the fact that there was fighting here, reduced the chances of Drusilla and Brian being in the village; Palfrey tried to prevent himself from dwelling on it.

The shooting grew fiercer. It seemed to be coming from beyond the village, on the other side of a hill, which was bleak and white. There was no sign of fighting in the village itself and no sign of occupation except a few plumes of grey smoke which were wafted southwards on the wind.

Beyond one side of the hill, Palfrey caught a glimpse of fur-clad men; only the flashes from their rifles as they fired enabled him to pick them out, and the shooting was rapid.

The launch drew nearer the deserted quay, which looked undamaged; Palfrey thought of mines, but the men seemed to have no fears, for as soon as the sides touched the quayside three jumped out and began to make the launch fast.

Adding to the noise made by the men, the cracking ice and the shooting, a distant drone made Palfrey look southwards. At first he saw nothing, but soon a flight of aircraft came in sight, twin-engined bombers which made the air quiver as they drew nearer. They flew low over the village, as if on a bombing run, and when they had flown over the hill, Palfrey saw the bombs drop from their bellies.

Explosions followed swiftly, reverberating through the air and drowning all other sound. Clouds of smoke rose up, peppered with darker pieces of earth or debris.

Stefan said, quietly: 'We were not first, Sap, but the attack is well-managed.'

'It's beginning to look as if the Huns drove the villagers away,' Palfrey said, grimly.

The words were hardly out of his mouth before he was confounded by the appearance of three men from one of the wooden houses. Short, fat; and clad in seal-skins which made them look grotesque, they came bustling towards the launch. By then, Palfrey and Stefan had joined the detachment on the quay. Four men stayed behind to guard the launch, while Ohlson, Palfrey and Stefan went ahead of the main party, to speak to the villagers.

The only man above medium height proved to be the spokesman. His dialect was different from any Palfrey had heard, and he understood only a word here and there, but he was able to follow the opening sentences from Ohlson's questions.

'Has there been a party including women?' Ohlson asked. Palfrey, studying the other man's face closely, judged that he was admitting that there had been. 'Where are they?' Ohlson demanded. The man pointed towards the fighting, and spoke very rapidly.

Stefan said in a low voice: 'They were here until quite a short time ago.' After a pause, he went on: 'There were two women and two or three men, together with a party of German guards. They have not been gone for more than half-an-hour.'

Palfrey nodded, thinking bitterly that they might have been in time. Now, he hardly dared allow himself to hope.

Ohlson was talking more swiftly, and Palfrey could only guess what he was saying, but within five minutes Stefan told him the whole story so far as it was known. The first Nordian attack had come over the hills to the south. As soon as it had started, the prisoners had been moved, but the villagers knew that they had not yet crossed the flat ground between the village and the mountains. The guards had not joined in the fighting, but had taken their prisoners a long way round, to avoid it.

'Come on!' Palfrey said, urgently.

'Wait!' Stefan exhorted, but Palfrey was already running towards the hump of snow-clad ground. His feet slipped on the frozen snow of the village streets and his breathing grew more laboured; two of three times his breath stabbed like a knife through his lungs; he knew that he was acting foolishly, but felt that he had to get to the top of the hill.

Stefan had joined him, and he reached the summit first. They stood together, looking on to a plain which stretched for some two miles and was unbroken except for a hut on one side. The opposing forces were half-way across the plain, with some hundred yards separating them. As there was no cover, any concerted rush would lead to disaster. Some were crawling forward on their stomachs, trying to outflank the Germans, who had their backs to the mountain and to a pass leading into them; and others were maintaining a distracting fire.

On either side of the pass, what looked like great blockhouses had been built, and heavy guns were mounted on them; smoke was still rising from the side of one, and it was obvious that the bombers tried to destroy the artillery. The blockhouses were more like great walls, perhaps twenty feet high and certainly as thick; and there was only a narrow gap between them. Beyond, the lower slopes of the mountains were cut in two by the pass, becoming little more than a defile as it reached the higher ground.

There was no sign of the party of prisoners.

'I was wrong,' Palfrey said, dully, 'we've wasted time.'

'No harm is done,' Stefan said, 'Ohlson will have finished interrogating the villagers by now, and will know the position.' The Russian's calmness was steadying, and Palfrey scrambled down the hill, sliding on the seat of his trousers most of the way. When he reached the foot, Stefan was already talking to Ohlson.

'There is a short cut to the pass,' Stefan told him, quickly, 'which the Huns are trying to reach the easy way, with the prisoners. The fighting is mostly an attempt to give them cover. The short cut is a difficult one. Will you stay?'

'I'm coming!' Palfrey said.

Ohlson's men were already on the move, and Palfrey went briskly with them. They appeared to be going a long way round, but as soon as they were in the foothills they turned left, towards the pass.

Palfrey's breath began to get short, and twice he glanced at Stefan. The main party was ahead of them and he knew that Stefan was deliberately slowing down.

'Don't wait for me,' Palfrey said. 'Yes,' he said a moment later, at Stefan's questioning glance, 'I mean it.'

'Take no risks when on your own,' Stefan exhorted.

Soon Stefan and the others were scrambling over snow-clad rocks and through scrub and small trees, always along a well-defined trail. They were half a mile ahead of him when they climbed over a high ridge and dropped down out of sight.

Palfrey was on his own amid that illimitable expanse of dreary whiteness. The shooting meant little, and occasional cracks did nothing to spur him to greater effort.

He reached the foot of the ridge and, after many false starts, began to climb it. When he reached the top, he looked along a defile through the rocks; no one was in sight. On either side were wide chasms, where a single slip, which might prove fatal, would be easy for an unpractised climber.

Ahead and all about him were only rocks and snow and silence. That lasted for so long that he began to fear that he had lost his way, for he was hidden from the mountains by the high ground on either side of him, but footprints were still visible.

He had been in the defile for perhaps twenty minutes when he heard a droning sound, which at first puzzled him. Soon, he realised that it was another flight of bombers. The roar grew louder, and turning his head, he saw them approaching. The reverberation brought snow tumbling down as the bombers passed low overhead.

Again, he saw bombs falling and heard the explosions. He knew that the bomb-aimers could not tell the difference between friend and foe, but he shut the thought from his mind.

When he reached a higher spot, he could see beyond the rocks, towards the plain. He was much nearer the mountain pass and could also see the fortifications clearly. As he watched, one of the big guns opened fire, but the cloud of dust from the bombs which had fallen, obscured great stretches of the pass; suddenly he appreciated the object of the bombing—a way was being made easy for a frontal assault.

He assessed the position on the plain quickly.

The opposing Nordian and German forces were half-way between the village and the pass, still on their stomachs and maintaining rapid fire. The big guns were silent. Nearer the pass, a file of men and women, dressed in ordinary clothes— the soldiers were all in furs—was hurrying on. Palfrey had no doubt they were the prisoners, and even imagined that he could distinguish Drusilla. There were five in all, chained or roped together. By their side were four armed soldiers, ahead were two more, and bringing up the rear were three who were backing from the scene of the shooting and occasionally firing.

Ohlson was right; the fighting was being done by a rearguard, protecting the withdrawal of the prisoners from the village.

Palfrey would have thought the position hopeless, but, ahead of him and approaching the pass—nearer to it even than the prisoners—were Stefan and Ohlson and their party. The Nordians and the prisoners were equi-distant from Palfrey, and both nearly half a mile away from him. As far as he could judge, Ohlson's men had not yet disclosed their presence; the guards with the prisoners were not shooting towards them. They were probably hidden by the rocks from the plain itself.

He heard another flight of aircraft.

That scared him more than anything else, for the prisoners were dangerously near the pass and a bomb would cause havoc among them. Hurrying on, he held his breath as he saw the bombs dropping, then paused, exclaiming aloud in admiration, for it was pattern bombing; not a single missile fell more than a few yards from the fortifications.

Palfrey was near enough to see other fortifications further up the pass, which grew narrower and was much easier to protect. He missed the full significance of it then, for his interest was only in the prisoners.

Brian was not among them, for no one was being carried.

He heard nothing, but saw one of the guards point towards Ohlson's party, now deploying into the plain. A sharp burst of rifle-fire followed. The leading guards pulled at the rope to which the prisoners were tied; one of the women fell, but was dragged to her feet and hustled on. Some of the Nordians, ignoring the shooting, were heading for the pass, to try to cut the prisoners off, while others, including Stefan, were making for the guards. Palfrey, desperate now, saw two guards fall, followed by two of Ohlson's men.

There seemed to be a long pause before the guards began to run towards the pass, *leaving the prisoners!*

The three men who had been behind the party had stopped, and Palfrey saw them turning their guns towards Drusilla.

A crackle of fire sent one of them falling, but they had already fired several bursts. The first man of the prisoners fell, dragging the others with him, so that one well-directed burst would injure them all. Stefan was covering the ground at amazing speed, but he fell once, and for a moment Palfrey thought that he had been wounded. The Russian was up again in a trice, firing from the hip. Palfrey's concern was for the helpless heap of men and women on the snow, the savage-faced guards who knew that there was no hope for them and might kill for the sake of it, and from the mouth of the pass a stronger party of men came running to oppose Ohlson's main force.

Palfrey hardly noticed them as he ran towards Drusilla.

28 : The Finding of Gagliani

The bulk of the German rearguard was cut off from the pass and had no chance of rejoining the main forces, which were further up the pass, and were in a well-nigh impregnable position. But Drusilla, if she were alive, would be saved; nothing else seemed to matter to Palfrey.

The five people on the snow did not move.

Only one of the guards was firing, and Stefan was approaching him and taking careful aim. The man fell, and lay still. Stefan reached the prisoners and Palfrey drew a deep, sobbing breath. Stefan took a knife from his pocket and began to cut the ropes, turning the prisoners on their backs. Palfrey could not be sure which of the women was Drusilla, but one was motionless and the other trying to sit up.

At last he drew near enough to distinguish the faces, *and saw that it was Drusilla sitting up,* only to fall back again.

She lay with her eyes open and her face expressionless, showing neither relief nor pain; she looked as if she were beyond feeling. Palfrey did not realise that the other woman was Madalena Gagliani.

The snow near them was stained red.

Palfrey went down on his knees beside Drusilla.

'She is not hurt,' Stefan said, quietly.

'How——' began Palfrey.

'She is just cold,' Stefan said, 'that is all.'

'Ye-es,' murmured Palfrey, 'yes, of course.'

She was stiff with cold. The blue tinge at her lips was evidence of that; and his first task was to get warmth back into her body. He began to massage her, slowly and gently. Others joined the party and Stefan came to his side, his large hands kneading and slapping Drusilla. They worked until they could feel the warmth returning, when Stefan looked up with a smile and there was recognition in Drusilla's eyes.

'There is a hut not far away, Sap, I saw it as I came,' Stefan said. 'We will take her and the others there. They will be better off, and we can perhaps make a fire. It is too far to carry her to the village yet.'

'Yes,' said Palfrey. He drew a hand across his forehead; it was damp with perspiration already freezing. He stood up, and others lifted her and carried her across the plain towards the hut. Palfrey followed, not removing his gaze from Drusilla.

The hut was near the edge of the plain, by the side of a stream which had frozen over. It was empty when they reached it, but a fire was burning in a circular iron stove, and the room, the first of two, was stiflingly hot. Palfrey loosened his furs as one of Ohlson's men stood on the threshold of the other room and beckoned them.

In the room, there were skin rugs on the floor, ready to serve as beds, and another warm stove. All the prisoners were soon lying down and their colour became more natural. The second woman had been wounded in the thigh, and one of the men, a short, thick-set, grey-haired fellow, with a very full face, had been hit in the chest.

The second man had been shot through the heart, the third in the stomach, but the latter was apparently in no pain, although his eyes followed them about piteously.

Palfrey attended to the wounds, longing for some equipment; he would soon have to get supplies if he were to save the lives of the more severely wounded. He was left alone until the door opened and a fur-clad soldier entered, carrying a box on which was painted a large red cross.

Palfrey cleansed the wounds more thoroughly, and dressed them. The flesh of the fugitives was flaccid, and there was no further danger from the exposure, although they were physically and mentally numbed.

Now and again, Drusilla stared at him, and although she recognised him, she could not speak. Palfrey kept smiling across at her, and even hummed a little to himself. What was happening outside did not seem to matter.

He went out and stood at the front door, buttoning his coat about him. The hut—it was the one in which Conroy had been interrogated—was on high ground, and he could see the whole of the plain and the pass. The fighting had nearly stopped, for the Germans who had escaped were already beyond the barricades. As he watched, another flight of bombers came over and dropped their load with fine precision.

Stefan came towards him immediately afterwards, smiling cheerfully.

'They are doing well, Sap!'

'What *are* they doing?' Palfrey demanded.

'The sides of the pass were heavily protected,' Stefan said, 'and the bombing is reducing the fortifications to facilitate a drive into the pass. It won't be long now.'

'You're sanguine,' Palfrey said. 'What else do you know?'

'The attack came more swiftly than the Germans had expected,' Stefan told him. 'They thought that they were quite safe—they believed that Conroy would never reach Sven, of course. How he did, from here, was a miracle.'

'Ye-es,' said Palfrey, smiling. 'Alex deserves——' He broke off abruptly. 'That can wait. Is there anything else?'

'The village has been in German hands for some time, and those villagers and authorities who were not friendly were taken away. The Finnish border is only a few miles to the west. The village is almost isolated, for there is little communication with the southern part of the country.'

'We knew that,' Palfrey said.

'Fienne isn't the main entrance to the fastness,' Stefan told him. 'That is on the other side, approached from the Finnish frontier. This way has been kept open for easy and regular communication with Sven, and the village was used as an advance post. No one was taken into the pass except those who were trusted. Even the prisoners were not allowed to go inside.'

'Conroy——' began Palfrey.

'Conroy ran wild, and was brought to this hut, where he overheard talk of the fastness. He was taken out to be shot, escaped, and was befriended by a villager. Of the stronghold——'

'Yes?' asked Palfrey, his voice sharp.

'As Conroy said, there are thousands of men,' said Stefan quietly, 'but not altogether in the way we expected. You were near the truth, Sap, about the slave-workers. Now we know the truth behind the story of Private Roshki!' Stefan went on, gently. 'You remember how he tried to find his family, who had been driven away with many other Russians and Poles? He traced them towards the north, but that was all. If the German prisoner whom I have interrogated has told the truth, there are many thousands of slaves working within the mountains. It is not hard to imagine what they are doing.'

Palfrey said: 'What kind of fortifications are there?'

'They will take much reducing,' Stefan told him, 'but the advantage of the surprise attack should make all the difference. I think it will be less costly than it might have been otherwise. Only the militia is here, but there is news that the regular army advance patrols are not far away, and the bombing is being done most thoroughly.'

Palfrey said: 'How did the Nordians know what to bomb?'

Stefan shrugged. 'I wondered that, also. Since daylight, scouts have been here and radioed reports. Oh, another thing! Brian is alive, he is in the village, still very ill.'

'Is there a doctor?' Palfrey asked quickly.

'One has just arrived,' said Stefan. He was silent for a while, and then asked: 'What are you thinking, Sap?'

Palfrey said: 'I don't like it. A straightforward attack—no, man, it won't come off! They've obviously been preparing the place for years, and they won't allow it to be taken by a frontal assault. They may have been taken by surprise, but they've got inside the fastness and they'll take some forcing out. There are two entrances, therefore two exits——'

'The other is known, and is watched by now.'

'It still isn't good enough!' Palfrey declared, sharply, 'they are well prepared for a siege, and we mustn't play into their hands. Thousands of men—doing what? Preparing the birthplace of another master race, perhaps, but also making sure that the people inside remain safe.'

'You are not often pessimistic,' Stefan said.

'I'm not pessimistic now,' said Palfrey, brusquely, 'I just don't believe that it's going to be easy for a frontal attack, although there's probably an easy way. Some of their agents outside probably know a third way in.' He eyed Stefan steadily.

Stefan said: 'Sap, I once suggested that Ingrid——'

'And one of those agents tried to stop us getting here, tried to send us to waste time at Staar,' Palfrey went on, 'it might have been Ingrid, but there's at least another bet—there's no need for pessimism from you, either!'

'Whom do you mean?' demanded Stefan, sharply.

Palfrey said: 'My mind actually began to work while I was following you! There were the second lot of plans, cropping up so conveniently, with the false trail to Staar, and the reception party at Staar—yes, I know!' he added hastily. 'We've been into all this before, but we've been blind. Who had the best opportunity to put the plans in the drawer after the house had been searched, thus knowing that it was considered empty of information? Not Ingrid—true, someone might have told her of it, but that means the person knew. A servant?' he shrugged his shoulders, 'I doubt it. I once thought that a servant left me a note warning me against the Gregarovs—remember that, Stefan? Against the Gregarovs, *no* against Sylva. Sylva, who gave me a key and then hurried away knowing that if we used it and reached the grounds, the three of us would be shot. Sylva, who spoke so convincingly of his non-existent sick daughter. Sylva, who looks a tired old man and who hates the Soviet because he thinks it robbed him years ago. Opportunity—motive—guilt in some degree, on Ingrid's own admission. A capable actor, our Mr. Sylva!'

Stefan snapped: 'You think it likely?'

'I think we were fools to let him stay at large,' Palfrey said, 'and I think he ought to be brought here at once. Is the radio working in the village?'

'One is, yes.' Stefan was already half-way to the door. 'I will send the message.'

Palfrey spent some time examining the map which Sylva had produced, looking at the letters and figures near Fienne, which he had not noticed before. He made nothing of them, and returned to the inner room. The wounded man was awake and staring at him, and Madalena was also conscious.

Palfrey looked across at Drusilla's corner; her eyes were still closed.

He approached the man, as the woman said:

'It has failed, as I always knew it would fail, father.'

Palfrey's smile faded; he realised that this man was Gagliani, who might possibly know a third way into the mountain stronghold, and would certainly know a great deal.

* * * * *

Stefan went immediately to the Militia headquarters in Fienne—they were at premises which had been used by the Nazis until that day. Ohlson was present, and Stefan had no difficulty in sending the message to Sven. Only then did he feel that he could relax enough to send off for the wounded, and he ordered a dray to be despatched to bring them back to the primitive comforts of the village and the facilities of a field-dressing station. Then he went to see Brian.

The military doctor was hesitant about the chance of saving his arm, but said that an hour would make no difference and decided to wait until he could consult Palfrey. Brian was in a fever and his arm was very gangrenous.

After leaving him Stefan began further inquiries about the German occupation.

The stories from the villagers were always the same. Loyalty had been bought or induced by threats—Stefan gathered that there had not been much opposition, for the Mayor had been pro-Nazi. The fact that the village was isolated for several months in the year and that the district—and the mountains—could be approached from Norway and Finland even more easily than from Southern Nordia, had set the seal to security. The majority of the men now within the mountain had been brought across from Norway, always after dark, although a few had come through Finland. Occasionally Bruckner, Schlessing and Zukmayer had come in person, but Kloeb had been a more regular visitor; the one-armed man was greatly feared in Fienne.

The villagers knew that machinery had been taken into the mountains, over a period of more than two years, but had little idea of what was happening there.

Before Stefan had finished, Palfrey arrived.

Without attending to the removal of Drusilla—who was now conscious—and the others, Palfrey hurried to Brian's room, spent ten minutes in consultation, and decided on amputating the arm; secretly, he was afraid that the infection might have spread too far. He operated himself, and when Brian was comfortable under a shot of morphia and on the way to Sven by air, he was glad of a cup of hot, sweet coffee and a rest in a primitive easy chair.

Drusilla was well enough to sit in another, and Stefan leaned against a table, and said quietly:

'I have sent for Sylva, who should not be long. I cannot get information about what is happening in the mountains, but Gagliani might know—there has been a quarrel, I understand.'

'We'll tackle him,' Palfrey said, 'but first——'

His words were drowned in an explosion so great that it deafened them as they jumped to their feet in alarm. Another and yet a third followed, then a roaring sound which continued for a long time.

Stefan and Palfrey hurried into the street, where the villagers were streaming from their houses in alarm.

A great cloud of dust was rising near the mountains and obscuring the lower slopes. It was being blown by the wind towards the village.

Militia were hurrying to and fro, emergency radio messages were sent to aircraft which were approaching and about to land with reinforcements. Ohlson soon joined them, able to give chapter and verse of what had happened.

The mouth of the path to the mountain fastness had been blown up. When the dust and smoke settled, not long before dark, it was possible to see the great tumbled mass of rock where once there had been the defile leading into the interior.

Word was received by radio that the entrance on the other side had also been blocked.

'Which means that we've no chance until we've found the third entrance,' Palfrey said soberly, 'they've kept the place for something like this—the thing that they didn't expect was that a lot of Nazi bigwigs would still be in Berlin. But there must be a means of communicating with the world outside, they won't have cut themselves off completely. Come and see Gagliani, Stefan. He's about ripe to talk.'

Now that Drusilla was safe, he was interested in the major problem; what and who were inside the mountain? Vague guesses were no longer satisfying, he had to know. Above all, he wanted news of the secret entrance in which he firmly believed. Yet he was not optimistic about Gagliani; the Germans would have killed him if he had known of any such entrance.

Gagliani, grey-haired and grey-bearded, was also thin, emaciated, bitter and sullen, but he talked freely.

Yes, there was such a passage through the mountains, but he did not know where.

. . . . .

Gagliani had been a party to the plan to build the fastness. He was consulted because he was a specialist in tunnelling—a German weakness since the death of Todt and several other experts. Gagliani had designed several of the tunnels which Mussolini had built through the Apennines and the Calabrian mountains. He had been a firm Fascist.

Palfrey asked: 'Did Biagni know what you were doing up here?'

'Yes,' Gagliani said, 'that is why he was killed when it was learned that you were going to question him. Gruvel, who worked for us, learned of that from other war correspondents. From the time Brett came to see you, Palfrey, you were watched. You have always been dangerous, and directly there was a suspicion that you were searching for Bruckner, it was decided to keep you in Rome, and if necessary, to kill you.'

'Go on,' said Palfrey.

'You, or those with you, worked too swiftly in Rome, making it necessary for me to hurry away,' said Gagliani. 'I would have done nothing to my daughter-in-law, but she had overheard a discussion and had stolen blue-prints, which were never found. She would have been killed, but it was necessary to try to find out where she had left the drawings. You understand?'

'Fully,' said Palfrey. 'The plans were——'

'Of the mountain stronghold, of course,' said Gagliani. 'The only thing missing was the map, saying where it was situated. That was found, so I was brought to Sven, then forced to hurry here, where I discovered that they had no intention of sharing the full secret. If I knew it, believe me, I would tell you!'

'I wonder,' Palfrey said, sceptically. 'Did you know of the faked map left in the Gregarov's house in Sven?'

'I knew of it, yes,' said Gagliani.

'After Gregarov died, who remained to work for them in Sven?' Palfrey asked. 'Ingrid Gregarov, and——'

'Gregarov's wife?' exclaimed Gagliani, showing more animation, 'she knew nothing, she is just a Nordian patriot. While we were trying to work with Nordia she was helpful, but after that she was worthless. Do you not know who——'

Palfrey said: 'So it was Sylva.'

'Of course,' said Gagliani, scornfully, 'he has been with us from the beginning.'

Stefan's face showed no change of expression. Palfrey glanced at and then away from him, and went on quietly:

'I hope you're not lying, Gagliani.'

'Why should I lie?' demanded the Italian, harshly. 'Lies would not help me. The truth—it might help, perhaps, but I am an old man, and all for which I have worked and for which I have dreamed has been taken from me. *I* shall not lie, Doctor! I will tell you this—within the fortress of Fienne, if you can find them, are some of the most brilliant men of Germany. Scientists—doctors—psychologists—inventors—oh, the Nazis have been clever! Within the fortress there is the mind of the German nation, all that is most clever, all that the Allies hate most. And it is safe—do you understand that—*it is safe from you*. Unless you find the one way in, you cannot reach them. And there is more——'

The Italian paused; there was a glare of fanaticism in his eyes, and Palfrey did not think that he was lying. He looked old, yet spirit burned in him; whatever else was wrong with Gagliani, he had followed his convictions, there was no hypocrisy in his make-up.

'There is more!' he repeated. 'There are workshops and factories, laboratories and offices. There are the materials for the manufacture of poison gases of great potency and which have not been used but which one day can be. There are bacteriologists within the fortress, who have a supply of bacteria and the means of multiplying them a millionfold. And there are those within the Nazi party who will not accept defeat. If you fail to get them, they will escape one by one, on deadly missions. *They will spread disease and death throughout the world, they will poison the cattle and scatter the seeds of destruction over your crops.* You and your talk of reconstruction! There will be none, Palfrey! Infection—poison—disease. Think of how it would spread in any part of Europe, think how it can be spread even in parts of the world which have not been ravaged by war. Oh, they will strike, if once they believe their position within it hopeless.'

Palfrey said: 'Their position *is* hopeless.'

'Then if you would save yourself and your countries, find a way in!' cried Gagliani. 'They have great ideas, these Nazis! Within the fortress there are the means for building a new Germany. The greatest minds in the Reich are busy on the specifications for new weapons of war, weapons which can be wielded by the few to destroy the many. There are enough men and women of the *Herrenvolk* to perpetuate the German race. While you may think that once Germany is beaten no one in the country will continue to work for the Nazis, you will be wrong. Do you understand me? You will be wrong! There are agents throughout Europe who hate the very word of Freedom, and they will work and plan secretly for a quarter of a century if needs be, until they can act again.'

He fell back, gasping for breath, while Palfrey and Stefan stared at him, believing that he spoke the truth and afraid of what might come of it.

29: Within the Fortress

Over a long period, all the necessary machinery and equipment had been brought to Fienne and assembled—everything needed for the excavating work and the tunnelling, to make the underground fortress impregnable and yet large enough for thousands of people to live and sleep, to procreate and to rear the future Hun. Palfrey had never believed that the leading Nazis would accept the arbitrament of force; now he realised that while there remained a way of access to the fortress, others would escape from Germany —possibly Hitler and his blood brothers, but more likely the lesser-known members of the party, who were determined to make every effort to perpetuate Greater Germany. If that could not be done, they would leave a terrible trail of disaster. There was nothing intrinsically impossible in what Gagliani had told them, even though it was an idea born out of a fanaticism. It was on a par with all the horrors which had been committed in the name of the Third Reich.

Gagliani said, hoarsely:

'There have been great underground factories in Germany and Russia and in England, there is nothing new in the thought of men living underground, but the Germans have perfected it—and I have helped them. The ventilation system is superb, a man can live there for twenty years and be no poorer in health than if he lived above the earth. The slaves who have built the fortress will remain as servants— those who are needed—but all who are superfluous will be killed off. Only the finest physical specimens will be retained for future service, and to rear offspring. But if the Germans think they can only hope to destroy the rest of the world, then not a single slave will remain alive, and the way into the fortress will be defended until the last German there is dead. It will be the most fiendish battle of the war, for they will use every weapon, every poison gas, every germ known to science!' Gagliani had his head, now, and went on, wildly: 'I do not think you will find the secret way in! They will stay there for years, sending out their messengers of death. They have dehydration plants and they have seeds which do not need soil. Nothing has been left undone. The laboratories and research shops will bring about new methods of destruction, new aeroplanes, new——'

Palfrey said: 'I think you've said enough.' He looked at Stefan with a twisted smile: 'The gestation chamber of the new Germany, but I think we've stopped that.'

'The lethal chamber for the world!' Gagliani shouted, 'the lethal chamber for——'

Then he choked, and lay back on the bed, gasping for breath, while Palfrey and Stefan stared bleakly at each other. other.

· · · ₁ ·

They went to the Militia headquarters and radioed a message to Sven, but found that there was no news yet of the arrest of Sylva. Even if he were caught, there was no guarantee that he could give the information, and uncertainty made the waiting worse. Palfrey, Stefan and Ohlson spent hours interrogating the prisoners, some of whom admitted having heard of a secret trail; others denied all knowledge of it. There was no hint forthcoming of the whereabouts of the entrance, and the prospect of searching throughout the foothills was a bleak one.

After two days, there was still no word from Sven, except the assurance that every effort was being made to find Sylva. Palfrey began to wonder whether the old man had come North and was now inside the fortress. As the hours of the third night passed, he knew that a mass attack from both sides could not be delayed much longer. He could not hold back the Militia; even had he wished to, he doubted whether the Allied Governments would have agreed. But once that attack started, and the men inside knew that their last chance was gone, what unimagined horrors would be let loose?

He had not even the comfort of hoping that Gagliani had lied.

The word for attack at first light on the third day had been given, and the men were massed and ready, while the bombers were already winging their way North. Palfrey and Stefan, sleepless and weary, went towards the plain where the first onslaught would begin, and they were there when a messenger came from the village.

The message was handed to Palfrey, who ripped open the envelope, and read swiftly. The others saw from his expression that the news was good, and before he had finished reading, he looked up and said:

'They've found Sylva, and are bringing him here.' He paused, and then went on: 'Action's postponed until we've had a go at him. It ought to be quite a party!'

•　　•　　•　　§　　▮

The aircraft flew in low, just before mid-day; it was a tiny speck at first, hardly visible against the bright sky, for the sun had broken through the clouds for the first time since Palfrey had been north. He was waiting with Stefan and a small party of officials. Further away, the troops were impatient at the delay, while the squadrons of bombers had been turned back to landing fields, to await another signal.

The bomber landed without circling, and had hardly stopped before the doors opened and a uniformed man stepped out, followed by the insignificant figure of Sylva. Wrapped in an astrakhan coat and with a fur hat pulled low over his forehead, he looked a timid, frightened little man. He was followed almost at once by a taller figure, and Stefan exclaimed:

'Ingrid!'

'A family party,' Palfrey said. He spared a glance for the Russian, and his smile was almost amused as he saw Ingrid staring at the giant. Then he went forward, two of the crew hustled Sylva after him, and the party went into the house which had been commandeered. Until they reached it, Sylva said nothing, but as soon as they were inside, he turned to Palfrey, and said, appealingly:

'Doctor, you of all people will not believe——'

Palfrey said: 'I not only believe it, I suggested it. Sylva, there'll be no fooling and no quarter. If you want to save yourself a lot of pain and suffering, you'll tell us of the secret entrance to the mountains.'

Sylva stared at him, his eyes suddenly different. They were no longer weak and watery and faded, but filled with cunning.

Softly he said: 'You have little authority here, Palfrey, but I might come to an understanding with you. You may know what will happen unless my friends are defeated quickly. Gagliani has talked, I think, he is an Italian——'

'He's talked,' said Palfrey, coldly.

'Then—give me a guarantee of my life against my information,' Sylva said. 'My life and a comfortable income, Palfrey! It will be so easy and if you choose, you can arrange it.'

Palfrey looked at the little man dispassionately, not surprised by this final effort of self-preservation. He wondered what the Nordians would do; if he had his way, he and Stefan would handle this man, and they would find a way to make him talk.

He did not think twice about it, for he was prepared to go to any lengths.

Ingrid said: 'Dr. Palfrey, I discovered much when I was at my home with my father. That is why he arranged for me to be carried off, although he did not realise that I learned he had planned that too. On the map which he said that he found at the house——'

'Be quiet!' cried Sylva. 'Would you, my own daughter, betray me?'

Ingrid did not even look at him.

'On the map, Dr. Palfrey, the entrance to the stronghold is marked by the figure 5.'

But for the guards restraining him, Sylva would have flung himself at her. She watched him screaming and struggling and writhing, watched him taken away, and heard the last obscene muttering from his twisted lips.

Palfrey was poring over the map with Ohlson and other officers, and Stefan stepped to Ingrid's side. Palfrey did not know what they said, but when he left for the place marked '5', Ingrid and Drusilla were talking together.

* * . . .

Within two hours of Sylva's arrival, the search party was ready—fifty picked men, with officers, Ohlson, Stefan, Palfrey and two guides from Fienne. The spot marked on the map was some ten miles to the West—difficult miles to cover, and likely to take them the rest of the day, perhaps even longer. Soon after they started, a few single bombers were sent over to bomb the pass, and sporadic attacks were made on both the known entrances, to keep the defenders confident of their security.

It was a nightmare journey.

Over rocks, needle-sharp and covered with ice, through defiles and narrow crevices, up the sides of the mountains and down the steep valleys Palfrey plodded on, determined not to be a drag on the main party. Frequently they rested, to allow the guides to make the trail. Dusk came, and when darkness fell about them they rested under the cover of a giant hill until the first pale glow of the moon spread enough radiance for them to go on again, stumbling, slipping, falling, cruelly burdened by their heavy equipment.

There was no indication that they had been observed.

Long before dawn, the guides stopped and whispered together, then reported that the place was near, and they were certainly within a hundred yards of it. After a while, they led the way to what looked like a sheer wall of rock, with boulders on the lower slopes. Some of the boulders were movable.

The guides led the way into a tunnel some three feet wide, obviously cut out of the rock by the men who had prepared this fantastic chamber of thwarted ambitions. Soon they heard the throb of engines pulsating within the mountain. It was much too warm for the heavy clothes they wore, and Palfrey began to perspire. Before long, they saw electric lamps hanging from the ceiling. There was a breathless hush, broken only by the throbbing note, which seemed to shake the air.

The tunnel widened. They caught a glimpse of the layout of a gigantic chamber, not quite finished. About the floor, men were lying prostrate, either exhausted or dead.

The slave workers, Palfrey thought.

There were hundreds of them; probably this part of the fastness had been the last to be built and the man had worked until they had dropped asleep; some still held their tools. All were in rags, and nearly naked. One or two stirred. At the far side of the chamber, which was a hundred yards across and a hundred feet wide, were German guards, wearing linen uniforms and with tommy-guns by their sides and whips across their knees. They could not see the file of men approaching from the shadows of the tunnel.

One of the guides halted the party by a gesture, and beckoned an officer. There was a whispered colloquy before the officer drew a long-barrelled automatic pistol—the 'barrel' was a rubber silencer.

The officer fired three times in quick succession.

The silencer was only partly effective, but the sound was not loud. The guards fell dead.

Some of the workers stirred.

The rescue party began to speak in urgent whispers, in Russian. The waking men, gradually realising what was happening, kept quite still; there was a hush as of death over the chamber; water dripped slowly from the walls, the high ceilings were carved out of solid rock.

The rescuers pressed on.

One false move would have betrayed them, but now they were guided by two of the workers, who knew where the leaders were to be found. Slowly, the ghostly column moved along passages and tunnels, across great empty workshops, many fitted with machinery. They passed deserted laboratories and great chambers stacked to the ceiling with stores.

It only compared, in Palfrey's knowledge, with a vast ordnance factory built underground, yet it had an air of grim fantasy. It had less effect on the engineers in the party, for, to them, there was nothing surprising in it except the location. The ventilation was good, although in all the passages were notices prohibiting smoking. In spite of the warmth, the air was not foul.

They reached a spot which might have been the interior of an office in any large building. Men were hurrying about their work, or passing through doors. Everything seemed normal. The inhabitants were convinced of their immunity.

One of the workers pointed towards a closed door. Palfrey heard Stefan whisper:

'Bruckner?'

'It is so,' the man said.

'So!' said Stefan, and shot Palfrey a quick, sidelong glance.

The party moved on, disgorging upon the passages, and two officers using silenced automatics. So complete was the surprise that there was little opposition, although other doors opened and there were loud shouts of alarm and incredulous voices raised in sudden fear. The worker-guides led the main force of the raiders towards the chief passages and exits. Beyond, were other great chambers filled with slaves, who were so exhausted that only a few seemed aware of what had come to them.

Stefan opened the door of Bruckner's office. Palfrey and Ohlson stepped through together. There were a dozen men in the room.

Bruckner was sitting at a large desk. He was a short man, with a heavy jowl, and he wore pince-nez. Palfrey recognised Zukmayer and Schlessing with him; a one-armed, dark-haired man, who was no longer important—Kloeb, of course. The other familiar faces were of men he could not name offhand.

Ohlson stepped forward. Palfrey and Stefan stood near the threshold as others crowded into the room. Bruckner and those with him stared in petrified silence. There was not a sound, but heavy breathing. Bruckner's eyes nearly popped from his head; Zukmayer's bald pate glistened beneath an electric light; and Schlessing's swarthy, ugly face was made grotesque as he gaped.

Palfrey's lips were curved in a faint smile.

'The gentlemen returned from the dead, I presume?' he said.

On his words, Bruckner made for a drawer in the desk, and two others whipped their hands to their guns, but the men behind Palfrey were too quick, and Stefan stretched out a hand and swept Bruckner from his chair.

  . . . . .

The principal entrances were opened soon, and the main forces came streaming in; but before they came the 'slaves' ran wild among their persecutors, and none could have stopped them, even had they wished.

30 : Differences of Opinion

'This,' said Dr. Stanislaus Alexander Palfrey, 'is London—the finest city in the world!'

'I would not say that,' protested Stefan, mildly, 'undoubtedly the second best, but——'

'It may possibly be the second best,' said Conroy, who looked thin and pale. He had told them how he had escaped from Fienne—he had found a small boat, rowed part of the way down river, obtained a lift in farm carts farther south, taking in all a little more than two days to complete his journey. 'Sure, it may be second best,' he conceded, 'but——'

'Moscow,' began Stefan.

'Hooey! Now New York——'

'Who was it told me that Shakespeare is adjudged the second greatest poet in every country in the world?' asked Palfrey, a little vaguely. 'I mean, one vote for first place and every other vote for second, makes him first—still, what *are* we arguing about?'

Drusilla admitted that she had no idea. She looked radiant in the sun, as they walked from Euston Station into the streets. Palfrey refused to look for a taxi until they had spent a few minutes afoot.

They had left Nordia two days before, a week after the capture of the fastness. They had had their fill of questions and reports. Stefan had flown to Moscow and obtained permission to return to England with Palfrey and the others. Ingrid was still in Sven, and Stefan admitted that he proposed to go there for a few days before returning to Moscow to take up a resident post under Madame Crikov. On the subject of Ingrid, Stefan's silence was voluble.

Brian, convalescent now, was in the Kirche Hospital. There were moments when Palfrey wondered how Brian, so much a man of action, would find life with one arm; he decided that Brian would not feel sorry for himself and would resent anyone else feeling sorry for him.

Madalena was in Rome with Amata.

Her husband had been among the *élite* at the fastness. He was one of the few Italians permitted within its gates, and he had been killed when the slaves had run amuck. There was one curious thing about Madalena's behaviour. She, not Drusilla, had nursed Brian in Fienne. When Palfrey had last seen him, Brian had said he could not face a winter in Nordia or in England, but if it were possible he would go to Rome. Palfrey, with his mind on other things, had thought little of it at the time; since, however, he had wondered what it implied.

They walked towards St. John's wood, where Palfrey was at last persuaded to get a taxi, and, with Stefan half filling it, and the other three squeezed together, they were taken to Brierly Place. There, Christian opened the door, and inclined his silvery head, smiling a warm welcome.

'I *am* glad to see you all,' he said, 'I am glad!'

'The pleasure is mutual,' Conroy grinned.

Palfrey smiled, while Christian beamed upon Drusilla, and went on:

'His Lordship is waiting for you.'

'Alone, I hope,' said Palfrey.

'Alone, sir?' asked Christian, slightly discomposed.

So Palfrey was not surprised to find Brett with a thick-set, round-shouldered man with a pale face, a button of a nose, and a cigar in his mouth, standing with his back to the fire.

The Marquis stood by his desk, smiling.

The Prime Minister looked at the new arrivals, and put his head on one side.

'I haven't long,' he said, 'but I wanted to be here to welcome all of you, and—' he smiled, and took his cigar from his lips—'to say thanks.'

'Good of you, sir,' murmured Palfrey, 'we hardly——'

'I suppose you're going to talk about luck?' said the Prime Minister, his smile widening.

'It wasn't *all* luck,' admitted Palfrey, 'it was largely Moscow.'

The Prime Minister positively beamed.

'I understand from Moscow that Andromovitch reported that it had been largely due to London and New York. An excellent compromise, I think, and a good augury. I mustn't stay,' he added, looking at his watch, 'you're later than I thought you'd be, but—' he shook hands with each of them, stood back, and added: 'Some people will tell you that the Nazi Nordian venture could never have succeeded, others will tell you that it might have succeeded beyond all dreams. *I* think that it would have been a source of grave and urgent danger had it not been destroyed.'

Palfrey said, quietly: 'Thank you, sir.'

'Other people,' said the Prime Minister, with a smile at Conroy, 'will say that our efforts might have gone awry if it hadn't been for Washington's representative. And well they might! At least all of you realise that it was not London nor Moscow nor Washington, but all three. As it should be! Now, I must go!'

He raised a hand in farewell, and hurried out as Palfrey opened the door. Palfrey watched him disappear, thinking that no man could have found so satisfying a way of saying 'thanks'.

They talked for a while with Brett, before going to Palfrey's flat. Palfrey and Drusilla reached the landing ahead of the others, and stopped abruptly as a man moved from the front door.

Palfrey's momentary alarm faded.

'You promised me a story,' said Charles Bright Murray, 'and you also owe me an apology.'

Palfrey regarded him, meditatively.

'If you haven't got your story yet, you're a poor correspondent,' he declared, 'and the apologies are due from Andromovitch!'

Murray laughed. 'You're always ready with an answer, aren't you?'

'*Am* I?' asked Palfrey.